2ND EARTH 4

Logistics

EDWARD & EUNICE VOUGHT

Dedication

This book is dedicated to those who seek to live a better life

and that do their best to help others do the same.

1

It's still pretty warm for this time of year. It makes the harvesting and canning a little more uncomfortable, but we still have a lot of fun when we get to work together like this. Oh, where are my manners. I am Jon Gorman. I hope you still remember us. Dayna and I along with all of our family here in Virginia have missed you even though we have only been away for a short time. When last we visited we had just received several new additions to our family that made Kathy and LT very happy and filled their home totally.

Those young adults and children have been a big help with every project that we have worked on since they joined us. The youngest ones fit right in with the other little ones in the family that specialize in making sure the quality of the fruits that we are canning maintains a high standard. They are always willing to help us by tasting every batch before it is canned, frozen, dried, or made into jelly or preserves. At first the older members of that group were afraid that we would get upset with them, but they have learned that to us our little ones are the most important members of our family.

They are the ones that will be the future leaders and will hopefully carry on the same as we have for the past fourteen or fifteen years. Today we are finishing off the last of the tomatoes, at least until more of them get ripe. Pretty much everyone working on the tomatoes today asks if we can keep some of them out to be used for fresh spaghetti sauce. The newest members of the family are not sure what that is, but they are all anxious to find out. As usual we are doing the canning in several groups. The ones that have been canning spaghetti sauce today just came over and made an announcement that they ran out of jars so we will have to eat spaghetti this evening.

Naturally everyone acts like that is the worst possible thing that could happen. Just about the time we get the mess from canning cleaned up, at least for today, tomorrow we will be canning more yellow and green snap beans. Anyway just as Dayna and I are starting to wonder where our hunters are we see three trucks heading to the yard where we are standing with about twenty other members of our family. Tim looks at the trucks and says it looks like the girls will get here first. I should probably explain that even though we are all family and we try very hard to avoid conflict, some of our young people still enjoy competing in pretty much everything they do. At least so far it has been good natured competition.

The girls do pull into the yard first, but they were not really racing, the young men prefer to have the girls in front of them in case something happens. Even though we maintain our vehicles well, there are still times when they break down and believe it or not, we have even had people forget to put gas in the cars and have run out. Today the lead car has Amy, Misty, Lillie and Izzie in it. The young men that went hunting today are Teddy, Tommy, Sam, and Matt. This is Matt's first time going hunting with the guys. He told us yesterday that since his wife Sandy eats as much as two of the rest of us, he feels that he should help with the hunting.

Naturally that remark got him smacked by Sandy and both of their lovely children Erica and Aaron. He was only kidding, but she has gotten much stronger since they joined our family. When Teddy asked him how much experience he has hunting he kind of talked all the way around the topic without really saying anything. Then Sandy told us that as far as she knows he has never been hunting before. They lived in a city up in Canada and never had the opportunity. The young men told him that they will make sure he has a story to tell when he gets home today.

As soon as the girls stop their truck they jump out and come running over to Dayna and me. The young men are right behind them. Sandy and the children meet Matt as soon as he gets out of the truck they are riding in. She asks him if her great hunter brought home something for dinner. Teddy answers before Matt can say anything, telling her that he hopes they have a very large frying pan if they are going to cook the steer that Matt shot today. We all rush over to the truck to see how our hunters did today.

The truck has two very nice bucks, a large pig, and one of the largest steers we have seen. The other truck has the fruits of the girl's labors today. They have three really nice deer, an equally large steer, and a pig that may even be bigger than the one the guys have. I start to tell them that they maybe should have left some of the game for another day when our daughter Amy tells us they mainly went for the venison today because all the groups have been asking for it. Unfortunately while they were field dressing two of the bucks they shot with the bow and arrows, the steer that Matt shot came out of the woods and charged straight at them. Fortunately Matt was coming to see how they were making out and was able to shoot the steer on a dead run with one shot.

They say if it would have taken two the bull may have hit one of them even though they were running. Izzie says that she was trying to get an arrow off, but she wasn't as fast as Matt. We can see where the bullet hit the bull through the skull and killed it instantly. We ask Matt where he learned to shoot like that. He smiles and says just because he never went hunting doesn't mean he didn't practice shooting in case he ever got to go. That explains the one bull, what about the two pigs and the other bull. Teddy, Tommy, and Sam say that is their fault. They were hunting about a mile from where the girls and Matt were. Pretty much the same situation happened to them only it was the pig that surprised them first.

The girls say that the pig they got came out of the woods while they were field dressing the steer and they had no choice but to shoot it. This one Misty and Amy shot. Izzie, Lillie, and Matt were busy with the steer. The guys say the bull came after them while they were field dressing the pig. Dayna tells them that accounts for two deer each and the other animals so how did they get the other deer. They all start laughing and show us a new dent in the side of the truck the girls were driving. Dayna asks if they hit the poor thing and they laugh again and tell us it ran into the side of the truck while they were on their way home.

The impact killed it so they dressed it and brought it home as well. We all agree that it was one of the more eventful days of hunting, but we still have to get the animals skinned, quartered, and hung in the meat cooler until we can do more with it. We have to call the other groups because our meat freezer can't hold as much as we have. The other groups have quite a bit as well, but we manage to get all the meat where it belongs. We have to make a couple large batches of both Italian and breakfast sausage with some of the pork and beef that has been aging for a few days anyway. That's never a problem because pretty much everyone in our group loves one or the other and most of them, both types of sausage.

The spaghetti sauce is great and so is the company we have helping us eat it. While we are eating supper the conversation turns to the large number of baptisms we had a couple of weeks ago. Wyatt, Max, Troy, Junior, Heber, Joseph, and Matt all tell us that they are still sore from the labor involved in baptizing all six hundred plus members of our groups that are over the age of eight. They are only joking. They are always telling us that joining our group is a missionary's dreams come true. None of them have ever heard of that many baptisms in a single area except maybe in some of the stories in the Book of Mormon. I always joke with them saying that I thought I would feel holier or something. I didn't even stay in the water long enough to feel clean.

Dayna and our children always smack me for being irreverent, but even the long time church members laugh about it. The evening is almost over when Tim comes running over to tell us that he has been talking to some people in the U.K. My son Timmy, who loves to harass his Uncle Tim, tells him he didn't think the University of Kentucky is in session this time of year. The only reason he knows that there was a University of Kentucky is because we went by there on one of our trips. We want to visit several of the colleges that were available before the war to see what we can find that may help us.

Tim tells Timmy that of all the traits he could have inherited from me, he chose to inherit my sick sense of humor. We start to get way off track so Sara lets out a very loud whistle and says that if someone in England took time to call us we should at least listen to what they had to say. We all couldn't agree more. Sometimes we just get carried away joking around. Tim tells us that it's nothing earth shattering, but they have been talking to some of the other groups and are wondering if there is any way we could possibly help them. We start talking about whether or not we feel safe enough to fly one of our planes all the way across the ocean.

Even Sara is hesitant to try that right now. It's one thing to fly over the ocean for a couple hundred miles and another for several thousand miles. If something happens and the plane goes down, those on board would have very little chance of survival. We agree to talk to the people there more in depth and see exactly what they need help with. We go over to the radio room and Tim tries to raise them again, but they must have signed off because there is no response. We do however hear from a group that has been making a go of it over in what was Mississippi in our world. We have no idea where they came from, but one day last winter Tim started hearing from them.

They seem to know what they are doing and we have given them a lot of advice in the time we have known them. Colonel Bob and his wife Marie went over there a couple months ago and everything seemed to be going okay. They were still in the early stages, but at that time they were optimistic that they could make a go of it. This evening they are asking if we may have room for the fifty-four people in their group. They say they hate to throw in the towel, but the latest storm to hit the coast where they are wiped out their crops and all but destroyed their homes. They are embarrassed to say it, but that storm messed up the only vehicles they had running and they can't get them, or any other vehicles running now.

We tell them that of course we can help them and ask if they have food at least until we can get a team over there to help them. They tell us that at least they have some supplies left from their food storage to last a few weeks if it has to. We tell them we will call them tomorrow morning and make arrangements to pick them up. When the call is over Wyatt tells me that we definitely have a Christian attitude, but what if those people are only trying to get us over there to take our vehicles and possibly any women that go with us.

I ask him if he really thinks they may be bad guys. He looks at me and answers his own question. We have not survived this long in this world by taking everything we are told, or even that we see, at face value. We will proceed on the assumption that this is a legitimate plea for assistance. On the other hand we will be ready in case their intentions are not what they say they are. We know that there are children in that group so we don't want to take too long to help them either. We form a team to go, planning to leave tomorrow after we talk to them again. This team will consist of LT and Kathy, Dayna and me, Bob and Marie, and of course Sara and Gary.

In the morning we get a call from Dave and Kimberly who are our friends that are some of the leaders in the Missouri group. They tell us that they heard the call for help last evening and if we don't mind they could use the people in that group to strengthen their group. We tell them that we really don't care where the people go as long as they are part of something substantial when they get there. We know that the Missouri group is very strong, but they are still fairly small and those new people could help them tremendously. The biggest problem is that the Missouri group doesn't have any vehicles big enough to carry that many people except the C-130 they have and they can't afford to have four or five men driving down to pick up the other group.

While we are talking the group from Mississippi joins the conversation. At first they ask if we are going to be able to help them. Apparently they overheard the part of the conversation when Dave told us they don't have the vehicles to help them. We tell them everything that we discussed and they say that they don't really care where they wind up as long as they are safe and welcome there. The gentleman on the radio tells us all that they are good hard workers and want nothing more than to be part of a group or family where the weather isn't quite so violent.

We agree that we will go down, pick them up, and take them to the Missouri group and if for some reason they don't feel comfortable there we will bring them back here to our groups. We are ready to leave within an hour of when we get off the radio. We decide to take one of the large busses that we have, a small box truck, and one of our fifteen passenger vans that we have. We have three of the large busses that will seat sixty people so we are planning to leave this one with Dave and Kimberly. The drive down is uneventful except for having to move several cars off the road so that we can get through. We harass Colonel Bob because he has been this way and didn't clear the roads.

He tells us he cleared them enough for them to get the jeep they drive through. They didn't realize we were planning to bring a caravan through here. The good natured arguing helps the boring miles go by a little easier. At least he knows where every gas station is along the way and we even find a couple of places that we want to stop at on the way home possibly. It takes almost two full days to get to the settlement and we can see the devastation and the look of total defeat in the faces of the members of this group. It doesn't take long to know that they did not call us down here to take advantage of us. These people are desperate and just about at the end of their hope for a good life.

There are actually sixty people in the group because they had six people join them after we talked to them yesterday. These people walked in looking for a place to stay and as bad off as the group is those people were worse off. Some of the people in the group have injuries so Kathy, who is a registered nurse, takes a look at all of them and does what she can to help them be more comfortable on the trip to the new group. The people have some belongings that they would like to take along, which is the main reason we brought the truck with us. Also if we find an outdoor store or something similar we can take a bunch of supplies to the other group to help them out as well.

We load the vehicles and start on our way. We start to take one road when Dayna tells me that she has a feeling that we should take a different road. It's all the same to me as long as they both lead to where we want to go so we take the one Dayna suggests. We go about ten miles when we see a small group of people walking the direction we are going. When they see us they run to get off the road and to hide. It takes a few minutes, but we convince them that we are not going to hurt them and they wind up joining us. They figure they have nothing to lose so they may as well. We always enjoy being able to find those that need homes, but on this trip if we find too many more we will have to get another vehicle running.

We find an outdoor store just before sundown and decide to spend the night here. We load what room there is left in the small truck and Sara, Gary, LT, and I find a nice truck a size larger than the one we have with us. The ladies find enough dehydrated foods in the store to fix a very good meal for everyone. We load that one as well and decide to post a guard in all of the vehicles just in case someone comes along. Along about midnight Dayna and I are awakened by voices outside the truck we are sleeping in. They sound like girls or women's voices so we wait to see what is going to happen. We don't have to wait long when one of the young ladies climbs up into the cab of the truck and starts looking for food.

Dayna and I are in the back of the truck so we work our way as quietly as we can up to the cab and stop directly behind three other young ladies that in the light we have look to be between thirteen and sixteen. The one in the cab tells the others there is no food and when she turns to look at the others she sees us standing there. We can see that they want to run, but we tell them we are not going to hurt them, in fact we would like nothing better than to help them if they will let us. They at least listen to what we have to say then they eat what appears to be the first meal they have had in a while.

In the morning they are with us when we start out again. We get to the group in Missouri about mid afternoon the second day. The reception we receive makes the new people feel very welcome and like they belong here. The people in this group are happy to see the treasures we brought with us from the store and are very happy to accept the large bus and one of the trucks we have with us. We have a very good celebration dinner and get a good night's sleep before we leave in the morning. The four young ladies that joined us last ask us if we could possibly take them with us. They tell us that when their parents were alive they heard about a settlement in Virginia and have been trying to find it since then. When they found out that we are from there they all hoped to be able to go back with us.

LT and Kathy want them to come and live with them and their new family. We talk to Tim on the radio before we leave and he tells us that he has talked to the people in England again and he will tell us all about their conversation when we get back. Something tells me that we are going to be going to England no matter how dangerous it may be. Most of us are riding in the fifteen passenger van so we have plenty of time to discuss the possibilities and to speculate some pretty wild scenarios on the long ride home.

2

After hearing all of the wild scenarios we have been going over on the ride home it's a wonder that our new friends believe anything we have told them. As soon as we get home Jon, Tim's son, comes running to tell us that his dad is on the radio with the people in England right now. LT and Kathy come with Dayna and me to see what they have to say. We were also met by Teddy and Nickie as well as Misty, Amy, Lillie, and Izzie. They take the new people to show them around and to drop their meager belongings off at LT and Kathy's house. We are sure that by the time the tour is over the new young ladies will have everything they need.

When we get to the radio room we can hear what is definitely a British accent talking to Tim. After a few minutes a ladies voice with the same accent comes over the radio. She tells us that they are fully aware of the danger they would be putting us in if we choose to help them. She also says that they are afraid that they may not survive if they don't get some help soon. Apparently they have no electricity where they are and they do not know how to grow crops in the quantities that they need. They have been surviving by scavenging and growing some vegetables. They say there are animals in the countryside, but none of them have ever hunted and even if they knew how to hunt, they do not know anything about guns.

Their culture is totally different than ours, but none of our people knew anything about guns or hunting either when we got here. I ask them some questions trying to get a feel for what we will be walking into. I guess I should say what we will be flying into because there is no other way to get there. Apparently the people we are talking to live in a city or town not far from London. Tim, LT, and I have been to England when we were together on the Seal team. LT and Kathy were there not long before they wound up in our world. Naturally Tim and I ask him why he didn't help those people when he was there at that time.

He starts trying to think of a good reason when Kathy smacks him and us saying that it wasn't the same world then. The woman on the other end says that they have been there all their lives so if they were here they should have seen them at least. Kathy starts to explain, but I interrupt and tell them we will explain everything when we see them. They are happy to hear that we will be coming to help them. We talk for another half hour to get a list of what we should take with us. We are sure that much of what we will need is available there, but we can't count it still being usable after all this time.

When our conversation with them is over we agree to take care of the things that have been neglected since we have been gone, and then meet together this evening with the group councils to talk it over with them. One of the first items on the agenda for today is help the newest members of our family get settled in with everything they need. They already have it picked out. All we have to do is carry it over to LT and Kathy's house. Dayna and I do not have much to catch up because our children do such a great job of taking care of the house whether we are home or not. Naturally the boys and the girls want to show us how the projects they are working on are coming.

They are all very impressive. Max, Troy, and Junior brief us on the progress they have made on the chocolate project. They say we should have some soon, but we could not pin them down on exactly what that means. Unless it is within the next couple of days some of us will miss the first batch anyway. Our cattle herd is growing steadily. It seems that every day now when they go out to check on the cattle there are more waiting patiently to join the herd. They are already over the hundred head that we discussed originally. This was going to be a project that all of the groups that make up the big group here were going to share. Now that it is far more successful than originally thought at least two of the other groups would like to have their own herds.

Our guys are helping them build their pasture areas and will help them move some of the cattle in the original pasture to theirs. I ask the question that I am sure at least one other person is thinking. I ask them why they don't simply enlarge the area they already have and all work on this as a team. My sons and the others that have been working on this project say they have no problems with that. I can tell some of the others are looking for a good answer why that is not a good idea. Finally they all laugh and say they can't see why that won't work at least as well as separating the herds. Personally I think they have already decided to do just that, but they wanted to make me think it is my idea.

Dayna and I have a little while to discuss the upcoming trip and we decided that we will both go. This is primarily because if something should happen to one or the other of us, neither of us would want to go on living. I know that sounds mellow dramatic, but that's the way we feel. When we get to the meeting, there are a lot more people here than the groups leadership. That's fine with us because a trip like the one we are planning could affect pretty much all of our lives to some degree. Even though there is a large group of people here the meeting goes on with little or no interruptions.

We decide to take some food supplies along with survival gear of all the types we have and some supplies to help with pretty much any kind of electricity they will need. We decide rather than deplete our stores that we will go to a couple of outdoor stores where we know there are still plenty of supplies to take with us. The next step is to decide who is going. I do not want to go, but just about everyone thinks that I should, so Dayna and I are on the list. Ken and Carrie want to go. At least Dayna will have one of her sisters along with us. Sara and Gary are going. Big surprise there, she is the one flying the plane. Besides Sara spent quite a bit of time in England before she came to this world.

James and Jenna will round out the list, which is what we feel is a very good group to help with any eventuality. Our biggest concern is getting there and not having enough fuel to return. Tim asked the people there about the availability of aviation fuel and they had no idea what he was talking about. We know there were military bases there before the war and there were also airports so we feel pretty confident that we will find what we need. If worse comes to worse, we can always fly over to Europe and check there for what we need. We are also taking enough guns and ammunition to start a small war. Or maybe I should say to stop a small war if we have to.

The hangars are still being worked on, but we are hoping to have them ready before winter. That is pretty realistic since we have a couple more months before the weather turns nasty. Even then it is not as bad as it is up north. We decide to leave in the morning by truck to get the needed supplies and bring them back here. We don't want to waste our aviation fuel landing and taking off if we can avoid it. In the morning we get an early start to get to the stores we want to go to. They are only a couple hours away and we have our trucks loaded in no time with the items we think we will need plus a bunch more that we decided to bring back with us rather than leave it here to possibly go to waste.

We have a pretty good sized crew working with us today. Just as we are loading the last of the supplies we are taking back, Sara's daughter Misty and our son Tommy come over and tell me not to look to my right, because there are some people over there watching us. Misty says she thought for sure she heard a small child crying a little while ago so they started watching closely to see if they could find the source. That's when they saw the people watching us. I start to work my way around them when Dayna, who heard us talking jumps off the dock and walks straight to the people.

By the time I get around them they are all standing near the truck talking. Sara asks me where I have been and before I can answer Dayna tells everyone that I was making sure we have everything we need from the store. The young man that appears to be the group's leader or perhaps co-leader would be more appropriate because he has a sister that is within a year or two in age from him, asks if we mind if they stay in the store and use some of the things they need from there. The young lady tells him that they have been invited to come back with us and join our group. She reminds him that it is most likely the group they heard about and have been trying to find.

We have just enough room to squeeze all of us and our six new family members. There are the two older ones I told you about and two boys and two girls that look to be between four and seven or eight. We found some unopened cans of chocolate candy in the store so our younger family members decide to give our newest friends a treat. The older girl who is about the same age as Misty asks if this is the same kind of chocolate that she heard us talk about on the radio. They are happy to hear that it is and we have six more volunteers to help make chocolate any time they are needed.

When we get home we tell our children that they are responsible for showing the new people around and helping them find a home. Kathy and LT are coming toward us and hear most of our conversation. I know that they are going to volunteer to take in the new people, but Heber and Joseph, along with their wives, come over to help unload the truck and they volunteer to take all six of our new friends into their home. They live together in one of the original homes from when we moved here so they have plenty of room. One of the little girls in the group asks if they might be able to get something to eat. The chocolate was good, but she is awful hungry.

The oldest young lady tells us they haven't eaten since yesterday or possibly the day before. They were on their way to see if there was any food in the store when we came up and they thought it might be safer to watch from a distance. Heber's wife Ruth picks up the little girl and the others pick up the other three little ones and tells them that they can have all the breakfast they want and they never have to go hungry again. She is naming off all the different foods that they can have when the little girl tells her she has no idea what most of those foods are, but she is willing to try all of them if it is okay.

Ruth and the others just laugh and tell them they will have plenty of time to try them all. Heber and Joseph stay to help us unload the truck. The young man we brought back stays as well. He says that if we are letting them stay with us, the least he can do is start earning their keep. I think these young people are going to be a great addition to our family. While we are loading the plane LT comes over and asks if he is welcome on this trip. He says that Kathy is staying home to take care of the children, but he has a feeling we will need his skills before this trip is over. I look at him kind of sideways and he smiles and says that his dad visited him in a dream last night and told him that he would be needed on this trip. That's the first time anything like that has happened to him so he doesn't want to ignore it.

Naturally I tell him he can't go, but he tells me that his bag is already packed and in the plane so I can't stop him anyway. Then he sticks his tongue out at me. I grab him around the neck and nuggy his head. That's where you rub your knuckles across someone's head. Not hard enough to hurt, just enough to tell him he is always welcome to come with us no matter where we are going. We finish loading the plane. This is not much of a load for a C-130 cargo plane. This is a good thing because it will not take as much fuel this way.

We hold a quick meeting with the leaders of the groups to show them the way we are planning to travel. This way we will have a better chance of being found if something happens. We say our goodbyes and those of us who are going board the plane. For some reason this trip doesn't seem like it is going to be as much fun as some we have been on. Sara taxi's the plane out onto our runway and we are under way. We are going to fly up to New York first and refill our fuel tanks. Karl and some of the others in their group assured us that there are airports in the area where we can get fuel.

We are flying fairly low, but since there is no other air traffic or ground traffic for that matter we should be fine. We are hoping to possibly see some settlements that we do not know about so we can send someone from our group to see if they would like to join us. They may want to stay where they are, but may need a hand and we can help them with that as well. Actually we do spot a group in north western Pennsylvania that is closer to Karl's group than ours so we will tell them about the people. We couldn't see individual faces, but we are pretty sure they were surprised to see a plane fly overhead.

At approximately 300 miles per hour it doesn't take long to get to New York and Karl is right. There are several places where we can fill the fuel tanks. We do that and let them know about the group we saw and we are on our way again. We would love to fly straight through to England now, but the plane only has a range of approximately 1400 miles. We are going to fly over part of Canada, land for fuel in Newfoundland, then Iceland, and Greenland. If we can make it from Greenland to England we may do it, otherwise we will be stopping in Ireland to refuel as well. We planned the route based on airports or military bases along the way. We should be able to spot any settlements that are within our range of vision.

Military planes like the C-130 were not made to carry passengers although they have carried many soldiers to their destinations. It is not what you would call a comfortable ride, but it is not terrible either. It is difficult to talk over the noise of the four 4,300 horsepower engines. We are about an hour away from New York when Gary comes back to where we are sitting. He says so far the plane is doing great. He says that Sara decided to try to stretch the fuel all the way to England. I tell him to do whatever they feel is best, but if we go down he and Sara will be paddling our survival rafts to shore. He smiles and says it's a deal. I'm not sure if I told you or not, but we are all wearing parachutes and we have several of the boats like we used when we were in the Seal group. Not that we think we will need them, but I have always found that if you are prepared for any eventuality, you have a much better chance of surviving in almost any situation. That doesn't mean you will always survive, but your chances are much greater.

We look out the windows, but all there is to see is water in every direction. Just like we always did when we flew in one of these planes in the other world, LT and I fall asleep. We must sleep for quite a while because when we wake up Dayna laughs and asks us how we could sleep with all the noise and through three landings and takeoffs. We are wearing earphones to protect our hearing so it really isn't all that bad. Before we know it Gary is coming back to tell us they think they can see the coast of England ahead of us. I ask him if our instruments are working and if they are does Sara know how to read them.

He laughs and says that they couldn't find that page in the instruction manual so they pointed us in the direction of England and figured we would find it eventually. We all laugh and tell him it sounds like the way we usually do things. James is checking the map that he brought with us and asks is it England or could it be Ireland. Gary tells us that we passed what they believe was Ireland a little while ago so they are pretty sure it is England. We all decide to look out a window and by now we are over land again. We fly over several small towns and cities, but we see no life at all. It seems like only a few minutes when Sara calls over the intercom that she can see London straight ahead of us.

We fly over London and again see no sign of life so we go a little east of the city and find nothing. We turn south and within a few minutes we can see the signs of life. At least we see some smoke from fires down there. We are flying low so that we can see what we need to. Apparently the people down there hear us and come out and wave. We are not sure if the sun is just coming up or just going down, but it is definitely not full light. Sara starts looking for a place to land the plane and there just happens to be an airport not too far from the settlement. Sara sets the plane down almost perfectly considering the shape of the runway, but we all have to ask her if she is trying to kill us.

Well, we are here now. Whatever lies ahead we will have to handle the way we always have. We decide to leave most of the supplies in the plane until we find out exactly what we are up against here. We brought a van and a couple of our multi fuel dune buggies and motor cycles. We unload the van along with some food supplies and head for the settlement.

3

It only takes us about fifteen minutes to find the settlement and as dark as it is getting we determined that it is the end of the day. That's no problem. Actually most of our group can use the sleep before we get started. These people are living just about like Dayna and the other families were living when Tim and I came to this world. The food we brought with us is dehydrated foods that we found at some of the outdoor stores back home. The people here are very glad to see us and the food we brought. They are not going hungry yet, but from the looks of them they haven't been eating very well either.

We get to talk to some of the people, but when we ask who their leaders are they say we will have to wait until tomorrow because they don't like being bothered unless it's an absolute emergency. James asks them what constitutes an emergency and they tell us they are not sure. They have gotten yelled at every time they bothered them. Sara asks them where these so called leaders live. She has no trouble bothering them. Then she adds boy will she be happy to bother them. I tell everybody that it might be better if we wait until morning when we can see what we have to work with, then we will have a visit with the so called leaders whether they want to see us or not.

I ask the people if they will be safe for the night and they say they should be. It's been a while since any roving bands have bothered them. That's not very reassuring. LT says he will stay here tonight and the rest of us should go back to the plane to spend the night. There are several small children that ask if we really came all the way from America in that flying machine. They say they would love to see what it's like inside sometime. We wind up taking about a third of the group back to the plane with us to spend the night. Luckily we have enough cots and blankets to go around plus a bunch more.

One little girl, who looks to be about four, along with her mother, seem to enjoy being with Dayna so they make their beds right next to her and me. The little girl gives us a hug before she lies down to go to sleep and tells us that this is the first time she hasn't been afraid going to sleep. I love listening to the people talk especially the little children. Dayna tells me quietly that if we can't help these people here then we will take them back with us if they want to go.

Since I slept quite a bit of the way here I am not really tired so I decide to go outside and make sure nothing disturbs those inside. Just before sunup the rest of our group comes out to join me. Dayna tells me the little girl, whose name is Genevieve, is sleeping and talking in her sleep. She and the other women say that children should never have to know the fear that these children know. Dayna, Carrie, and I are thinking about how the children had to fear living the way they did before Tim and I came to this world. Apparently Sara and Jenna are thinking the same thing because they say it must have been terrible living the way they were.

We are all just happy that way of life is behind them and hopefully will be for this group as well. Ken asks the question that we are all thinking. Do these people really want to change the way they live. There is a certain amount of comfort in letting others make all the decisions for some people. That way they never have to feel responsible if things don't work out for them. Personally I couldn't live that way and I will do everything in my power to help others avoid that trap as well. James asks if we think the person they have for a leader is a member of the royal family. We all agree that they could very possibly be just that. But in this world there is no place for someone that doesn't pull their share of the load.

We hear a small cough behind us like someone wants to get our attention without interrupting. We turn and it's Genevieve and her mom. Her mom tells us that the leader is part of the royal family. He has one of the rings that the royal family always wears. I don't know if the royal family always wears a certain ring or not and I don't really care. There is nothing to stop anybody from going through Buckingham Palace, if that's what it's called in this world, and take a ring and claim he is royalty. I am thinking this, not saying it, yet, when the mom tells the little girl to tell us what she did.

Little Genevieve has tears running down her cheeks and can barely speak she is so scared. Dayna picks her up and tells her there is nothing she could have done to us that would require her to be afraid of us. She chokes out the words that she stole food from us. Dayna asks her if she took one of the bagels in the bag on the little table in the planc. She shakes her head yes still crying. Dayna smiles and wipes her eyes and tells her they were left there for her and her mommy and anybody else that stayed with us last night. So she doesn't have to feel bad because the food is for them anyway. We all go in to let the others know they are more than welcome to eat the bagels. They were fresh when we left home, but they are still pretty good.

The others are up by now and nobody is complaining that the bagels may not be as fresh as they could be. I don't think any of them have ever eaten anything quite like it before. We brought what we felt would be enough for the entire group and it looks like there should be enough for everyone and two for the children. We take the bags of bagels back to the settlement and LT reports that all was quiet under his watchful eyes. The rest of the people are happy to try the bagels, some of them say they should probably wait until the leaders have had their fill before eating any.

I ask them what this leader does for them besides take their food and anything else he wants. One older gentleman tells us that His Majesty is part of the royal family and should not have to do anything other than lead. I know Sara wants to go get this guy badly, but we will wait for him or them to show up here, within reason. I figure another half hour will be long enough to wait. Sara asks how many leaders this settlement has. Jenny's mom tells us that there are six men and six women that are leaders and His Majesty has two bodyguards. She asks if any of those people help gather food or fight off the roving bands. The people shake their heads and say that they don't.

Well that's all I need to hear, it looks like their half hours up. We men almost have to run to keep up with Sara, Dayna, Jenna, and Carrie. The leaders are living in what appears to be a small mansion that probably belonged to some very rich people before the war. We men have caught up by the time we get to the large front door that the ladies simply open and walk in. Sara starts yelling for the big shot in charge. Two men come from a room off the main hall and start toward the women. LT steps in front of one of them and I step in front of the other one. The one in front of me takes a swing at me, which I was hoping he would do, and I put him down at about the same time LT's guy hits the ground.

Four or five women come out next and ask us what we want. Sara tells them that we want to talk to the guy who calls himself the people in the settlements king. One of the women tells us she will see if he has time to see us today. LT and I just walk past the women into the room beyond in time to see some men ducking into rooms that run off the big room we are now in. I tell them that we mean no one any harm. We came here from America because the people in the settlement told us they could not survive for very long if they didn't get help soon. I am talking loud enough to be heard outside so I know they can hear me.

After a few minutes all seven men and the rest of the women come out and ask if we are really from America. It may be my imagination, but the one talking has one of the worst English accents I have ever heard. I really don't think this guy is British. I assure them we are, I add that we flew here in a C-130 jumbo jet. The one who asked if we are really from America tells me that a C-130 is a military cargo plane. Not a jumbo jet. The others look at him and ask him how he knows that. Ken asks him how long he has been in this world and how did he come to be here.

He tries to bluff his way out of answering us, but we already know he is not what he claims to be. Finally he tells us that he was on leave from the army where he was stationed in Germany. He came to England about six months ago by ferry across the English Channel. The fog was so thick you couldn't see other people standing right next to you. He went below to at least try to stay warm and when the fog lifted he was the only one on the ferry, which had docked by the way. He looked around and was able to find the royal palace where he found the ring he wears. He didn't think about the royalty bit until the people here mistook him for being part of the royal family.

He met the people that are his cohorts here in London and a couple of them were in the group here. They tell us that there was no settlement until they came and got several small groups together to make the group we see now. He asks how we came to be in this world. We tell them our stories, but we also tell them we didn't expect the people to support us. We are all equals and we all share the work and the benefits of that work. One of the guys says that he is hungry. He wonders what the people in the settlement made them for breakfast. Gary has to catch Sara before she beats the crap out of that guy.

The bodyguards are sitting up when we go back out the way we came in. Carrie tells them they better find a new line of work because they are not very good at what they were doing. We all walk out and meet up with the people of the settlement. Some of them bow and call the leader Your Highness. I have to laugh because it reminds me of a book I found in an airport one time back in the world we came from. There was a guy doing a comedy softball routine and he was always calling the umpire Your Highness. It was probably more appropriate then than it is here now.

Our new guests see some of the settlement people eating the bagels and ask where they got them from. The only one who knows what they are is the guy from the other world. Some of them reluctantly offer their food to the former leaders, but we tell them they have to earn anything they eat from now on. We tell everyone that we want to have a meeting with everybody in the settlement to decide how they want to go forward. We overestimated how many people are in the settlement so we have enough bagels for the workers and the children to have two each and we even have enough for the leadership to have one each.

Their first question is where we got them. We tell them we will explain everything in our meeting. This is one of those times when it would be great to have pictures. We do have pictures of the original homes we lived in, but those were from before the war. We found them in boxes in the homes. We have tried to take pictures, but so far all the film we can find seems to either be too old to develop or the radiation from the war destroyed the film. Learning how to make film is on the list of things to do, just not at the top of the list at this time.

It is a pretty dull looking day, but the settlers tell us this is kind of average for this part of England. We decide to move our meeting inside the mansion that the leaders were using. There are a couple of rooms big enough to hold the entire settlement comfortably. We went back to the plane and brought back some of the drink we make that is similar to coffee only we make it from Chicory and some grains that make the drink not only good, but good for us. We know the English have traditionally enjoyed tea so we brought some of the herb teas that we grow and dry the leaves. Many of us enjoy peppermint tea. It's tasty and it can help settle an upset stomach.

While we are talking Ken, Gary, and James are exploring the mansion and the area around it to see how we can put it to best use. Dayna and Carrie are telling the people about how we were just like them in the beginning, but that with the proper leadership we were able to change our lives totally. Whenever they talk about being victimized, by what we called predators, every person in the room except a couple of the former leaders nods their agreement. The girls explain how we did everything that has made our groups what they are today. Naturally when they tell the people that we now have over six hundred members in what we call our family, Sara has to tell them that just about five hundred of those are my children from my thirty wives.

I think some of them even start to believe her. Actually Jenny's mom and one of the other women that spent the night in the plane, say that if I want numbers thirty-one and thirty-two they will be happy join the family. Everyone laughs and Dayna tells them that she is my only wife and it is going to stay that way forever. We do explain that when we first got started there were several more women than men, so some of the men had more than one wife. Now that we have pretty much an equal number of men and women, no one has more than one wife.

When the women get through telling them how we got started, LT and I tell them about the things we do for recreation and to relax as a family. We keep stressing that we have no leaders that do not have regular jobs as well. We also stress that we feel it is important to change the leaders periodically to give everyone the chance to lead and so that no one feels left out. While LT is talking, James comes in and asks if they know where we could find a propane truck. The guy who was the leader says he remembers seeing at least a couple of those in London when he was there. No one else has any idea what we are talking about.

James is ready for this because he has drawn a picture that actually looks like a tank truck that actually resembles a tanker. One of the little girls that looks to be about eight or nine, says that she saw a truck like that the last time they went to the city. She and her mom go with James to look for the truck. I assume that they have found a generator, but need propane to run it on. The rest of us are going to take a vote to see if this group even wants to make a go of living like we do. We leave them alone for a short time to let them discuss their options amongst themselves. We told them we will wait outside until we are called, then we can make plans to do whatever is necessary.

The little girl must have known where a truck is because she, her mom, and James get back while we are waiting. The girl's mom tells us that she has no idea how the rest of the people will vote, but she wants to live like we do. She asks if the rest of the group wants a king or other leader is there any chance of her and her daughter going back with us. We tell her that we prefer to have the groups become self sufficient and prosperous, but we cannot force people to live the way we choose to. However we will not waste our time trying to help people that don't want to be helped.

She says she will go back in and make sure everyone knows what we just told her. We assure her that we made everyone aware of how we feel. We also made sure that the people know that this is not our plan. We found this way of living pretty much spelled out for us in the Bible and some other scriptures that we have read and continue to read so that we understand them, better. The scriptures are full of stories that show us how people prospered when they worked together for the good of everyone and how societies fell when people were divided into classes for whatever reason.

It is getting to be lunch time and we are still waiting. It really hasn't been that long, but we are getting hungry so we assume that our new friends are as well. A couple of us go back to the plane and get enough food supplies to feed everyone along with a small propane stove and a small propane tank that we brought with us. James and LT went back to get the truck with the propane in it started so they could get it back here where it is needed. We decide that if they can't get it running for whatever reason we will tow it back using the van we brought with us. Actually they get back just minutes before we are called back into the room to hear the results of the vote.

We go in expecting to hear that they feel the need for a leader. Instead it is unanimous or at least very close to unanimous to try making a go of it our way. We are sure that the smell of lunch cooking on our portable stove may have had at least some small effect on the outcome. While we eat we outline a plan to get started. One of the first questions came from one of the previous leaders. He asked what if someone does not want to be part of the group. I tell him and everyone listening that we do not want to hold anyone back. If they would rather leave than live the way we do then they are more than welcome to leave. I also stress that if anyone comes looking for trouble by stealing the groups food or trying to take women, they will be dealt with severely.

One of the bodyguards asks what that means. He has a smirk on his face so I don't like him much anyway. I start to answer when Sara tells them that we have a fairly large graveyard for the people that tried to take our way of life away. No one else seems to have any concerns about at least trying to live the way we do. As soon as lunch is over James asks if LT, Sara, Gary, and Ken can give him a hand getting the generator in the mansion working. The rest of us go over the entire mansion to determine how many families could live here if they choose to do that.

4

We determine that the entire settlement, the way it is currently, could live comfortably in the mansion. At least those that were the leaders of this group seem to be resigned to the fact that they are no longer getting a free ride. The mansion has stone walls most of the way around it and a large wrought iron gate and fence that joins the stone walls to enclose the entire building. There are also some individual houses within the walls of the fence. Even these would be very comfortable and much easier to defend than the places they have been living. The people show us what they have been using as a garden. It is a garden, but nowhere near large enough to feed the number of people they have here.

While we are talking one of the women in the group mentions that there are still a large number of people living in the city. Another young lady says that she has seen people looking at them at night, but she was too afraid to invite them in and they are probably too scared to ask to join them. It appears that this settlement could potentially double or possibly even triple in the next few days. We start looking at the area in a different way. It still looks like a very good place to have a settlement, but that will depend on what they have to defend it against. We may have to move farther from the large city to reduce the chances of attack from the roving gangs that seem to live in the large cities.

Since we still have quite a bit of daylight left, Dayna, Carrie, Ken, and I take one of the dune buggies we brought and the large van to go looking for people. We take Genevieve and her mom, whose name by the way is Kristine, she prefers to be called Kristi and Genevieve prefers to be called Jenny. We are hoping that with the girls along, the good people will not be quite as afraid to talk to us. The girls are leading the way with the van, while Ken and I follow closely behind. We don't go very far when we see what looks like a group of women and children run into a vacant store.

Dayna pulls up outside the store and we can see several of the people hiding, but still trying to see us. Carrie and Kristi get out of the van and tell the people in the store that they will not hurt them. They tell them that they are forming a new settlement outside the city and they are looking for people who would like to be part of it. There is at least one man with the group because he stands just inside the door and asks if we are the ones that came in that flying machine they saw yesterday. Little Jenny tells them that we sure did and she got to go in it and got the best food she has ever had from there.

Dayna tells the people that we have a settlement much like the one we are trying to help get started here. We have been together for many years and have learned how to survive better than most people did before the war. One lady actually comes out of the building and says that she heard that there was a member of the royal family in that settlement and he and his friends took whatever they wanted, including women. Kristi tells them that we changed that this morning. Now everyone has to work together or they will have to go somewhere else.

The man asks if we are strong enough to over throw the old leaders what makes them think we won't be just like them or worse. I have gotten out of the dune buggy and am now standing next to Dayna. I tell them that we brought our wives with us and we are intending to stay only long enough to help them get started and to teach them how to sustain life in this world. I continue telling them that we know from experience that the food supplies and safety are disappearing quickly in the cities. The only way to survive is to learn to be self sufficient and how to defend themselves. I add that our offer to join us stands as long as we are here. After that it will depend on the people in the settlement. I add that we are going to continue looking for people that may wish to join us. They can come with us, they can stay here, or they can go to the settlement, it's totally up to them.

I turn to go back to the dune buggy when the people come out of the store and ask if they can come with us. There are seven all together, the man, three women, and three children. The children are very close in age to Jenny. As soon as they get in the van they ask Jenny what she got to eat in the flying machine. I don't hear her answer, I do hear the others saying that they hope to get some food like that. We do not go very far when we find another group of people. When they see the others in the van they must figure that it is safe because they want to join us. The problem with that is the van is full and we have to take them back to the settlement.

When we get back the others have the generator working enough to have at least some electricity working. It is still daylight so we want to save the generator for when it is dark. The biggest improvement, at least to me is that they have the stoves and ovens in the kitchen working so we can cook on them. This in itself is a miracle to these people. Gary and LT are planning to take the other dune buggy and try to find some game for supper. Our supplies were meant to augment, not carry the entire settlement for an extended period of time. One of the older gentlemen in the group tells us it's not legal to hunt on the royal family's property without written permission.

I have to hand it to LT. He handles the situation better than I was going to. He takes out his diplomatic identification from the other world and tells the gentleman and any others who may be interested that he received permission from the queen herself. Fortunately none of them can read very well, but they recognize the royal stamp on the document. One of them says that the queen was killed during the war, how could she have signed that paper. LT tells them that this document was handed down to him by his father who knew the queen well before the war. That seems to satisfy them at least for now.

One of the young men from the settlement asks if he could possibly go with them to learn how to hunt. They head one direction and we go back looking for more potential members for the settlement. I notice that some of the former leaders including his majesty are nowhere around. Sara tells me she will bet me ten to one that we wind up shooting that guy before we leave. I won't bet against it, but I was hoping he would use the knowledge he brought with him to this world to help these people. We make three more trips out and back bringing a full van load every time. Sara went on the last trip and we decided that tomorrow we will try to get one of those double-decker busses running.

While we were looking for people we also looked for food in all the stores that we came across. The people in the settlement were accurate when they said that they could not survive for much longer the way they were going. With the people we brought in today we have more than doubled the number of people in the settlement. We brought plenty of food, but we are still hoping we can find some to augment what we brought. While we are pondering what to do Gary, LT, and the young man who went with them pull into the yard. LT jumps out of the dune buggy and comes over to where we are talking.

He tells us he bets that we are wondering what to feed these people tonight. We have to tell him he is absolutely correct. Then he gets that smug look he gets and says daddy LT has to come to the rescue again. We go over and they have three very nice deer strapped in the back. He tells us he had to track these animals for miles then he had to sneak up on them to even get a shot. The young man that went with them says he thought they saw the deer on the edge of the woods and shot three of them before they walked away. LT looks at us and says they were several miles from here.

We tell our hunters how grateful we are for the great job they did today. Now we have to see if our new friends even like meat because only a few of them have even tasted it. LT and Gary also show us a large basket of potatoes, carrots, and onions that they picked in a garden next to a small deserted cottage. They tell us that it is only a little over two miles from here and it looks like a great spot to build a settlement or to at least grow one.

The women in our group and some of the local ladies cleaned the kitchen in the mansion this afternoon and found a bunch of very useful, very large pots and pans for cooking. Dayna, Carrie, Sara, and Jenna would like to make a great stew for dinner, but it is a little late for that. Instead we cut a bunch of the fresh meat up into small pieces for everyone to try. We will cook enough for dinner for those that like it and for those that don't we will make some soup from the dehydrated meals we brought with us. Some of the people are not sure whether or not they really want to try the meat, but when they smell it they all decide to at least try it.

They all say they like it, but some would still prefer to have some of the soup we are making. Actually we make enough soup for everyone to have some and some of the meat. The women are going to make a stew tomorrow, but with the number of people we have we are going to have to find a source for food quickly. Our new friends are very much impressed with the electric lights we now have in the mansion. It is dark outside, but in the courtyard and in the house we have lights. Dayna and the others are putting what soup and meat that got cooked and not eaten away. It's a good thing we have the refrigerators in the mansion working. James was busy pretty much all day today.

Many of the people have found rooms they would like to use, at least temporarily and are checking them out to get used to a little comfort for a change. I hear a noise out in the darkness beyond the big gates here. The gates are not closed so it's just a large opening. LT hears it as well and we are both pretty sure we know what it is. I walk toward the opening and tell whoever is out there that they are welcome as long as they are not intending to hurt anyone. I am not too surprised to see a group of ten come walking up out of the darkness. There are two men, four women and four children.

One of the men says that they saw us picking up some of the other people in the city and they followed us for as long as they could before losing us. Then they started smelling something they have never smelled before and followed it here. They were trying to get up enough nerve to ask if they could come in when I called to them. There is a little girl in the group about the same age as Jenny. She says she would be pleased to help us eat any of that food that smells so good. We all love to hear the little ones talk. Dayna tells her that we would be pleased to have them eat all that is left from dinner.

Luckily there was still quite a bit leftover and we can cut some more meat and cook it for them. One of the men tells us that he has seen the deer and other animals in the forests near here, but he doesn't have a gun and couldn't find any to hunt with. He jokes and says it's probably a good thing though because he has no idea how to shoot a gun or what kind of ammunition it would take if he found one. We tell them that we are going to teach them how to shoot guns, how to hunt, and how to be self sufficient. The other man says that there are not many guns around here. Before the war only the aristocracy was allowed to hunt.

We couldn't have planned better timing than this. The young man who went hunting this afternoon comes running out to the area we are sitting. His name is Neville by the way and he is carrying a shotgun that he says he found in the basement. He was checking out the rooms down there when he opened a door and found several guns hanging on the wall and in cases around the room. We decide to check it out and sure enough it looks like a room where the people who lived here used to keep their guns and ammunition in. It looks like they may have used this room as kind of what was called a Man Cave in the other world.

This will be a very good start for our new friends. These along with the ones we brought will get them started very nicely. I still think we will be able to find some guns somewhere. Our newest friends are not sure what to do about living arrangements. We apologize and tell them that they are welcome to find as many rooms as they need and make themselves at home. Some of us will stay here tonight and some of us will go back to the plane and stay there. Jenny and Kristi ask if they can come back to the plane with us. They found a room, but they really enjoy being with us. We don't mind a bit, in fact we enjoy their company as well.

There is so much going on in my mind that I have a hard time getting to sleep. The situation here is worse than I thought and now we have to hurry to get some of the things done that we thought we would have more time to do them. One of the items at the top of the list now is to get some crops in the ground and to look really hard for other sources of food. I must finally fall asleep because before I know it there is sunlight coming through the windows on the plane. Dayna and the other women already made a list of things that they want us to bring back to the mansion today. We load the van and head back over there.

There is so much to do that we men simply grab some jerky and get started on our day. The women are making pancakes for the people of the settlement. Our new friend Neville along with one of the men who came in late last night want to know how they can help us today. The other young man's name is Dean and he is in a hurry to get started. The other young man that came in last night would like to go, but they are not sure that they should leave their wives alone here. When we start loading into the van we have several more men and women that want to get started as well. We tell them to wait for breakfast and we will be back for them in about an hour.

Ken and Carrie are staying here this morning just in case something unforeseen happens. The rest of us are going into London to check out some places to see if we can find some edible food. The stores are almost empty of anything worth using, but we notice that the restaurants don't seem to have been bothered so we decide to look there. It's not exactly a jackpot, but we do find several cases of canned goods that are still sealed in the cans. We also check some homes and find small amounts of canned goods. It all helps plus we are hoping to find more when we check the rural areas. At least we have a van full of canned goods to take back with us.

We decide to break into two groups this morning. One of the groups will go to the small town that LT found yesterday and the other group will continue checking out the big city. As much as I would like to go to the village I have the feeling that I need to go to the city today. Gary and Sara want to go with me to look for a bus that they can get running. That will make our projects go a little easier. Actually everyone that is old enough to help is helping today. Of course some people have to stay at the settlement to watch the children who are too young to do what is needed at this time.

The settlement people who came with us today are going through houses looking for food or anything else we may need. We find a bunch more restaurants and get enough canned goods to fill a good sized truck if we had one. I am looking for a truck to work on when we hear a bus coming down the street. We have to move some cars off the street in order to get the bus all the way down it. We are getting ready to load the food into the bus when Sara says that she sees a nice sized truck in a garage a few doors down. She is standing on the top level so she has a better view then the rest of us.

Naturally we go to check it out and find that it is a diesel, which makes it even easier to get running. Now all we have to do is find a place that sells diesel fuel. We still need to find one that sells gas, or at least that did sell gas and diesel fuel. We find that just a couple blocks away. Luckily we brought a small compressor that runs on 12 volts direct current. We can plug it into the cigarette lighter and use it to put air into the tires. We go to the gas station or to be more correct we should probably say petrol station where we find both gas and diesel fuel. This way we can fill up the van again and the truck and bus.

When we have the truck running good we decide to look for more food supplies and people. At least with the local settlers they are not quite as afraid as they would be. We are going through an area that looks to be more of a commercial area than residential. We see a sign on a warehouse that sounds familiar to those of us from the states. For some reason I associate the name with food. It won't hurt to check it out at least. We have to pry the door open and none of us are ready for what we find. This is a warehouse that was used for shipping dehydrated and freeze dried foods from. The main headquarters is in Utah back home.

There are thousands of boxes full of food here, but we have to find out how much of it is still good to eat. The boxes and cans say that this food has a shelf life of up to twenty-five years. It has been here longer than that, but we have had very good luck with this kind of food lasting even longer than that. We decide to take a case of several different types of food and try those before we go to the work of hauling it all back to the settlement only to find out it is no good.

We are carrying the food out to the truck when I hear a voice behind me that sounds very familiar. I know without looking that it is the guy who was the leader of the settlement until yesterday. One of the settlement people is walking next to me. He turns to look and tells me that's Harry. I never heard his name, but I have no reason to believe that this is going to be a friendly visit. I am stalling, trying to figure out how I can drop the boxes I am carrying and get my gun out of the holster I keep it in.

5

I can hear either him or someone else walking toward me from the rear. Just as I am about to turn and throw the boxes at them I hear Harry's voice asking me if I can use a hand. He says it looks like quite a load of food. The settlement can really use it. I tell him I have this load, but if he would like to help there is plenty more inside. He looks behind him and tells someone to come and help load the truck. As they walk past me it looks like the group that we overthrew yesterday. We get more than we were planning to get, but it is beginning to look like we may need it.

When the truck is loaded Harry comes over to me and extends his hand to shake mine. Naturally I shake his hand and ask him why the sudden change of heart. He tells me I will never believe it. He tells us that when they left yesterday they were thinking of ways to get even with us, but they saw how easily we handled Guy and Sam so that kind of made them think twice before starting something. They spent the night in a store that was totally empty and didn't really get much sleep. But once Harry got to sleep he says his grandma came to him in a dream and yelled at him good for taking advantage of those people. She told him that if he didn't straighten up she would come back and tan his hide good.

He looks at us and sheepishly says that he told us we would never believe it. We all tell him we have no reason to doubt him. Sara asks him if he left any family behind in the other world. He thinks for a minute and says not really. He never had any real family after his grandma passed away when he was thirteen. He never knew his parents and he was put in foster homes after grandma passed away. He wasn't treated badly, but he was never loved either, so when he turned seventeen he lied about his age and joined the army. They didn't look too closely at the birth certificate he gave them.

Since then he has been going wherever he was stationed until he wound up here. When we are in the bus they show us where they found twenty more members for the settlement. They board the bus too quickly for me to tell how many men and how many women there are, but I do know there are several children in this new group. We stop at several restaurants on the way back and find canned foods in every one. We also find eight more people that would like to join us. We decide to head back to the settlement and make sure that there is enough time to cook the stew for this evening's meal.

When we are back at the mansion we can already smell the stew cooking. Carrie and Ken got it started while we were all gone. Now the other women will help Carrie make it a complete meal. Ken has the venison all cut up and in the refrigerator to keep it fresh. We figure that now is as good a time to try some of the dehydrated foods that we found. Harry and the other men that rejoined us smell the venison and mention that they haven't eaten since yesterday morning. Dayna takes pity on them and cooks some venison and we also try some of the freeze dried vegetables to go with it.

Everything we open is good so far. Even the powdered milk, although you will never convince me that any powdered milk is good. Our new group members think everything they have eaten is great and the children love the milk. I can't wait until they get to try fresh milk from a cow. I always tell Dayna that if Heavenly Father had wanted us to drink milk from a can he would have put udders on the cans. Naturally I am only kidding and she doesn't hit me too hard when I say it so she knows I am kidding. We unload the truck into the mansion and ask for volunteers to go back to get more food and perhaps more people.

We are happy to see that just about every able bodied man and most of the women volunteer to go with us. Some of them can't go because they have children to watch over. Ken says he would like to go with us so Gary stays here to make sure everything is okay. There are some projects that need to be done anyway so Gary gets some of the men and women to help him while we go back to town. We load the truck to capacity again and load the bus with as much as we can and still leave some room for people if we find them. One store we found that Sara was very excited about is one that sold commercial cooking equipment like stoves, grills, wheat mills, and pretty much anything a restaurant would need.

We cross a large river, which I think is the Thames. Sam, one of the young men who came back to the group tells us that he has caught a lot of fish in the river and they are very good to eat. That is very good news because fishing can be a great way to relax and catch a great dinner while doing it. We are on our way home when I see two things that I have been looking for all afternoon. One of them is a small group of people who hide in a building with a sign that says Fish and Chips. Ken says that sounds like a great idea. He would really enjoy a plate of fish and chips right about now.

Some of our new friends convince the people in the store to join us. While they are doing this I am checking out the other thing I saw. It's a sporting goods store and if nothing else it will have fishing gear and probably bows and arrows that we can use for hunting. We do find a bunch of archery equipment and fishing equipment, but what I am interested in is seeing if there is a trap door in here some place. Actually one of the children we just found finds what I am looking for. There are a bunch of books about fish and animals that are on the floor in piles. The children want some of those books so they can look at the pictures. One little girl about eight moves one of the piles and tells me that there is a handle on the floor and points to it.

We find a couple of empty boxes to put the books in and then we open the door in the floor. We almost always carry flashlights with us, so we can go down the stairs leading to a room below. Now this could just be a basement or it could be where the owner kept items he didn't want just anyone to see. It turns out to be the latter. There is a pretty decent stash of guns and ammunition for them. We haul as many as we can get now up and load them into the bus. We hide the opening again and plan to come back tomorrow to empty the place out.

When we get back to the mansion we find that the others have returned and they are about as excited as they can be. For one thing they shot a large bull, several pheasants, rabbits and two more deer. They also have a very nice stake body truck that they found. We take the opportunity to teach some of our new friends how to skin the animals and birds and how to quarter the large animals for hanging and how to cut up the rabbits to be cooked. The pheasants we cleaned and put them in the refrigerator to be roasted probably tomorrow. When that is done we can finally sit down to eat the delicious meal that we have been smelling since we got within a mile of here.

The ladies not only made the stew today, they made some great biscuits with some of the flour we brought with us and some from the food we found today. It was in cans that were still sealed so they tried some of it and it tastes as good as the fresh flour we brought with us.

The only thing missing is the butter, but from what the other group is telling us we may be able to fix that soon. While we are eating we have six more people come up to the gate and ask if they could join us. This is two men, two women and two children. They are surprised when we have food enough for them as well. They tell us they saw the bus and the truck coming this way, but when they smelled the food they started praying that we would have enough for them as well, at least enough for the children.

Most of the people here tell us that this is the best meal they can remember having. We tell them that they can eat like this every night if they are willing to work for it. Gary tells us that leads perfectly into what he wants to show us. It's still light enough out to go out the gate and around the fence to an area that at least I have not seen yet. We can see that this used to be farm land or at least land where crops were grown probably back before the war. There is a section of about three acres that have been recently plowed. When I say recently I mean this afternoon. I ask where they found the equipment and who did the plowing. That's one job that Gary does not like to do back home.

Gary points to an older lady named Minerva. She says all she did is drive the tractor. Then she says that is after she showed the men how to hook up the plow, but that was after she showed them how to hook up the brush hog. She says it's a good thing they found more than one tractor. She showed one of the young men how to drive the tractor with the brush hog to cut down the weeds so she could plow it. After it was cut the grass was moved to the outside of the field and put into large piles to possibly feed any livestock we may get. She says she will disk the ground tomorrow if it doesn't rain too much.

The other group that went to those cottages we spoke of yesterday say that they didn't have as good a day as they did here, but they did find at least three barns where there is farm equipment and they also found at least twenty houses in what appears to be a village along with several farms around the village. They started cleaning out some of the homes and they were surprised at how well they have held up against the elements here. That starts some conversation that we were planning to have anyway. We tell the people that what we are proposing is that they break up into two groups that form one settlement.

They are afraid to split their numbers in two even though most of them didn't know the others existed until yesterday and today. We point out the advantages of being in two places even though it may be more difficult to defend. We also remind them that we will be here with them to teach them how to be self sufficient as long as they need us. Minerva and some of the others say that they lived on farms before the war and they can't see why they can't do that work again. A couple of them say that they can't believe that they didn't think of doing that earlier. They have grown small gardens, but didn't plant enough to sustain them. We tell them that starting tomorrow that is going to change.

Before we turn in for the night we tell them to think about it and tomorrow we will start making our settlements real homes for them. Some of us go back to the plane to sleep. Kristi and Jenny come with us as well. They say they just feel much safer with us so we don't mind. Sara tells me that we really need to find some aviation fuel to make sure the plane is ready to go if we need to. We can't think of any reasons why we would have to leave quickly, but there is no sense putting it off any longer. We decide that we will go looking for a truck or a tank of fuel that we can use.

During the night I wake up and I could swear I heard someone or something trying the side door on the plane. It is locked so I am not overly worried, but I am concerned because we have no idea what the roving gangs are like here, yet. Dayna and I have discussed this topic and we are both sure we will find out soon enough what they are like. We only hope we can be as successful against them as we have been back home. I hear the noise again and this time Dayna reaches over and touching my arm she points to the door, then to the window where we can see a face looking in.

We cannot see it clearly because it is dark and we are sure they cannot see in for the same reason. I have my 9mm automatic in my hand in case someone tries to break out a window. We hear more than see them go from window to window trying to see in, but finally they go away and we can go back to sleep. This is when I revert back to when I was on the seal team. When we were on a mission, if we got to sleep it was always with one eye open. In the morning Kristi says that she heard someone around the doors and windows last night. She says she knows Dayna and I were awake so she didn't worry about it too much.

When I go to open the door she tells me I may want to look around before going out. The gangs have been known to wait for people outside where they are living. I was going to do that anyway, but her statement makes me doubly careful. When I open the door there are people waiting outside alright. There is a man, a woman, and two children wrapped up in blankets sleeping against the rear wheels of the plane. The man wakes up when I tell Dayna and the others what I have found. He tells me that he hopes they are not being too forward coming to us this way.

He says he and his family came to London hoping to find a settlement. They have survived with another couple north of here, but they woke up two days ago and their friends were gone. We invite them to join us and while they get warm in the plane Gary and I go looking for fuel. We don't have to go very far. There is a truck full of aviation fuel not a hundred yards away, but it was hidden behind one of the hangars. Again it is a diesel truck so Gary says he can probably have it running within the hour. While he is tinkering with that, Sara comes out and joins me looking for whatever we can find.

It isn't long when we hear the sound of a diesel engine coming to life. It sputters a little, but straightens right out after a few minutes of running. Sara and I find a portable gas powered compressor that we get running so we take it over to the truck to see if the tires will hold air. If they don't we will probably just drive it over anyway. Luckily they do and we are able to drive the truck over to the C-130 and fill the tanks again. We also found some gas pumps inside the hangar we were looking in. That will help with the van and the other vehicles we brought with us. As soon as we have completed our tasks we head over to the mansion.

Apparently our new friends have decided that everyone should get to see the other option before they make up their minds. That sounds fair to me. This morning for breakfast we cook oatmeal that we brought with us, but there is also a bunch of it in the dehydrated foods we found. I like mine just with sugar on it, but there is powdered milk to put on it if someone wants to. Most do along with the sugar, this is the first time many of them have ever tasted sugar. When we finish eating and cleaning up we decide that some of us will stay here and work on getting some crops in the ground.

Another group will take a bus load of the people who have not been to the other site to see which they prefer. Minerva asks if she can go to see the cottages because it sounds exactly like what she has always wanted. I tell her to go ahead. Ken and I can handle the disking and possibly even plow a couple more acres. We put the people that are left here to work raking up the long grass and piling it in piles like yesterday. Ken is going to drive the brush hog and I am going to drive the tractor with the plow after I disk the already plowed ground. When that is done we hook up a planter that we find in the barn and try our luck with some winter wheat seed that we brought with us.

When that is done I hook up the plow and do a couple more acres. Harry and two of his friends took the van today to look for more people and to hopefully find some more food. Some of our other friends spend part of the day scouring the area around us looking for more cottages or anything useful. They come back with baskets of vegetables that they found in gardens around just about all the cottages they found. The good news is that they say there are a lot more to be picked yet. When we finish plowing and disking the acreage that we wanted to for today we start looking for ways to maintain electricity to the mansion without using the propane generator.

We can pretty much rule out solar energy except possibly as a way to augment the power. We have gotten great results from windmills using some of the newer technology thanks to our scientific people. The more we talk about it the more we feel that we have to try using windmills. One of the young ladies in the group who is about ten had been reading a book and when she hears us mention windmills she brings over the book to show us the pictures in it. Several of the other group members come over to see what windmills look like. Several of them tell us they saw things that look like this at the cottages they went to today.

We are happy to hear that, but not really surprised. To generate enough electricity to keep the mansion maintained will take either several windmills or perhaps we could do it with just a few if we separate the circuits. We agree that it will be better to wait to talk to James and Jenna before we start doing something that may be a waste of time. While we are talking Harry and his group pull into the yard with four more people and the van packed with more canned foods. I was half expecting him to take off with the van and not come back. When he comes over to tell me about their adventures he asks me if I am surprised to see him.

I smile and tell him not as much surprised as relieved. I tell him honestly that these people are going to need someone with his experience to sustain them after we leave. I add that the best way to lead people is by example. If they see that he is willing to do any of the jobs that will become necessary, it takes any excuses they might have had for not wanting to do them. He tells me he has been thinking quite a bit about how we can get away from being dependant on the propane for electricity. He says that he is sure we have already thought about it, but we could do it with windmills if we do it correctly.

Tim and I are getting his opinion of how we may be able to use windmills when the rest of our group gets home. The bus is quite a bit emptier than it was when it left this morning. LT tells us that he is glad that Kathy is not here or they may be staying for good. He says that when most of our new friends saw the cottages they decided that they were going no farther. James laughs and says that right now thirty-four of our group members are living in three of the cottages until we can get more wind mills and electrical wiring functioning properly. We will discuss that over dinner. It looks like we are starting to be a group.

6

Our wandering friends return with a nice bull that they shot on their way back. They wouldn't have shot it, but it was standing right in the middle of the road and when they beeped at it to move, it charged the bus. They take us to the front of the bus to show us where the bull hit them. It's not as large as some of them we have back home, but I bet it weighs well over a thousand pounds field dressed. I can see that the shot that killed it went in right behind the ear. I ask who shot it and James points his thumb at Jenna. Jenna is not exactly our best hunter although she has gone hunting and has brought back meat.

She laughs and tells us that she is trying to figure out how we can get one of these busses home and she didn't want that beast to wreck this one. We all laugh about that. Our friends ask if this kind of meat is as good as the other kind. Jenna, who is not really fond of venison, tells them that it is much better. Now we all start teasing her saying that we know why she shot that poor bull. She wanted some beef rather than venison. We have been so busy talking that we forgot that some of our friends are not here with us.

We start looking for them when we start to smell meat cooking. We find them in the kitchen and they are cooking the pheasants and rabbits that were brought in the other day. They tell us they may not know how to cook large animals, but these they know exactly what to do with them. It appears that we may not have quite enough to go around so those of us who know how to shoot a gun and hunt go looking for some more rabbits and pheasants. We don't have to go far although we don't like hunting this close to where they will be living. The additions to our dinner get cleaned and put on the spit to roast.

I didn't notice it before, but the mansion has a large grill right in the kitchen. It is designed for use with wood or charcoal. Obviously someone who lived here enjoyed their food cooked this way. They will not get any complaints from me or anyone else in our new family. When we start eating Sara says that this would be even better with some of our barbeque sauce on it. Harry asks if we really make our own barbeque sauce. Sara tells him that we make pretty much everything we had in the other world including hot dogs and pretty much any kind of sausage he could want.

He says that he has a pretty mean Buffalo chicken sauce recipe. The same little girl who showed us the windmills goes over to another book and turns to a picture in this one. She shows it to us and asks if we really have chickens in America that are that large. She has a picture of a Buffalo in the book. At first LT tells her that would be a small one. When she looks shocked, he laughs and tells her that the chickens are normal size. The sauce that Harry is talking about kind of originated in a city named Buffalo. She says she would love to have some chickens for eggs and they taste really good as well. She has only tasted it once and she has never had a real egg, but she just knows they would taste wonderful.

The other children agree with her. Dayna tells them that after dinner we will see what we can do about getting some chickens. She told me earlier that she saw some signs of them and that she is sure she saw at least a couple of them while we were raking up the cut grass. The mansion has a large barn that is just outside the fence near the back of the property. Dayna says she saw what appeared to be nests where chickens could have lived. Several of the young people and even some of the not so young people eat in a hurry so that they can go out to learn how to catch chickens. Just about all of us go out to the barn to get started. Dayna shows everyone how to clean out the nests and how to put new grass in them to make them more appealing. Then she takes a can and dips some seeds out of a bag that says of all things, Chicken Feed.

Several others do the same thing then follow Dayna out toward the wooded area not far away. We go right into the woods and look to see if we can find any tracks or other signs of where chickens may be. When we find what we are looking for Dayna starts trickling the feed as we walk out of the woods. The others were going to do the same thing until Dayna explained that they will drop their feed along the path leading to the barn and right into the coop where we cleaned the nests. The children are really excited about this. Surprisingly three of the girls that are either wives or girlfriends of the former leaders ask if they can help take care of the chickens when we get some.

Several of the younger children, mostly girls, ask if they can help as well. Carrie tells them that she has had a lot of experience with the chickens we have and would love to help them get started. We drop the feed all the way back and into the barn and coop just like we wanted to. Some of the people want to stay out here and watch to see if any of the chickens follow the trail in. The girls explain that it may take a while before the chickens even find the food we left so it would be better to check it in the morning. They reluctantly come back into the house. It is getting dark out so we fire up the generator and have lights for a while before bed time.

Just like when we first started we are using this time to teach our new friends how to read. It is even easier than it was then because several of our new friends can already read. We realize that we have to find at least one good library to get books from. Another thing to add to our to do list for tomorrow. This evening we find out that some of our friends are of the same faith that we are. The young man and his family that we met this morning are reading from the Book of Mormon, which is one of the books we use. I ask him about it and he says that they are hoping to find a new Bible because the one they had somehow got lost in their travels.

There are at least six others that say they are Latter Day Saints as well. The new families ask if they should sleep here in the common room tonight. We are embarrassed that we didn't show them the rooms that are empty so that they could choose one. They are all impressed that they will be able to have the privacy of their own rooms. So far every room that I have seen here has its own bathroom as well. When everyone has gone to their rooms for the night, Dayna and the other women in our group mention that we have to get some hot water heaters working soon so that people can shower and clean up. We agree that will be at the top of the list of things to do in the morning.

Some of us are getting ready to go back to the plane when Jenna reminds me that she is serious about trying to take one of those busses home with us. She asks me if I could measure the opening in the plane to see if one of those busses will fit. I was planning to do that anyway, Dayna already asked if it would be possible to take one home with us. She laughed when she said it earlier. She told me that she has read in many books about people taking souvenirs home from vacations. She wants a double-decker bus for a souvenir is all. Just looking at the cargo door of the plane I am pretty sure we will not be able to just drive one in. We will have to see if we can take one apart.

We have no unexpected visitors tonight. In the morning we go back to the mansion and get started on our day. The young people are excited to show us that they now have twenty-six chickens sitting in the coop and they don't seem to be in any hurry to leave. The important thing is that there is at least one rooster with them. That's how they found out the chickens are here. That rooster crowed early this morning waking many of the people up. Now that they have some chickens we need to build a pen for them to move around in, but so that predators can't get at them. The young lady with her books shows us a picture of a chicken pen so we tell some of the young men that is their project for as long as it takes.

These are very busy times as we try to do everything we can to help our new friends become self sufficient. We make trips to the library, to different stores in search of food and other necessities. We also find a record player and a large bunch of records that we take back to the mansion. We also found one for the people that are settling the cottages. Whatever we get for this group we also get for the other group. Harry and the other guys that were the leaders are proving to be very valuable to the settlements getting organized. It seems that we only have to show them something once and they learn how to do it to help others.

Apparently Harry was in the same group in the Army as Ken was, which is the Army Corp. of Engineers. He has had a lot of experience with electrical work and helped James rewire the mansion so that it could be broken up into four zones that are covered by windmills now. There were some electrical problems at the cottages that he was able to help with as well. James is usually very good with electrical problems, but over here they use totally different voltages and frequencies. Harry was stationed in Germany for a while and had the opportunity to work with it as well as having been trained in the difference.

Sam and Guy, who if you remember were Harrys bodyguards, love driving the tractors and getting the ground ready to be planted. Since it is fall we can't plant any crops other than winter wheat, but that is not stopping them from plowing several acres of land in both locations. We have had several groups of people come to us and we have found several other small groups that have been living in the northern part of London. We found a family of four in one of the libraries we visited and it turned out to be the friends of the family that we met outside the plane a few mornings ago.

Apparently they got separated one day when they went looking for food and couldn't get back to the others because a group of guys on motorcycles got between them and they had to hide until they went away. When they finally got back to where they had been living their friends were gone and they were afraid that the group of what we refer to as predators got them. We are on a heightened alert because we know sooner or later we are going to have to deal with at least some of the predators. I have already set up a spot on the roof of the mansion where I have a good field to fire from if it comes to that.

I almost forgot to tell you that our chicken population has increased greatly in the last couple of days and it doesn't appear that the chickens are interested in going back to the wild. We have a good group of young ladies and even a couple of young men want to help out with them. Some of our new friends were very much surprised because the other morning when they woke up we had four cows with calves standing in the yard at the mansion. At first some of our new friends were afraid of them, but we put them into the enclosed area behind the barn, fed them plenty of the cut grass we have an abundance of and they seem to be about as happy as they can be.

Luckily some of the people in the settlement know a lot more about cows than I do because now the children have all the milk they want and we even have some left to make butter with. The people settling the area we now call The Cottages tell us that they are doing the same things we are and having as much luck as we are. These people have had a settlement before, but they didn't know how to go about becoming self sustaining. Now they are learning that part of it and they are really excited about it.

We now have a radio set up in both locations that they can communicate long distances with and we also showed them about using the Citizens Band radios to communicate over relatively short distances like when they are away in the city or even between groups. They have base stations in many of the cottages and the mansion has several base stations located where someone can hear them in case there is some sort of emergency or even just to let each other know what is going on during the day.

We noticed that many of our new friends were wearing clothing that was not sufficient for the changes in the weather so we brought the clothing we brought with us for them to use. You would have thought it is Christmas when we showed them the cases of clothes that we brought. The camouflage clothing is very popular back in our groups and it is here as well. We also brought several cases of military uniforms that the people seem to really enjoy wearing. It's great watching everyone walking around now wearing new clothes and shoes or boots. They also have very nice cold weather gear as well now.

One of our groups that were out looking for more people found an outdoor store here that was loaded with clothing and other supplies that they will need as they grow. It took two days to empty that store, but we did it and now we have a couple warehouses full of extra clothing and other supplies. Right now we are using trailers from large trucks for warehouses because we don't have any outbuildings that are clean enough for the purpose. We are showing them how to take metal buildings apart and set them up where they are needed. That excites some of our people as much as it does some of us back home.

We have been traveling around a little in pretty much every direction. We found at least three more nice places for the settlements to grow if they need to and it looks like they will need to in the not too distant future. We finally found some pigs here. The ones we found are not quite as big as the ones we have back home, but they are still quite large for a pig. The one that we shot dressed out at just about six hundred pounds, which means it probably weighed around eight-fifty to nine hundred pounds on the hoof. We have been here now for two weeks and it is difficult to remember how inept these people seemed when we first got here.

The elected leaders of the settlement at the mansion and the leaders in the cottage settlement asked us if they could go fishing to catch their supper this afternoon. We tell them it's their settlement, we are guests in their home, but we would love to try our luck fishing as well. As soon as the young men who are assigned to clean the stalls of the cows heard we are going fishing and we need some worms for bait, they dug through the pile of manure and straw that they have cleaned out. Luckily their moms taught them about germs and staying at least somewhat clean. They have rubber gloves that they wear anytime they have to clean the stalls then they wash their hands.

Each settlement now has their own double-decker bus. We need both of them to get everybody that wants to fish to the river. When we get to the river Sam and Guy tell us they can show us the best places to fish. Some of the other people have fished here as well and they have their favorite places. Most of us just spread out along the bank and try our luck. Pretty much everybody from our group loves to fish. Some of the local people like to use lures, but the majority of us are using worms.

It doesn't take long before people are catching fish. Some of the fish being caught are familiar to us, but they are catching some that I have never seen before. A couple of the children brought books along that have pretty much every species of fish that are in British waters, so they are busy finding out what the different fish are. Dayna hooks a very large pike that puts up a good battle, but Dayna wins. LT hooks a very large eel that we think is a snake until Minerva tells us that is probably the best eating fish we caught today. We tell her we will take her word for it, if she wants it, she can have it.

It doesn't take long to catch enough fish for a good meal for both groups. When the fish are all cleaned and ready to be cooked several people ask how we cook fish. Some people like it grilled or baked, but most of our group back home likes it deep fried. We made lard by rendering the fat on that pig we got so we show the groups how to dip the fish in flour and deep fry it, at least some of it. It appears that everybody tries at least some of the fish cooked all three ways and all of them like it at least enough to have it again sometime for supper.

During supper we discuss the need to go farther in pretty much every direction looking for people as well as things that they either need now or will need soon. It's decided that LT and I will take a small group and go north since that's the direction the predators were last seen. None of us can believe that we haven't had any trouble with the roving bands, yet. Not that we are complaining, but if they are leaving us alone it probably means they have easier people to go after. Harry, Sam, and Guy want to go with LT and me. Naturally Dayna says she is going wherever I go. I know better than to argue about it. Besides I enjoy having her with me and she is as good a fighter as most men I have known.

Our new friends have been learning how to defend themselves and are doing quite well at it so far. Each group that is going out looking will be taking guns and supplies to last several days in case they are needed. We discussed having all the groups go out at one time, but we decided that it might be better if we go out one or two at a time. That's in case they run into something bigger than they can handle. There will be some of us home to help. The first group going out has Sara and Gary and James and Jenna going with them. We found some satellite phones in some of the outdoor stores we have discovered. The groups are taking one with them so that they can communicate if they get out of range for CB radios.

7

The weather has changed from having temperatures in the mid sixties to being in the mid to high forties and it is overcast and drizzly out quite a bit. The first group is going to go south and then go east along the coastline looking for whatever and whoever they can find. The first day out they run into three small groups that were headed for London because they thought there would be more food available there. There are enough people with the group for them to send one of them back with the new people and rejoin them tomorrow.

It's a good thing that we started getting those new settlements ready to be inhabited. We have volunteers to move to the new settlements to assist the new people that will be settling there. The first group makes it to the coast and heads back going close to the shore line to find any settlements along there. They are taking a criss-cross pattern to make sure they don't miss anybody. This turns out to be a good strategy because they do find some people struggling to survive not more than ten miles from the settlements. They also find several places that look very good for the settlements to obtain some much needed supplies.

The next group goes west and follows much the same pattern of criss-crossing the area until they reach the west coast and then work the area that they haven't seen yet on the way back. They are only gone a little over an hour when we get a call that they have found a military base. We knew there was one southwest of London, but we didn't know exactly where until now. They are going to continue looking for people and other important items so we are going to make a trip over to the base and see what we can use. I don't think I mentioned it earlier, but the settlements now have a couple of box trucks to haul our treasures in.

We are taking both of them and we will not be surprised if we have to try to get another one started. One thing I know Harry and the other young men are looking for is a couple of military jeeps that they can mount a machine gun and if possible a rocket launcher like our dune buggies. We have been joking around about that for the last week. We get to the base and it is one of those that had both American soldiers and British soldiers stationed here. This particular base was an

Air Force base. When Sara sees the huge hangars on the base she is thinking about another C-130 or possibly maybe even a bomber.

There is one bomber in the hangar along with several helicopters and some smaller planes. We were hoping to find a plane that has more range than the C-130 for the trip home. The one bomber here is an HS-780 Andover which has just about the same range as the C-130. We leave Sara and Gary to check out the helicopters while the rest of us look for other treasures. We see some warehouses and that seems like a good place to start. We find pretty much what we expected. There are cases of uniforms, bedding, cold weather gear, weapons and ammunition, and all the necessities of life in the military and civilian life.

There is a very nice truck in the warehouse with a twenty-six foot box on it that would carry a whole bunch of stuff for us. LT and I start working on the truck while some of the others head over to the Base Exchange and the commissary to see what may be available there. They find lots of treasures there. There are clothes, uniforms, K-Bar knives, candy, food, pretty much anything a soldier could want. LT and I get the truck running good enough to get it back to the settlements so we start loading this one with the items we need from the warehouse. The other trucks are being loaded with items from the Base Exchange and the commissary.

Dayna has been helping the settlers get the most important items first and we can come back for the other items. She comes to the warehouse and tells me she found another warehouse on the other side of the base that is marked top secret on it. She tells me that she knows she shouldn't have, but she went in and found a large number of guns that they must have been testing or something. I ask her if they happened to have one of the fifty caliber guns like the one I have back home. Actually I have more than one back home, but I will take another one if I can find it. She tells me that she is pretty sure there is a case of them along with enough ammunition to fight a small war.

LT and I have to see this. When we walk in both of us say that we will take one of every gun in the building. Actually we are going to take every gun on this base. It will not be today, but we will get them before someone else finds them. This base has dozens if not hundreds of Quonset huts on it and they seem to be in good condition. We tell the local people how much our people enjoy living in those and they say that they can see why. We go looking for a flatbed truck to haul the huts back on sometime in the future. There are several warehouses on the base so we go to them one at a time.

It appears that some of them were for the Americans supplies and some were for the British soldiers. Either way there are enough uniforms and other clothes to last the settlements for years to come. It may not seem important to some people, but there is also enough toilet paper, light bulbs, cleaning supplies, paper towels, mops, buckets, and even paint. Sara and Gary get the helicopter running, but there is no hurry so they concentrate on getting another box truck running. I almost forgot to mention that in the top secret warehouse we also found some of the dune buggies and motorcycles like we have.

We will work on getting those running probably tomorrow or the day after. As it is we have four fully loaded trucks full of supplies that the settlements can use desperately. Both settlements have at least one cottage that they have cleaned out to be used as a warehouse for extra items that they obtain. We have also stressed the importance of having someone keep track of what is in the warehouses and keep a record of who takes what and when. Most of the people in the groups only want what they absolutely need, but there are always some who like to have things just for the sake of having them.

It takes the remainder of the day to get everything cataloged and put away. Some want to go back today for a second load, but it will be dark soon and we prefer not to travel in the dark any more than we have to. We get a call from our friends that are traveling to tell us that they have found some people who would like to join the group. Today they made it to Stonehenge and Bath. They could have gone farther, but they spent time in both places looking for people and for supplies. They found both. They are taking the time to get another vehicle running and will send the new people back with the supplies while they go on.

The next morning we go back to the military base and load all four trucks again. When we get back home the new group has been here for about a half hour. The local people are proudly showing them around. The new people are very much impressed. They help us get the trucks unloaded in time for us to go get another load. With this load we should have pretty much everything that we need right now. The rest can wait until we have more space to store it. Our group calls again this evening saying that they found more people and more supplies. They went to more cities today, but the only one I am familiar with is Bristol.

Again they are going to get a vehicle running and send the people and supplies back with it. They still have a lot of area to cover, but they think they can be home either tomorrow evening or the next day fairly early. With the new addition to the groups we decide to open the third group which is just a little over a mile from both of the other groups. They form kind of a triangle which works good for them because they can plant crops in between the groups. They can also fill in the edges of the boundaries and possibly be touching to become one large group geographically as well as spiritually.

As with our settlements we go in and get the places cleaned up, get the electricity working properly, make sure the well works and has good water, then make sure the stoves and refrigerators work properly. I know that sounds like a lot of work, but with the people we have we can do as many as three or four houses in a day. One of the reasons we can do that is because as soon as we find out what houses we are working on, each group of specialists goes to work doing what they do best. At least what they do best for this week. They all agreed to switch jobs every week if they are busy and whenever makes sense when they are not busy getting homes ready.

Today we added a new crew. They are the ones who will start dismantling the Quonset huts and moving them to the settlements as homes. Harry is heading this group up because he has already had experience putting the huts together on bases and stations in other places. I am also helping with this project at least for today. Some of the guys start taking the nuts and bolts off by hand when we show them the air tools that were in the base maintenance area. All we have to do is bring in three or four gas operated compressors. The people working on them are trying to keep all the nuts and bolts until I show them several large boxes of the right size nuts and bolts to put them back together.

LT, Sara, and Gary get a flat bed truck running well enough for us to use when we get the first one down. We are pretty close to that when we call it quits for today. From experience we know how much of one of the huts we can get on a single truck. We start loading at a point we know well and load the panels on top of each other until the rest of the hut is on the truck. Then when we get it back to where we are putting it, we can start assembling as we take the panels off the truck. We put them on a cement slab that we pour ahead of time. We measured a couple of the huts to make sure they are the same and another crew started working on the slab today as well.

Our wanderers did not get back yesterday, but they do get back just after lunch today. We are all excited to see the level of success they had on their journey. Some of their success is very tangible and can be seen by the number of new friends they brought and sent back. They also had some very good luck finding supplies that will be very welcome during the coming winter. The rest of us are planning to leave in the morning for our trip. We have divided the northern part of our adventure into three parts for now. We realize that there may already be a settlement or possibly even more the farther north we go. We will give anyone we find the opportunity to join this settlement, but if they already have one of their own they may not want to.

We finish the afternoon helping take down the last of the first Quonset hut, then we go back to the settlement and help them pour the foundation. LT and Harry were able to get a good sized excavator and a back hoe running so the work on the foundation went very smoothly. Sara and Gary found a very large cement mixer truck along with some huge piles of top soil, sand, and gravel not far from the settlement. After some looking we found where they used to load the cement into the truck from these huge silo-like bins that are still almost all full. We had to break through the outer shell, but then it flowed perfectly. That will save dumping about two hundred bags of cement mix into the mixer by hand.

Once the cement is mixed, all that is left is to pour it and level it. Naturally we have to wait for it to harden then we can put some expansion cuts in it to prevent it from cracking. This settlement is a little bit ahead of where we were at this time in our development. They have people that did most of the work that has to be done before the war. They are getting older, but they are excited to be using these skills again and being able to teach younger people their craft. We spend the evening listening to the adventures of those who just got back. There are still several truckloads of supplies over that way. They are planning to go back for them while we are gone.

We spend the rest of our evening getting ready for our adventure. There is not much to get ready. We are only planning to be gone three, maybe four days. We are planning to take one of the dune buggies and one motorcycle along with the van and one of the double-decker busses and the twenty-six foot box truck. I'm not sure whether or not I mentioned it, but we are not going to be able to take one of those busses back with us. It won't fit on the plane, but someone found an old newspaper article that said two authentic busses were sent to an amusement park in Florida before the war obviously. I'll give you three guesses where we are going when we get back to the states.

As tired as I am you would think I would sleep like a baby tonight, but I am lying here wide awake thinking about what we may run into in the next few days. We are all aware that we will probably at least see some of the predators that have attacked the settlement in the past. Since none of the others did, it stands to reason that we will. I am not afraid to meet them, but with Dayna and Sara along I worry about them getting hurt, especially if there is gunfire. I am bringing my fifty caliber and a very nice .308 that I have used for hunting quite a bit and I trust it totally. I am also bringing my Sig Sauer and a .44 magnum revolver. LT is bringing pretty much the same arsenal with him so we should be ready for just about anything.

I must fall asleep because the next thing I know is Dayna waking me up with a kiss and telling me that I can't sleep all day even if it does sound inviting. We loaded most of our supplies last evening so we just throw the rest of them in the van and get ready to head north. LT comes over and tells me just loud enough for me to hear him that he wishes Tim was with us on this trip. I know what he means. It's always nice to have people that you can count on when there is impending danger. I know Gary and Dayna and Sara can both shoot as well as any man I ever saw. I assure LT that everyone in our group can fight, even the local members of our adventure have been doing very well with their self defense classes and can all shoot a gun.

We start out heading into London and pretty much starting this adventure at the northern most point we have been in the city. London is such a big city that it would be very easy to pass people less than a block or two away, so we are looking for smoke to possibly show us where some people may be. It is a cold overcast day so there is a good possibility that some people may build a fire to stay warm. LT is driving the dune buggy and I am riding the motorcycle at least to start the day. We have some very good cold weather gear that is also waterproof so we are not uncomfortable.

We find some supplies at a couple of restaurants that we load into the truck. We decide that since we are still fairly close to the settlement that we will save our space in the truck for when we are farther away. We find some places that we definitely want to look into further, but in the interest of time we decide to mark where they are on the map and come back. I am out in front of our little parade, we turn a corner and I see what appears to be a man, a woman, and some children duck into a building up ahead.

Rather than have me go after them and probably scare them even more, I call Dayna on my CB radio and tell them what I just saw. She is driving the van today with a couple of women from the local group. They drive past me and up to about fifty feet from the building the people went into. The three women get out and call to the people inside that we do not want to hurt them, we are here to help them if they would like us to. The woman in the building recognizes one of the women with us so she asks how we can help them. She explains about the settlement and invites them to join us.

They say that if what we are telling them is the truth, they definitely want to join us. Sara spots a car dealership that sells cars called Mini Cooper. She says if we can't take a bus back with us, she is taking one of these cars back with us. There is a whole showroom full of them so we feel fairly confident that we can get at least one running. Harry is with us and he wants one for the settlement. We mark that dealership on our map and continue with our new friends riding in the van. Dayna calls me on the CB and tells me that the man we just picked up with his family told them that they had to make their way around a band of men not too far from here.

I am glad he told us, now we know approximately where we may expect to run into them. I am watching ahead and to the right and LT is also watching ahead, but he is watching to the left to make sure we don't miss too much. LT signals us to halt and tells me that he saw some smoke coming from a chimney about three blocks over. I decide to leave my motorcycle and check it out on foot. Harry wants to go with me to make sure if it is a trap at least one of us can go for help. It makes sense, but we also have some small short range radios that we can communicate with for about a quarter mile or a little more.

The blocks in this area are not very long, but they are filled pretty full of houses and apartment buildings. We get to the spot that LT told us he saw smoke and we can see it coming from a small apartment building across the street from where we are. I tell Harry to wait here and I will get a closer look. I get to a window that looks into the ground floor and I can see a woman and three children huddled around a fireplace in the building. I look around closely to see if there is anyone else around and do not see anyone. I let Dayna know what I have discovered and she is on her way to see if we can help these people.

Dayna and the local women get here and we knock on the door to talk to the young lady. I am still watching through the window and can see the young lady gather the children and try to hide in another room. Dayna opens the door and tells her that no one is going to hurt her or the children. She explains about the settlement and introduces her and the children to our newest friends. I think what finally seals the agreement is the biscuits and preserves that Dayna offers them. The children who range in age from about four to eight ask if there is more of this kind of food at the settlement. We tell them they can eat them every day if they want to. We now have four more friends to add to the settlement.

8

Approximately an hour after we find our new friends we find a military base. This one shows signs that someone has been here, but they didn't take very much from it. Or at least if they did take a lot, it isn't readily noticeable. We go to the Base Exchange and we can see where someone broke some of the display cases to get at certain things, but the stock room doesn't look like it has been touched. We tell the new people to find as many new clothes as they would like and to be sure to get some cold weather gear. Since there are so many children, Dayna and Sara help them find what they need and some things that they just like a lot.

Sara finds several cases of canned chocolate candy and says she has to make sure it is good enough to give to the children. She wouldn't want them to get sick from eating bad candy. We call the settlement and ask them if they think it's worth it for us to load the truck we have with us from the base and bring it back before proceeding or if we should wait until the way back. In one of the warehouses we find literally thousands of institutional sized cans of food. There are vegetables, meats, grains, cereals, powdered milk, you name it and it is probably here. There are also several hundred cases of dehydrated and freeze dried foods.

This added to what we have already found will give the settlement enough food to get them through the winter even if they double in number. We load the truck we brought with us, while Gary and Sara work on getting another large military truck running. This one is an eighteen wheeler with a sixty-two foot trailer. Actually there are several trucks and trailers in the hangar we found this one in. We must all be thinking the same thing because we all say that perhaps we should take some of these trailers back to the settlement to use as warehouses at the same time.

We agree to get the big rig running and to take the trailer back to the settlement and then bring the truck back to pick up another trailer. Sara and Gary have the truck running before we can load the box truck we brought. LT and Harry have the fork truck in the warehouse running at just about the same time. Once we can back the semi-trailer up to the dock we can load it in no time compared to what it would take trying to do it by hand. Since it is almost dark we decide to wait until morning to take the trucks and our new friends back to the settlement. We also decide to set this load down and back another empty trailer into place so we can load it as well.

The warehouse has some offices so some of us decide to spend the night in those while the others will spend the night in the Base Exchange which is only about seventy-five yards away. There are plenty of cots so we will sleep comfortably plus those that need them can get all the new clothes that they need. We open a couple of the cans of food to try it and to make sure it is worth taking back. The ones we open are a big hit with pretty much everyone. We opened some of the freeze dried beef and the other is a macaroni dish with sauce on it, so it is kind of like skillet lasagna. Dayna likes it so much that she says she wishes we could take some of this back with us.

Our new friends tell us how much they appreciate us coming to look for them and others. The young lady with three children tells us that she didn't tell us earlier because she was afraid we wouldn't help them, but her husband went looking for food two days ago and she is afraid that the devils got him. Apparently the devils are the same ones we call predators. All of our new friends tell us that we are in the area right now where the predators are known to take people from. After the others have gone to bed, Harry tells LT and me that he knows some of the predators. When he first came here he ran into them and they wanted him to join them. I ask him to assess their strengths and their weaknesses for us.

He tells us for strengths they have guns, they have some transportation like motor cycles and some cars, and they are totally ruthless and have no conscience when it comes to the people they take. Their weaknesses are that they are not very well organized and that they are not very good with the guns they have. I ask him if he knows where they live or hang out. He says he never got that far. He says that being around them reminded him of watching some of the really nasty movies about motorcycle gangs. He was afraid that he may become one of their prisoners at any moment. He was definitely relieved when he got clear of them.

We decide to post a watch during the night. LT says he is awake anyway so he will take the first two hour watch. When it is my turn Dayna gets up with me and we sit up together. Neither of us are very tired tonight so we take a double shift and wake up Harry just a couple hours before time to get up anyway. As we decided last evening some of our group will drive the trucks back and take our new friends with them to the settlements. Those of us that stay will go back to London and continue looking west of where we left off. Unfortunately none of our new friends know how to drive so we have to send some of us, which leaves us pretty weak if we were to get attacked before they get back.

They leave and promise to be back as soon as they can get here. We already discussed it with the settlement and they are going to send more people with them to drive the trucks back after they are loaded and to pick up any new friends we may find. We still have the double-decker bus along with the motorcycle and the dune buggy. We start out looking for people and the day seems to suit my mood perfectly. It is overcast and it keeps raining on and off all day so far. Again we are looking for smoke as well as for signs of life. Dayna and Carrie spot the first signs of life in the form of seeing two young ladies crossing the street about two blocks to our right. If the building in the spot we are going past was still standing they wouldn't have seen them.

It isn't difficult to convince this group of people to join us. They heard about a settlement south of London and they are on their way to find us. They have been living in a city named Ipswich, at least that's what I think they said. There are seven people in this group. One young man, three young ladies, who are his sisters and they have three children with them that they say they found on their way here. The oldest little girl, who appears to be about eight to me, tells us that the devil people took their parents three days ago. Their mom told them to hide when they heard the devil people coming. They also say that they heard their mother scream when they took them.

The more I hear about these people the more set I am on going to look for them and make sure they never bother anyone again. The problem is so far no one knows where they live or even which direction it is. We continue looking for people in the northwest part of London. We see some smoke coming from three locations that appear to be just a few blocks apart. We decide to check them out as we get to them. I won't bore you with the details, but after checking the three locations we have twelve more friends to join the settlement. Just before dark we find an outdoor store that we can spend the night in.

Our friends get back with the empty trucks just a few minutes after we stop.

The plan is to go back to the military base and pick up another trailer and load the other truck with supplies. Then the people that came with our group will drive them back. We are still on watch for any sign of the predators. Dayna and I got to serve our shift at the end of the night. When the sun comes up we get started fixing some breakfast for everyone. We are in the process of making some oatmeal when Dayna tells me that she can see some people out in the street. She says it looks like a mom with a couple of teenage daughters. She says she is going to invite them in so I ask her to wait until at least one of the men can go out with her.

She calls Sara and her sister Carrie to come with her. I decide to go with them, but I am about thirty yards behind them when they get out to the street. I can see the woman and the girls motioning them to go back, but before they can react a pickup truck comes up between me and them. Three men jump out of the back and grab Dayna, Sara, and Carrie and throw them into the truck. I can see them fighting, but they were caught totally by surprise. The woman and young ladies were left behind. They are crying and saying that they were forced to lure the women out.

LT is already in the dune buggy, Gary is in the van with Ken and I am on my way to grab the motorcycle. LT takes off yelling for us to follow his noise. He doesn't want them to have time enough to hurt the girls. I am so angry and scared right now I cannot remember ever feeling this way before. Gary is off after LT, he yells that he has my fifty and my .308 in the van. I have my Sig Sauer 9mm in its holster on my belt. Finally I get the motorcycle running and am off after them. I catch Gary in no time and can hear the engines racing ahead of me. It takes a few minutes to catch up to LT. I didn't notice it before, but Harry is riding with him.

We are only a couple hundred yards or so behind the pickup as we head into the streets of what appears to be a small town. They go right through the town and drive into the yard of a large house that looks like it may have been an inn before the war. They drive right through a large set of gates then the gates are closed behind them. We stop short of the gates and discuss whether or not we should ram our way in. We can see inside the gate and now they have the girls with guns held to their heads yelling that they will kill them if we drive through the fence.

The guy who appears to be the leader has a nasty smirk on his face when he talks. I yell at him that I will fight him for the women. Harry told me that might interest him because he fancies himself to be a very tough man. Harry also says that he knows these guys so maybe he can talk some sense into him. He calls to the leader and asks if he can come in alone. They tell him if he tries anything he will be as dead as we all will be soon. Harry goes in and is talking to the leader while I stand out in the open where they can see me. The others, of which there are now seven more followed us and want to know what they can do to help.

There is a double-decker bus right outside the fence about fifty yards to the right. It looks from here that we would have a clear field of fire from the upper level of the bus. The predators are telling us what they are going to do to the women. Luckily the predators can't see how many people we have out here now. I think they are convinced that it is just me and Harry. The others have their orders and their guns and are moving into position as we speak. The woman that drew the girls out earlier is telling LT and Ken that they have at least fifty more people in their compound that they have pretty much made into slaves.

We want to make sure we protect them as well so she goes with Ken to show him where those people are kept. The men holding the girls are treating them pretty rough. If they could fight back they could do a good job, but they are bound both hands and feet so they can barely move. The one holding Dayna slaps her because she bites his hand. I have had enough, I walk right up to the fence and tell them to let the girls go or we will kill every one of them. They start laughing and telling me to go ahead and start shooting. The most I will get is maybe one or two before they kill me. One of them says that they will not kill me quickly. They want me to see what they are going to do to the women.

Harry starts to say something and the leader shoots him saying he never did like him. Our people take that as a signal to open fire. They have all picked at least two targets ahead of time and their gunfire sounds like a continuation of the leader's gun. Our girls knew what to expect and dropped as soon as the leader fired his gun. I shoot the lock off the gate and am running in to get to the girls. I am shooting anyone that I see standing. Finally there is no one standing, there must be some of the predators over toward one of the outbuildings because we are hearing shooting coming from over there.

I help the girls up and cut the ropes that are binding them. Our guys are now making sure that the predators will not bother anyone else. When the girls are up and okay we go over to see if we can do anything for Harry. Luckily he was hit in the shoulder and not in the heart. We start to help him up when he looks beyond me and tells me to watch out. The leader is getting up and is raising his gun to shoot at us. I turn and covering the short distance between us I kick the gun out of his hand. He asks me if I still want to fight him. I tell him absolutely and hand my gun to Dayna.

I happen to glance toward the out building where the shooting was coming from and see a couple of our people along with a large group of what were apparently prisoners. I almost forget what I am doing, but when I get hit from the side by the leader I remember quickly. I am so angry at this guy and what he and his pack did to all these people that I barely feel his punches. I am exchanging punches with him feeling the strength leave him. He is not a very good fighter and is in even worse shape. He stops and holds up his hand asking for mercy, I hesitate for just a few seconds and I hear the report of a gun right behind me.

I see the blood spreading out across his shirt and a fairly large hole in his chest. He looks around and falls face first in the mud of the yard. I look around and see one of the women that came with our group with a gun in her hand. She looks at me and tells me that an animal like that doesn't deserve to live. She won't get an argument from me. I finally get the opportunity to look at Harrys shoulder. The bullet went through and we can clean it out with some of the first aid supplies in the van. When it is all sorted out we find out that there are sixty-two people that were being held here, but that includes the children whose parents were taken.

We tell the people about the settlement south of here, but while we are talking some of our people have been looking around and they tell the people that they could start their own settlement right here. There are plenty of houses in the vicinity, there are already crops that are mostly harvested now, but we could show them how to get started. Some of the people from the southern settlement tell us that they can show them how to get started if that's what they would like, while we continue looking for others that can use a large family to help take care of them. We like that answer even better.

We contact the settlement and let them know what has happened. There are several members of that settlement that want to know about their loved ones who were taken by the predators. We let them talk as long as we can then we have to get busy finding supplies and new family members. The first order of business is to go to the military base and swap trailers and to fill the box truck they brought back. A couple of the people that came back to drive the trucks back are from this area. They tell us there are at least two and possibly three more military bases north of here. They say they have no idea what there is at those bases, but they know they are there.

Sara and Gary get to work on another diesel truck to pull another of the trailers to the new settlement and if they decide not to stay there they can always take the food with them. We use the truck that is running to move another trailer up to the dock so it can be filled. Another warehouse has cases and cases of uniforms and other supplies that both settlements can use. Since the settlement to the south already stocked up from the base we found down there we will load a bunch of other items on this truck as well. It is not even noon when both trucks are fully loaded and ready to move out.

Harry was going to go on with us, but he is in too much pain from the shoulder wound. While we were getting the supplies and the trucks he asked me how we can be involved in a fight like that and just go on with the day as if nothing happened. I asked what we should do. I told him that we have had to fight like that and even much worse since becoming a family. I also tell him that we all wish that other people would catch the vision for the world that the bible and other scriptures tell us is the best way to live. It is never easy to take a life, but unfortunately some people will kill you, or your loved ones, or both, if you don't. He told me he and Ginny are very happy that they decided to join us rather than fight us. Ginny is his wife.

After the trucks leave we decide to continue looking for people who would like a home. We are driving through a town called Oxford when we see a couple of children run across the street a couple hundred yards up the street we are on. We pull up in front of the building and Dayna along with Carrie and Sara start to get out of the van when we hear the report of a gun and a bullet hits a car that is parked in front of the building. That's not exactly what we are expecting.

9

The girls jump back into the van and close the door as quickly as they can. Gary, Ken, and Sam ask if we should return fire. I tell them to wait until we see if they are just scared or if they really don't want company. I tie a white handkerchief to a stick and with my arms raised I walk toward the building staying far enough back to dive behind one of the parked cars in front of the building. A man's voice yells out that I am close enough. He asks me what the white flag is supposed to mean. I explain it to him and to whoever else is listening. I also tell him that all we want is to give them the opportunity to be part of a settlement where they will have plenty of friends to help each other survive.

He asks me how they know that we are not from the devils that have been taking people to work for them as slaves. This time one of the women that came with us tells them that we wiped out the devils this morning. A woman's voice asks how we did that, they were protected by the devil himself. The woman in our group, whose name is Emma, tells them that we have the Lord on our side. She asks the woman if she has heard of the Mormons. The lady answers that yes they have, they are Mormons, but they haven't seen any others of their faith in over a year.

The man asks me a couple of questions about the church and luckily I can answer them to their satisfaction. Finally the family comes out of the building, but he still has that gun in his hands. He apologizes for shooting at us, then asks if we might have something for his wife and children to eat. They have not been able to find any food in two days. Dayna, Carrie, and Sara are taking care of that right now. The three children are very polite and wait until a blessing has been asked on the food before they will eat. The man tells us that he will work to pay us for the food if that is okay with us. Then he mentions that we talked about settlements with a lot of people in them.

I start to answer when Sam and Emma start telling them about both settlements. He looks at his wife and she nods her agreement. He tells us they will visit both settlements if that is acceptable, then decide where they would like to settle. They both say it sounds like a dream come true to them. They also tell us that they have been smelling smoke coming from the west when the sun goes down so we head west. We go less than a mile when we find two more families trying to survive in a world where they are running out of food and other necessities of life. At first they are afraid that we are from what they call the devil people, but Emma and Sam tell them about the fight this morning and they are happy to join us.

Our new friends tell us that they were coming south and smelled smoke when they came through another small town that I have never heard of. That doesn't matter. We will go there to see if there is anyone else that we can help. We are just inside the town when a group of ten comes out into the street and waves us down. We find out that they have a short wave radio and have been listening to some of our conversations. They have been very excited when they heard we are headed in their direction.

They have everything packed and it only takes a few minutes to disconnect the radio and bring it with us. We ask them if they are hungry and they tell us they ate just this morning so they are good until tomorrow. Dayna and the other women do not agree with them and make sure that they have plenty to eat. It is getting toward sundown so we decide to look for a place to spend the night. One of the men in the newest group tells us that there is supposed to be a military base just a few kilometers to the northwest. We head that direction and sure enough there are signs saying that the base is straight ahead.

We drive right onto the base and look for a good place to spend the night. There are several hangars on this base as well as several very large warehouses. We pull right into one of the hangars and it is just as I thought it would be. There are planes in here, but there are also several large rooms that look like they were used as conference rooms and some look like they were used when people had to spend the night here. We tell everybody to make themselves comfortable and we will go looking for some cots to use tonight.

I am happy to see all the men follow us to look for the supplies we need. I am looking for a certain warehouse where I know we will find bedding as well as clothing and other essentials. It only takes a few minutes to find it and even less time to find what we are looking for. Ken brought the van with us so we load it up and head back to the hangar. LT and I excuse ourselves and head to the Base Exchange. We find a bunch of the great K-Bar knives here and we also find military issue handguns. We take enough for our new friends to have some and we also grab a couple cases of sweatshirts and sweatpants that should fit all of our new friends.

When we get back to the hangar the ladies have fixed supper for us all. The new people all say they couldn't eat our food after already taking so much from us. We tell them that we are sure we will find enough food on this base to feed the entire settlement for the winter. When I show them the new clothes along with the knives and guns they can't believe that anyone would care enough about them to give them these treasures. All the men turn down the guns because they do not know how to use them properly yet. They stress the yet because they are looking forward to learning how to use them safely.

LT and I saved one surprise until after everyone has eaten. We found several cases of candy in sealed cans that tasted fine to us so we are able to give a couple cans to each family to share. Dayna has fallen in love with a couple of the children already. There are two little girls that are about three years old. They never saw each other before today, but now they are great friends. Dayna gave them each a piece of chocolate before their parents could. Both little girls looked at it, then smelled it, and finally licked it to see if they would like it. The lick did it. They popped the entire piece of candy into their mouths and asked if they could have more.

Their parents told them that it is not polite to ask for such valuable treasures, but Dayna and I both asked them if they don't ask how will they know if they can have more or not. The new clothes are a big hit as well, especially when we tell them they can pick out plenty of new clothes in the morning. Even though we have defeated the predators we do not feel safe not posting a guard. This is when I wish we had a dog to warn us if someone comes around. Again Dayna and I take the shift that lasts until daybreak. We spend most of that time talking about how close we came to losing each other yesterday.

Today we are going to call home and see how everything is going. When everyone is up and had breakfast we take them to the Base Exchange and let them find some new clothes. They also get some uniforms, but the exchange has civilian clothes as well. This base also has several of the motorcycles and dune buggies like we have. The only thing we can figure is that maybe they are here to be shipped to trouble spots somewhere on this side of the world. Either way just about everybody with us wants one or the other and in some cases, both.

We are walking around the base checking out the warehouses and the other buildings when Dayna and I round a corner and come face to face with a dog that looks a lot like the ones we have back home. In case you have forgotten our dogs seem to be an Alaskan Malamute and a Siberian Husky, but that was determined by looking them up in a book about dogs, so we are not totally sure. Anyway the dog standing in front of us looks very much like ours. She is not growling or threatening us in any way so I talk to her while I am walking toward her. I am able to pet her without any threat so Dayna comes over to pet her as well.

Some of our group is following us and as soon as the children see her they are petting her and hugging her and she doesn't seem to mind at all. In fact she is wagging her tail all the while. She has been looking behind her since we came up and now she turns and walks toward an open door in the building we are next to. She looks back at us before going in so it looks to us like she wants us to follow her. We go inside and lying in a cot in the room is a woman that appears to be in her late forties, early fifties and she doesn't look very well. The dog goes up beside her and nuzzles her hand so she starts to pet the dog, then opens her eyes and sees us standing here.

She says hello and then thanks the dog for finding some help for her. We say hello, then ask her if she is injured or ill. She says that she is pretty sure she has caught a touch of pneumonia. She says she has been coughing a lot lately and she feels hot, which she is pretty sure it isn't because of the weather. She has a stethoscope right here with her so I listen to her heart and lungs and I can't be sure without an x-ray, but her lungs sound quite congested. She tells me that if I wouldn't mind going, I can find some antibiotics in the base hospital and probably some in the first aid rooms in most of the barracks.

I find some in the building right next to this one, but we have to hope they will still have any potency left in them. When I get back and give her some of the medication Dayna tells me that she has to show me something. We go to another room farther into the building and there are nine puppies having a great time playing with some of the children. Both the puppies and the children's mommies are watching to make sure no one gets hurt. We ask the lady if she feels up to being moved to a settlement where she would have a large family to help her if she should get sick again. Every family with us tells her they would be honored if she would like to live with them.

She says that she is well enough to travel as long as she doesn't have to walk very far. As far as moving in with a family, she winks at Dayna and tells us that given her choice she would move in with me, if I wasn't already married. We all laugh and get Maggie ready to travel. She told us that her name is Maggie. We bring the van around because we believe that it will be more comfortable for her. When she gets in the dog just stares at us like she is asking where she and her children are going to ride. The van has a cargo area where the big fluffy mat, that the puppies seem to be living on, will fit perfectly.

We have plenty of volunteers to carry the puppies out to the van under the watchful eye of mama. When the last one is placed on the mat, mama looks around for a moment then barks and jumps in with her family. A few seconds later another dog, very similar to the mama comes running up and stands in front of me, just staring at me. I look at him and tell him that I am happy to see that he is respecting the responsibility he has for starting a family. As long as he is willing to be a good daddy to his children he is welcome to come with us. He barks once and follows mama into the van.

All of our new friends are looking at me like I have lost my mind. Sara tells them that they will get used to the strange things I do, then this will not seem odd at all. Maggie laughs and tells me that it is refreshing to meet another person who talks to their pets. Sam and guy are going to take our new friends back to the northern settlement. That's how we are distinguishing between them. Those of us that are left continue to check out the warehouses and find the one with the food supplies very similar to the other one we found. We are running out of time so we have to get going and continue looking for more people.

We don't get to call home until the day is almost over. We have been crisscrossing all over the country and have found some new friends. Our last stop for the day is at a museum that Sara really wants to go to. We have visited several museums back home, but we have found very little that we can use in them. It is very interesting for the younger people and for the people from after the war because it gives them a perspective on what life might have been like before they were born. Sara doesn't know why she wants to see what's in this particular museum, but she asks for so little for herself we really don't mind stopping.

This is a really large museum compared to some of them we have visited. They have several exhibits of early British air planes. James and Jenna would love to see the display they have for the history of golf. We take several of the golf exhibits for them and for the people back home. We also decide we should visit a sporting goods store or possibly even a couple golf courses to see what we can find. We are checking out the rest of the place when LT, Gary, and I see a display that makes it more than worth the time we are taking in here.

There is a display of American guns starting with the old flint locks, cap and ball, and a really nice selection of weapons. I am mostly interested in the display with the Sharps Buffalo guns. Most of them are of the 45-70 caliber. We are taking every gun in the collection and will sort out what they are later. There are cases of the rifles as well as handguns of all kinds and calibers. There is also a very nice display of knives as well. They are not staying either. One of our newer friends tells us that he and his wife have gone to some of the museums farther north and they have a lot of the same things in them.

I'm not sure what city we are in, but we find a sporting goods store where we not only find all the golf equipment we could ever want, we can spend the night in the store using some of the camping equipment here. We can hook up to an antenna right next door to make our call home. Tim is waiting for us when we get through. He tells us that all is going well back there. He says to tell Sara that they are starting their third batch of chocolate. The first two are good, but they are learning more with every batch and they can't wait until she is there to help them. It's really great to get to talk to our children and grandchildren for a couple of minutes anyway.

Tim, Wyatt, and some of the others that came from the other world remind us that the later into the winter it gets, the worse the weather over the north Atlantic gets. We are well aware of that fact, that's why we feel we have to leave no later than two weeks from now.

Sam and Guy catch up to us just as we are finishing the call. They tell us that Harry told them to remind us that if we don't leave in the next few weeks we could be in for trouble flying home. We spend some time talking about it and our friends tell us that we should concentrate on going to Scotland and possibly stopping in Ireland to see if there are any settlements there.

They tell us that they can continue doing what we are doing long after we are gone. The important thing is that now they know how to survive and how to do it well. We explain about the items we found today that we would really like to take some of them back with us. They tell us that we are welcome to anything we want or need. There is plenty left for them, all they have to do is go get it. Sam and Guy are going to take the small truck we filled today back and unload it into the plane for us.

In the morning we all decide that it would be best if we get the rest of our group and then head up to Scotland. We do swing farther west on the way south and find some more friends for the settlements. We get to the northern settlement in the afternoon and the others are already here to meet us. We are all happy to see that Maggie is doing better and the dogs and puppies are a huge hit with everyone. Dayna told me after they left yesterday that she has fallen in love with one of the puppies. I think it is the smallest one of the litter and looks almost exactly like either Cricket or Biscuit, two of the dogs we have back home.

Anyway today when we got to the settlement we were walking through the area where the dogs are staying and the same little puppy ran to meet Dayna as happy as she could be. We notice that Sara seems to have a little furry friend as well. I tell them both that it would be advantageous to take a couple pups home with us to cut down on the inbreeding of the dogs we have. I think we will be having at least two more passengers on the way home.

Since our friends are ready we take off for Scotland with some of the settlers along with us. Under normal conditions Scotland would be about an eight hour drive from where we are. But the conditions are far from normal so we don't expect to get there until sometime tomorrow. We are really enjoying the beautiful countryside and our new friends are enjoying it as much as we are. We find some people along the way and of course we invite them to join us. We find some places where we can replenish our food supplies and then some.

We get a call on the radio from the southern settlement telling James and Jenna that the wheat grinder they helped the settlers set up is working brilliantly. That's a term they use here to describe something good. The northern settlement wants to know what they are talking about and the people from the southern settlement tell them they know where there is another big set of grindstones and they will be happy to help them get them working. It is starting to sound like our trip here has been a complete success.

We get to Scotland around noon on the second day. The first city we come to is named Edinburgh. We drive into the city and we are met by several armed men and women. Naturally we stop and tell them what we are doing here. They tell us they have heard us talking our fool heads off on that infernal radio. The gentleman talking is about sixty years old and has such a strong accent that we can hardly understand him. A lady that looks to be just as old smacks him on the behind and tells him to mind his manners. He smiles and tells her that we know he is only joking with us. But if she will hit his behind again he will yell at us some more.

We all laugh and Sara says that he must be related to me because we are both dirty old men. A younger man and woman come forward smiling and tell us that if we would like to see their settlement that we are welcome. We follow them through the streets to a place on the outskirts.

10

Their settlement is very impressive. It looks like either a mansion or a castle. It is located not far from the ocean on kind of a bay. We enter the settlement through the wrought iron gates and we can see that they have done a lot of work here. The one thing we don't see is vehicles of any kind. They explain that they don't have anyone that knows how to get them running. We can help them with that. Then the leader at this time whose name is Will tells us that they have been having trouble with the electricity as well since the last big storm hit. It just about wiped out their windmills.

One of the people we met on the way here tells them that he was an electrician before the war so he might be able to help them out. Will and the others tell him it will be greatly appreciated if he can. I notice James and Ken looking around the shore line very carefully. They ask if there are any caves that might run a ways under the shoreline. Will says he is not sure, but Angus, that's the crusty older gentleman that we met, tells us that the shoreline is full of caves. Many of them were used to smuggle goods in so that the English couldn't tax them.

James asks if any of them come in under the mansion. Angus tells us that as sure as we are standing here, there are caves under the mansion. James doesn't have to ask to be shown, Angus sets out at a pace that is difficult for some of us younger men to keep up. We go through the mansion, which is divided up into small apartments for the people who live here. There is also a very large common room that may have been used for balls and fancy parties at one time. You would have to have one heck of a big windmill to run this place.

Angus takes us down a dark corridor then opens a huge wooden door that must be four inches thick. He takes a lantern off the wall and after lighting it he leads us down the stairs. We go down into a room that is very large and has some large casks against one wall and several large boxes down a corridor a little ways off the main room. Angus tells us that the casks contain wine from before the war and the boxes are full of guns that were brought in by patriots. We continue past the boxes and find ourselves in another room. This one has a very large generator that looks like it might have been used to supply electricity to the mansion.

James is getting more and more interested the farther we go. He is checking out the wiring to see which direction it is coming from. He and Jenna both say that they can't believe it at the same time. He grabs another lantern and runs on ahead until he comes to a closed door. He points out that the wires run through the wall over the door to the other side. The door takes two of us to open, but when we do we find that the people that owned this mansion before the war were into the tidal generation of electricity. The equipment is somewhat different than what we have been installing, but it is the same type of system.

The electrician says that he heard of this technology before the war, but never actually got to see one working. We follow the cave until it ends on a ledge over the water in a cave very similar to the ones we found in Cuba and in Florida. We can see that the cave is about a hundred yards deep. James asks several questions, but the only one they can answer is that we are at low tide now. We can see on the walls that the tide probably rises somewhere around four feet, at least inside the cave here.

We cannot see the paddles that are necessary to turn and generate electricity so LT and I volunteer to go swimming to see if we can find them. Even though we are strong swimmers we tie a rope around our waists to make sure we can be pulled out if necessary. As soon as we jump in we know that we would be in big trouble if we had not used the safety ropes. There is a very strong under tow or current running just about two or three feet below the surface. We find the remnants of what once was the paddle wheel. It was made of wood and it looks like it simply rotted and fell apart.

The part that the paddles were fastened to is still intact and feels like it is still strong enough to use. The water is cold so we can't stay in for too long, but we found out what we needed to know. Now James and Jenna have a mission to accomplish. We have most of the supplies we will need to fix this, but they want to go into town to see if there are any supplies they can use. That way the settlement will have a way to fix it if something happens. Most of us are going into town, some to look for plumbing and electrical supplies and some of us to help them get some vehicles running.

We find a military base, which is a surprise at least to us. Will tells us that they have taken most of the supplies that were good from here. Sara asks him if they took any cars or trucks from here. He has to admit that they didn't so there may still be some that we can use. We are mainly looking for vehicles with a diesel engine because that is much less complicated than a gas engine. There are several hangars and warehouses on the base that look promising, at least from the outside. There are also dozens of Quonset huts that look to be in good condition. We explain to them how we use the huts and they tell us they never thought about doing something like that. We take a few minutes to show them how we do it just in case they ever need more housing.

We find several really nice stake body and box trucks in one warehouse and they are all diesel. The building has a generator and a large compressor so LT and I attack those while Sara and Gary work on the truck engines. We get the generator running just about the same time they get the truck to turn over. The people from the settlement are smiling and shaking their heads because we are able to accomplish so much in so little time, at least according to them. We have had to do this since the beginning so we had to get at least pretty proficient at it. The compressor takes about another half hour, that darn thing is just being difficult because it can.

We can finally fill all the tires and make sure they hold air before we drive the truck that is running. It's a nice fifteen foot box truck that the settlers here asked for first. We head to another warehouse where someone told us there are several jeeps and staff cars. There is even a van here that must have been used for transporting people before the war. Sara and Gary get two jeeps running while LT and I tackle the van. Now that they have a truck, Dayna and Carrie are helping some of the women from the settlement gather up some of the things that they simply could not carry all the way back to the settlement.

When the vehicles are running it is getting close to the end of the day. James and Jenna join us with the settlement people they were with and tell us they didn't have any luck finding what they wanted. Dayna, who has had a smug look on her face since they joined us, tells us all to follow them, meaning her and Carrie. They take us to a small warehouse almost hidden in the jumble of buildings. When we get there the name Special Projects is written on a sign above the door. I think I know what we are going to find in here. I am right. There are several paddles of varying size and configuration. They are all paddles, but some of them have straight fins and some have different helix fins. Our guess is that they were experimenting with the different shapes and even materials before the war.

James finds some that are very similar to the ones we used in Cuba and Florida, but he suggests that we bring all of them back to the mansion as soon as we can. That will have to wait until at least tomorrow because I refuse to carry them back to the settlement and the truck is full. When we get back James can't wait to get the new paddles set up and to try the generator. We all tell him that we may as well start tomorrow because there is no way that generator will work after so long. He tells us that he will set the paddles himself if he has to so LT and I put on the wetsuits we found in town today and check out what we have to do to get this done.

We are shocked to see that we can simply pull a large pin on each paddle, there are two of them next to each other, and slide the old paddle frame off and slide the new ones on. Replace the pins and get out of the way of the turning paddles. There is a device on the side that will lock the blades in place if they need to be worked on. The tide is coming in as we work and the water is just about three feet higher than it was earlier. The paddles will be completely underwater even at low tide, but then they will only be a few inches under the water.

The paddles are spinning very well, so James and Jenna along with the electrician are going back along the wires to make sure there are no breaks. When they get back to the generator they say there is no time like the present to try it so they flip the switch turning it on. It takes a couple of minutes for it to start up and it isn't generating electricity when it does. James knows what to do, but he asks the electrician for his opinion first. The electrician is thinking about it when he says he knows what they have to do. I am glad they do because I don't.

Anyway, whatever they do seems to work because the lights in the basement are coming on. The bulbs are not too good because they start to glow then blow. The people in the settlement say they can fix that and change the bulbs that we know are not good. It does not take long before the entire Mansion has electricity running through it. The tents that we brought to sleep in are set up and ready whenever we are ready to call it a day. We are very much relieved that the people here are doing as well as they are. It looks like we can give them some advice and a little training and move on.

Now that they have some vehicles the settlement people want to go looking to see if there are any people out there that would like to join them. They tell us that there is another settlement on the west side of Scotland as well. They have never seen it, but they have talked to them on the radio a couple of times. We decide to visit that settlement in the morning. We are looking for a small town or city named Oban, which is on the coast. There are dozens of inlets and bays over on this side. We have a welcoming committee similar to the last one. This time we have five people that we picked up on the way here.

Once they know who we are they are as friendly as the others were. This settlement is living in what appears to be a small town. There are approximately sixty people here, which is just about the same size as the other settlement. They are similar in that they don't have a mechanic either so they have no transportation to go very far at all. They have some young people who really want to learn so we take them into town to find a couple of vehicles. As it turns out there is a military base not far from here as well.

We go through much the same steps as we did the other day and when we are through they have a truck and a couple of jeeps to use. Tomorrow our students are going to get the chance to get a vehicle running. I don't think they will have much trouble at all. The people here are using wind mills for electricity. Looking around it would be very difficult to try to install the tidal generator. Their wind mills are very efficient and they have learned to make the vanes on the wheels so that they can remove them if there is a big storm coming. Their homes are made of stone and should withstand anything they may encounter.

They show us the fields where they grow their crops. Naturally there is nothing growing now because it is almost winter. They had a good year and have a good supply of food put away plus they have some supplies that they found and carried back to the settlement. Now that they have a truck they can go farther away to find food and people. The only suggestions we have for this group is to perhaps have more recreation in their lives. We tell them about the obstacle courses we built as well as the golf course and the miniature golf.

They told us that they do play golf. At least some of them do. James and Jenna and Sara and Gary along with LT are going to play in the morning. When we get up it seems to me to be much too windy to play golf. The people from the settlement tell us that if you wait until there is no wind here, you will never play. The rest of us decide to walk along with them while they play. The course looks to me like a wheat field that hasn't been harvested yet. If you look close you can see the fairways and the greens.

Those of us walking along find several golf balls in the deep grass and some not even in deep grass. Our guests tell us those are balls from before the war. We ask them if they would like to keep them and they tell us that we should, to have a small part of Scottish history. Our golfers tell them they would like to take some genuine Scottish golf clubs and balls back to the states with us if they don't mind. They take us to a building in town that looks like it was once a house. We go in and the entire place is filled with different kinds of golf clubs and cases of ball. They help us load the van and tell us not to worry. There are at least a half dozen more places like this within walking distance.

We go back to the settlement to see if our students from yesterday can get a vehicle started and are surprised when we get there and there are two more trucks, a van and three more jeeps in the yard. There is also a diesel fuel tanker parked a short distance away from the settlement. One of the young men is proud to say that when they got the van running they took a short drive to make sure it would run okay and found a family of four living not five kilometers away from here. Now that they have transportation they are going to go out to see if they can find others to join their group.

It's sad to be saying goodbye to our friends even though we have only known them a short time. We did help them find a new radio and showed them how to hook it up so that we can keep in touch after we go home. Dayna loves the children here. Their accents sound so cute when they talk. We go back to the other settlement and they are proud to show us that the generator is still working even though they had a breakdown. They were able to figure it out for themselves. They are also proud that they now have three more vehicles added to their fleet. The young people that we showed how to get the vehicles started learned well. They also have a tanker full of diesel fuel outside their settlement.

They see the golf equipment that we got in the other settlement and not to be outdone take us to a store that is very similar to the one on the west coast only larger. We don't want to hurt their feelings so we fill the remainder of the truck we have from there. We have an excellent meal of smoked sausage before turning in for the night. We make sure this group has a dependable radio before we leave. They promise to call to let us know how they are doing. Even our old friend Angus says he may even learn how to talk into that infernal contraption to talk to us again.

In the morning the entire settlement is here to see us off. I am shocked when Angus comes over and gives me a big hug. He starts to hug Dayna when his wife tells him she is the only woman he gets to hug. He gives Dayna a quick hug and says it is worth getting smacked by his wife for that. She just laughs and tells him he is hopeless. I almost forgot to mention that both settlements took us into town and showed us where we could get some great Scottish wool sweaters. We wondered where they got them when we saw everyone wearing them. They look like they are handmade and are so beautiful and warm.

We also found cases of military issue sweaters at all the bases we visited. We have enough for everyone in our settlement back home plus a couple dozen cases. We head down to the northern settlement first. Today we are taking the coast road instead of going inland like we did on the way up here. Actually we all just decided to do that at the last minute. The road is kind of rough and there are places where we have to get out and move cars in the way. We don't mind going a little slower because the scenery is breathtaking. We are coming up on a small town that seems to have some docks that reach out into the water.

We can see several boats that were crashed up onto the shoreline and we can also see some boats that are in buildings up on the shore a ways. We are watching the shoreline when all of a sudden Carrie tells us there is a young woman walking down the road. We pull up beside her and ask her where she is going. She tells us she is not sure where she is going or where she is for that matter.

11

We tell her that we can probably shed some light on that topic if she is interested. That is probably a poor choice of words on my part because she snaps back that of course she is interested. If you don't know where you are or where you are going, who wouldn't be interested. I apologize for putting it like that. What I should have said is that we can hopefully make some sense of her predicament. She apologizes and tells us she is sorry for snapping at the only people she has seen all day. She adds that we sound like we are from the United States. She asks if we are here on holiday or business. Then she asks where everyone else is.

We tell her we will take this a step at a time. First we ask her if she is hungry. She answers saying she is famished. She was hoping to find a pub open, but she found one that didn't look like it had been open in thirty or forty years. In fact every building she has seen looks like that. Sara gets her some things to snack on, then tells her she is not going to believe what we have to tell her. First Sara asks her how she came to be here. She tells us that she went on date last evening. At least she thinks it was last evening, now she is not so sure.

Sara asks her if she was out on a boat and ran into the densest fog she has ever seen. She tells us that's exactly what happened. She was on a date with a doctor she met at the hospital where she works. He took her for a boat ride and proved that he is no gentleman. She says she actually had to slap him to stop his advances. She also says when she woke up this morning she was concerned that she may have been drugged, but then she remembered that she didn't drink or eat anything. After she slapped him she went below and locked the door. It was already foggy at that time, but around here you get used to fog.

She must have fallen asleep because the next thing she can remember is going on deck and finding the boat next to the dock. It wasn't tied up or anything and there was no one else around. Sara asks her if after she left the boat did she go back. She says that's even more confusing because she is sure she knows exactly where that boat was docked, she even tied it there herself. But when she went back there was nothing there, even the dock had broken and fell into the water. She asks how anyone can explain that and have it make sense.

We kind of laugh and tell her we are not laughing at her, we are laughing with her because we all went through the same type of event except for a couple of us. Sara tells her about how she came to be here, then the rest of us give her the short story of how we got here. At first she doesn't believe us, but as we drive through a small city on the coast and she sees what it looks like, she is starting to. Dayna asks her if she had a large family where she came from. She smiles and says she didn't have any family and no, what you could call close friends.

Her parents passed away when she was young and she went to live with a distant aunt that didn't like children. Her aunt met a guy that liked children even less than she did, and our new friend Emma got sent to an orphanage to live. When she was sixteen what appeared to be a nice older couple took her in, but she learned very quickly that she was there to act as the man's wife when his wife didn't feel up to it. She hit the guy with a lamp and took off. Sara tells her she would have gelded him. Gary tells her that she would too. He saw her do it to a guy that was attacking a twelve year old girl.

Emma says that he definitely deserved it. She asks if Sara got in trouble with the law. We tell her that the only law is what you can do to protect yourself. That's why we believe so strongly in people living in settlements where they can take care of each other and help each other when it is needed. We like to think of it as an extended family. Getting back to Emma, she continues telling us that she worked at odd jobs, lying about her age until she saved enough money to go to the United States. There she worked hard and went to college and actually won a scholarship to medical school, then served an internship at a hospital in Utah until she became a doctor.

She asks us some questions about the settlements. When we answer them she says that it sounds like we are living what her church calls the United Order. All the women are excited now. They ask her if she is LDS, which is short for Latter-Day Saints. She says she is and it sounds like a teenagers pajama party, all of the women are shrieking and hugging each other. When they settle down enough to talk we ask her how she came to be back in England. She smiles and says that when she ran away from home she lived on the streets for a time and she has never forgotten how desperate she felt. She came back to London to help those that are not able to afford to help themselves.

We tell her that we have two doctors in our settlements back in America and they have trained several others and they are always busy helping someone. There are always babies being born or someone gets injured and there are always the simple cuts and bruises. We tell her about our settlement the rest of the way back. When we get to London we are going past a hospital so she tells us to stop so she can get some instruments and maybe even some supplies. I am able to help her a little in picking out the supplies she will need right away and we find several of the instruments she needs.

We also take an autoclave to sterilize instruments and enough bandaging materials to cover half of the country. It's a good thing we left some room in the van in case we found something we couldn't live without. When that is all loaded she sees a department store and says she needs some clothes to wear. She can't wear the same jeans and blouse every day, not to mention the unmentionables that she needs. Dayna and the other women help her while we men look for some new styles for ourselves. We decide we already have enough stuff going back with us.

When the women get back we can now head to the settlement. We only go about three blocks when we see what appears to be a family of four until we get closer then we can see that the man is carrying a small child in his arms. They try to run when they see us coming, but we call to them telling them we mean them no harm. In fact we would like to help them. Emma takes the child from the man and asks if she is hurt. The man says she was playing while they walked earlier today when she fell. The trouble is that her leg was caught and twisted badly. She says she is in quite a bit of pain. The poor little girl can't be more than four years old.

Emma is already checking the little girl out on the way to the settlement. When we get there we are treated like some kind of conquering heroes. We can see that they have been very busy plowing fields and they even have a Quonset hut sitting inside the fenced in area. It looks very nice where it is. We introduce everyone to Emma and tell them that she is a real doctor. Sam tells me that Harry and Maggie could use a visit with Emma as soon as she feels up to it. Emma continues the examination of the little girl and declares there doesn't appear to be any broken bones, but she should stay off the leg for a few days. The father asks if we might have a tent that his family can use. Sam and Guy, who apparently are part of the leadership at this time tell him that they don't have any tents, but they have a nice little cottage they can live in.

Emma tells them that if nobody else has moved into the Quonset hut yet, she will take that for her quarters and the hospital. She tells them that after she sees Harry and Maggie they can come with her back to the hospital to get some beds and linens. Sam looks at me and smiles, he says it's like having his mum around again except Emma is much prettier and he's pretty sure she's not as mean. We brought a bunch of the walking sticks down from Scotland with us. Emma asked if she could have one. Now she is brandishing it like a club asking Sam if he is looking for mean. She is smiling when she says it so we all know she is kidding. Sam tells her if she was as mean as his mum she would have hit him with that stick already.

We all laugh and she goes to visit Harry and Maggie. Dayna and I go with them and when that little puppy sees Dayna she comes running over and whines until Dayna picks her up. We can see the other puppy looking to see if Sara is coming as well. She does and that puppy makes a mad dash for her. Harry is doing very well considering he was shot in the shoulder. Maggie is doing much better than she was when they brought her down. Doc Emma tells Harry that he should be able to go back to work as long as he doesn't try to use that arm too much. He tells us that he has had enough bed rest to last for quite a while.

His wife Ginny says she will remind him of that next time he starts complaining that his arm hurts too badly and he needs a nap. We all laugh about that and Harry says he may have said that once, but he is feeling much better now. Emma tells them to stop back at her hut slash hospital in a couple hours. She is going to go looking for some herbs that will help that wound heal nicely. Maggie is still pretty weak, but she tells Emma that as soon as she can get around again she will be happy to help her find some of those healing herbs.

The people in this settlement are very happy to show us around. We can't blame them, they have made so many changes it's difficult to recognize this as the same settlement it was just a few days ago. Everyone tells us that even though Harry was not able to do much work, he was out there every day explaining what they should do and how they should do it. They even have about ten or twelve acres of farmland plowed for the spring planting. We tell them that we have some seeds that have worked good for us back in the states. We will be happy to give them some when we get back to our plane.

James and Jenna tell us that won't be necessary because they gave the seeds to the southern group while we were away. One of the leaders tells us that the southern settlement sent them quite a bit of the seed that we brought. They are planning to use it in the spring, then when the fruits and vegetables are harvested they will capture all the seeds they can and share those with the Scotland settlements. They also have several acres of winter wheat planted so that they should have a good crop to get started. They show us how much they have already accomplished in getting a large wheat mill set up.

There is a river running only about a hundred yards from the main building and they are building a very nice cinder block building close to the river so they can use the river to drive the wheel. They already have the concrete slab poured and they have pallets full of cinderblocks all around the slab. To me it looks like the slab is pretty big just for a wheat mill. They tell us that it was Harry's idea to make it almost twice as large as it needs to be so that they will have an area to store the wheat waiting to be ground and the flour after it is ground. Actually we did the same thing. I was just seeing if they had a reason for building it so large.

They show us where they are storing the extra goods that they find so that they have something to share with when they find new members for their settlement. They tell us that they have found some very nice steel buildings and they have two members of their settlement that are experienced masons so they are planning to use some of the huge supply of cinderblocks that they found. They even got a truck running that has a hoist like the one we have back home. We tell them we use that when we go hunting as well. That saves a lot of back pain from trying to lift the large animals.

They agree whole heartedly and say they figured that one out for themselves. They tell us that's about everything they can think of, but we are walking down past one of the larger barns on the property and we can see that they have quite a few chickens and some other birds that are like chickens. One of the young ladies that is taking care of this area says they are called Guinea hens. I will have to take her word for it, but it is still very impressive what they have done in so short a time. We go a little further and we see that they have several cows and calves in the barnyard. They tell us that they are thinking about raising some cattle for the meat away from the milk cows.

They also want to keep some sheep and goats. They tell us that the woods are full of them and they have been able to walk right up to them without scaring them at all. I tell them there is no reason for them to be afraid of sheep so that is not that surprising. Even our new friends roll their eyes and tell Dayna to smack me. Dayna, Carrie, Sara, and Jenna start talking about how great it would be to have some sheep back in our settlement. James and LT both say they could go for some roast lamb. I personally have never acquired a taste for lamb, or any meat that comes from sheep or goats. I do like the sweaters that they make out of the wool though.

We promise to go looking for some sheep when we get home, but the women ask us if we have ever seen any sheep around the settlement in the past fourteen years. We have to admit that we haven't, but then we weren't really looking for them either. Some of our new friends volunteer to help us catch some to take back with us to start our flock. Dayna asks them how many they think we should take back to start a flock of our own. One of the men says he thinks we should take at least a hundred head. I tell him he is fast becoming a former friend rather than a new friend. He and the others laugh and say that they think we could get a nice start with six or eight ewes and a couple of good healthy rams.

It looks like we are going into the sheep business so I will leave it up to the experts to catch us some sheep to take back with us. I ask when we are going to start gathering our flock so we can get the flock out of here. I get smacked by all four of our women and at least two or three of the settlement women. I was only joking, well sort of. Anyway we are informed that the southern settlement already has a small flock ready for us to take with us, but if we want to help them start their flock we are welcome to come with them in the morning. Actually we would all like to help. This is as good a time as any to start learning about sheep.

We have a very good meal and sleep well. In the morning we head for the woods around the settlement looking for sheep. We don't go very far when we see a bunch of what appear to be lambs. They are probably the lambs that were born in the spring, but they are still not full sized sheep. A short distance away we see a large flock of sheep. There must be over a hundred here, I ask the guy next to me how we are going to catch them. He smiles and says we aren't, the dogs will do that for us. In a matter of seconds we see the mother and father dog chasing the sheep toward the settlement.

The sheep pretty much just follow once the ones in the lead start going in that direction. The lambs follow what are probably their mothers and before we know it they have a large majority of the sheep going into a large fenced in area near one of the barns. The people say they are going to fence in a couple of acres more for the sheep to graze on. Once they get used to being here they will be able to take them to different areas to feed. Apparently these people know something about this, but we have learned most of what we know from books and experience so we are not too worried about it.

We are getting very close to our deadline for leaving. We reluctantly say goodbye to our new friends and head back down south. We have two more members of our family in the form of Dayna's and Sara's puppies. I honestly think those puppies would have tried to follow us to the southern settlement if we didn't bring them with us. Harry and Ginny ride down with us as well. When we get to the settlement it is much like the northern settlement is. They have come so far in such a short time. We go to the other group in this settlement and we can see that they have grown by at least fifteen people and their settlement is looking very nice.

They have several more acres of land plowed and ready for the spring. They have even painted some of the houses. We thought it was too cold, but they told us they worked hard whenever they got a day that is warm enough. Their generator is working great. They have had a couple of small problems, but they have been able to fix those problems themselves. We are very much impressed with the progress they have made and that they are continuing to make. They have done the same things with the chickens and the cows. Both groups have. Now they are talking about filling in the space between the two groups with houses. Those will be for new members that they are sure will keep coming.

We are down to just a couple of days left before we really have to be going. We are at supper when we get a call on the radio from a group that says they are very close to the coast in France just across the English Channel. They say that they are doing okay, but could use some advice and could use some help with their electrical and with getting vehicles. We tell them that we could come down there, but it will only be for a couple of days. We are willing to teach them all we can in that time, but we will have to leave. I don't even know what day it is so I can't tell them what day we will have to leave. We will only have two days to help them.

12

We discuss our options and decide to take the helicopter that Sara and Gary got running earlier. A couple of the local people want to go along. I am happy that Dayna, Carrie and Jenna want to stay here and learn as much as they can about raising sheep. Harry, Dean and Neville all speak a little French. LT and I speak enough to get us into trouble. At least he used his knowledge of the language when he was on diplomatic duty. The last time I even tried to speak French was at least a year before Tim and I wound up in this world.

We are ready to leave before sunup in the morning. Hopefully we can get there early and help them get whatever they need done quickly. Dayna tells me that I better be back in time or they will leave without us. I know that is her way of telling me that she is worried about me and can't wait until we get back. There was a time when a trip like this would have been fun, but anymore they all seem to keep Dayna and me apart longer every time. I am glad however that she and the others decided not to go. We never know what we will run into until it actually happens.

It does not take long to cover the approximately twenty-five miles across the English Channel. The directions the settlement down here gave are very good. We find them shortly after getting to the continent and finding some familiar landmarks. When we land just outside the settlement we are greeted by what appears to be the entire settlement. We are a little surprised because they seem to have plenty of vehicles running and there are windmills and solar panels pretty much at every home we can see.

I turn to the leaders of the settlement and ask them what they really need. They tell us that they have plenty of guns and other weapons to defend themselves, but they do not know how to use them correctly. They continue saying that they have lost several members of their settlement to people who come and take them away. They are ashamed to say this, but they do not know what to do to stop them. They have heard on the radio that we are experts in defending ourselves and in stopping others from attacking them. We decide that Sara, Gary, James, Harry, and Ken will begin by teaching them how to use the weapons they have. LT and I will take Neville and Dean with us and we will try to find where those people are taking the people they abduct.

We brought plenty of firepower with us just in case it turned out to be something like this. Luckily there is not much traffic in this area so it is not difficult to follow the trail being used by the people coming and going. The trail leads us to a small town about an hour from the settlement. We can see smoke coming from a couple of chimneys in the town. One of the buildings looks like it was a hotel or inn before the war. There could be several people living in both buildings so we will have to check this out carefully before barging in and possibly getting people killed, including us.

We park the vehicle we are driving a couple hundred yards from the buildings hoping that we have not been seen yet. We brought radios along so that we can keep in touch while we check this out. There is a church a short distance from the places with smoke so I am going to get in there to see if I can get a clear view into the buildings. The others are going to stay put until they hear from me. I make my way through the back alleys that I always heard about in France. They may be romantic in other circumstances, but with what we are here for they look like any other alley behind rundown old buildings. I get to the church and inside without being seen or heard, I hope.

I work my way up to an area of the church that looks out over the buildings we are concerned with. I stop at every level to see what kind of view I have. I am near the top of the building without going into the bell tower itself when I can see into both buildings. In the one building there are just a couple men sitting at a table. It looks like they are talking, but from this distance I can't hear anything. The other building is another story. In this one I can see several men and women. The women and at least two of the men are bound to chairs in the room. There is another woman that appears to be fixing a meal of some kind.

I have my fifty caliber with the heat sensing scope on it so I can see that there are at least two more people one floor above the people I saw first. I am talking to LT all the while I am checking out the buildings. We decide that the best way to handle this is for them to go in the front and for me to stop any interference from where I am. They are moving into place while I keep an eye on the buildings. It looks like one of the women asks one of the others a question and he goes over and lets her loose long enough to probably use the bathroom. The prisoners do not look to have been beaten or being treated badly.

I am starting to wonder just why they were brought here. I definitely don't want to kill someone that doesn't deserve it. I am communicating this to LT and the others as I am thinking it. I ask them not to shoot unless they have to until we see what is going on here. They are in the building on the ground floor when someone inside realizes that they are about to have company. I can see them talking and being very animated about it. One of them picks an automatic weapon off the table and is checking it to make sure it is ready to fire I guess.

I can't let our team walk into automatic weapon fire so I decide to see if they really want to fight or not. I take aim at the wall where I can't see any people and fire that big fifty. It has the desired effect in that it blows a big hole in the wall, which looks like it scared everyone inside that room. The men in the room holding guns toss them on the floor and raise their hands above their heads signifying they surrender. LT and the others get there just as this is happening. I look at the other building and I can now see at least four men looking toward the other building. They look like they are heading that direction with guns in their hands so I fire into one of the walls in the room they are just getting to.

They drop their guns and look around for someone to surrender to. Neville and Dean are on their way to gather them up with the others. LT is talking to the prisoners and their captors. He calls me Zeus and tells me I can come over now. When I get there everyone is sitting in the room and talking. What little I can understand sounds like the people taking the others simply wanted to start a settlement of their own and didn't know how to go about it. The people that were being held prisoner say that they do not have the knowledge that is required to start a settlement. They had only lived in the settlement for a short time.

With that knowledge their captors didn't know what to do with the people and have been trying to figure out how to take them back without getting shot. LT tells them we can take the people back where they belong, but if they want to be part of a settlement why don't they come with us and join that one. Apparently they can't see anything wrong with trying that as long as we promise that they won't be shot when we get there. With the vehicles they have and the one we came here in we have just enough room for everyone to ride in. By the time we get back to the settlement it is getting to be late afternoon.

When some of the settlement people see the guys that took their friends they start to get their guns. Apparently they think they are back to take more people. Things get a little hectic for a few minutes, but we finally get everything straightened out and the new people are welcomed into the group. In talking to them, it seems that they have a lot of skills that will help this settlement quite a bit. There are some other areas that we can help them with so we do some odd jobs and teach others how to do them. One of the areas that the new people can help the most in is hunting. The settlement has been struggling with that primarily because of their lack of prowess with guns.

The settlement must have had a very good crop of vegetables this year. The meal we have for supper is very good even without meat in it. Some of the new people vow that tomorrow they will make sure that they have plenty of fresh meat to eat. The group does have some milk cows and some chickens, but not enough yet to use them for meat. They are going to start raising some cattle for beef as well as hunting for it. They know enough to go a ways off from the settlement so that they don't either shoot all the game close up or scare it off. We wait until after we help them get some fresh game before we head back to England.

Our new friends in France wish us well and thank us for helping them. We will keep in touch with them using the radio as we do with all the other settlements. We wish we had longer, but if we are going to get back to the states we have to leave as soon as possible. As it is the weather could create some real problems for us and that C-130. When we get back to the settlement in England the plane is packed and we are just about ready to head back home. Our friends from when we first came here, Kristi and her daughter Jenny, are afraid that we will not take them back with us now.

There is another mother named Jill and her daughter named Tiffani, who is Jenny's best friend who would like to join us as well. We make sure they realize that this will not be a smooth ride and there is always the chance that we may not make it back. They say that they are willing to chance it. They feel that they will enjoy living in the United States better than here. Harry tells us that he hopes we will come back in a couple of years so he can go back to the states as well. He says that they need him too badly now, but by then they will be self sufficient. Doctor Emma even came down with Maggie, Sam, and Guy to tell us goodbye. She tells us that they stopped at the royal family's castle and found the crown jewels. They are going to hold them in case there is ever another royal family.

We are taking a bunch of stuff back with us. The plane has to be loaded so that it is balanced. Sara looks at the load we have and tells me to sit on the side opposite all the other stuff and people and we should be okay. James and Jenna had some experience loading planes in the other world and they assure us that the load is balanced. If it is not quite right we are stopping in Ireland so we will have a chance to fix it. Almost everyone in the settlements is here to see us off. It's always difficult to leave the new friends we have made. Unfortunately we would miss our families and old friends even more.

The plane seems to be flying as good as ever for the short trip to Ireland. We are only supposed to be here for a few hours to look at what they have done and maybe make some recommendations on what they can do better perhaps. When we land at the prearranged point there is a welcoming committee there. They take us to see their settlement and tell us that there are four settlements in Ireland and they are all about the same size. If they are all as nice as this one, we are sorry that we can't visit them all. The people here seem to be doing very well. They are doing some things differently than we are, but this is a totally different culture.

We spend a very interesting morning with them, but now we really have to go. We find a former military base where we are able to top off the fuel and we are on our way home. The weather is everything we thought it would be and more. I think our guests are not quite as sure as they were on the ground. I have no idea how Sara keeps us on course, but we are coming up on Iceland just as we planned it. We stopped here on the way to England so we have a good idea where to get the fuel we need. There is already snow on the ground here, but not enough to keep us from landing.

Sara pulls up right up to the place we filled up on the way here. The only difference is that this time there are seven people waiting at the base. Luckily one of them speaks English and we are able to find out that they are hoping we can take them with us. They also tell us that as far as they know, there are no other people here. We help them get settled in for the trip while LT and Sara make sure the fuel tanks are topped off. Once in the air there is more of the turbulence that we have had for the entire trip so far. We are hoping that it may calm down after we turn south from Greenland.

I must fall asleep because before I know it we are getting ready to land in Greenland. We taxi up to the place we filled up on the way and LT and I get out to fill the fuel tanks. It sure is cold here, LT and I are talking about some of the coldest places we have been when we hear the splat of a bullet hit the door on the fuel truck. At first we think we may be imagining it when another bullet hits the truck door near the other one. We are starting to get concerned because if they hit the fuel tank on the truck, we may all be on a permanent vacation. When a third bullet hits I tell LT I am going to find who is shooting.

I grab my rifle from the plane and head in the direction from where the bullets are coming. The shots sounded like they were fired from a pistol so the shooter can't be too far. I climb the tower here at the base and start looking around. LT has his radio on as usual and I am talking to him while I scan the area. All at once I see a man sneaking around one of the warehouses here and I am sure he is carrying a gun. I have my scope on him, but for some reason I do not want to pull the trigger. I still have him in my sights when I see a woman and two children approach the man.

It looks like there is an argument going on and it doesn't look like the guy is winning. While this is going on LT calls me on the radio and says that we are fully loaded and can leave any time now. I tell them to start the engines and pretend that they are leaving. I think I know what is going on here. Sara starts the engines and the plane starts moving just a little when several people come running out of one of the warehouses straight into the path of the plane. The one man still has a pistol, but no one else appears to be armed. I am on my way to the plane with my rifle at the ready. I have been wrong before.

I come up from behind the people and I walk straight up to the man with the gun and tell him to drop it. I have the rifle pointed straight at his chest. The woman I believe is his wife must tell him something to that effect only in their language because he sets the gun down on the ground and raises his hands. By now the plane is no longer running and several people are coming to join us. Our new friends from Iceland seem to understand the language because they seem to be carrying on a conversation. Our new friend tells us that they saw us when we came through here on our way to England. They have been waiting here hoping that we would come back and take them with us.

He also says that if they stay here they will probably starve to death before the winter is over. I ask him why they shot at us and didn't just come up and ask to join us. I think the woman understands a little English because she makes a motion with her hand that at least to me means that her husband is not all there. Apparently he thought he could scare us into taking them with us. It is really cold here so we tell them that we can take them, but we have to be getting out of here quickly. Luckily we still have room for people to sit. They run back into the hangar to get their meager belongings then board the plane.

I can tell that some of them are afraid of the unknown, but where they are the known is a pretty scary thing as well. I count them as they board the plane and we now have thirty-seven new friends. We take off without further incidents and we can all sit back and try to keep from being thrown out of our seats by the bucking and tossing of the plane. It seems like one minute we are being tossed around and the next the ride isn't bad at all. We stop for fuel in Nova Scotia where we pick up seven more new friends, then take off with the next planned stop being in New York.

We get to New York and land near the settlement that we know very well here. Karl and several others of our friends from this group meet us at the airport we are filling up at. He sees the group of people we have with us and invites any of them that would like to stay here to join their group. Some of them actually enjoy the cold weather if they are prepared for it. We tell them that if they decide to stay here and find that they do not like it they can always join one of the other settlements here in the states. Everyone decides to see what our settlement looks like first. We told them that if they decide they want to come back up here we will help them.

Karl and his wife ask me if we have room for them and a couple other people that just don't like the cold anymore. Naturally I tell them absolutely not, but I can't say it without smiling so they know I am only kidding. We ask them if they want to join us now and they say that they will wait for the next bus. With all the livestock we have on board we are beginning to look a lot like Noah's Ark. Besides with Sara flying they like their chances better staying on the ground. They tell us they will see us in a week or two.

The flight from New York to Virginia does not take very long now that everyone is excited about finally getting home. When we land at our settlement Dayna and I can finally relax. The crowd that comes to meet us at the plane must be at least a little intimidating to our new friends. Teddy and Nickie are the first ones to get to us along with our grandson, Little Jon. Our new puppy must know she is home because she jumps out of the plane onto Little Jon who is more than happy to have a new friend to play with. It is so good to be home.

13

There are people from all the settlements in our group to welcome our new friends. Teddy and our sons Timmy and Tommy tell us that they had a feeling we would be bringing home some new friends so they have been busy bringing in Quonset huts. Naturally those get taken as quickly as we can set them up, but that opens a house for the new people. They tell us that they found a new farm that has six houses and four barns on it about a mile from Doc Betty's group. Timmy tells me they tracked some small steers into some deep brush and when they came out on the other side there were the houses.

Apparently all of those houses have already been filled by some of the people that have been in the settlements for quite a while. Being apart like they are they need at least some people that know what they are doing if they are attacked. They really like the two Mini Cooper cars that we brought back and the guns, at least what they can see, causes quite a stir especially with my sons. The sheep are more of a question mark, but the people we found in Greenland seem to really like the sheep. We may have found just the right people to take care of them. Kristi and Jill have both said they would like to help with the sheep.

At least our family knew that we were bringing back sheep so they have a pasture all set up to keep them in. We are trying to get them to go to the new pasture, but they seem to have other plans because they are going everywhere except where we want them to. One of the women from the Greenland group gets a large handful of long grass from the side of the path we want them to go down and just about pushes it into the face of one of the sheep. Then she starts walking down the path showing the grass to the sheep again. The sheep she did that to starts to follow her and the rest of them drop in behind that one. She leads them all the way into the pasture.

When the plane is totally unloaded and we have homes for everybody we go back out to tackle the unpleasant task of cleaning the plane especially where the sheep spent most of the last eighteen hours or so. We have plenty of help, even the newest members of our family join us when they see what we are doing. When that is done we are pleasantly surprised by being able to sample the last three batches of chocolate candy that has been manufactured by our family. As far as I am concerned it is the best chocolate that I have ever eaten, but some of the others think there is something missing.

We have plenty of books on the subject of making chocolate candy so I am sure that they will figure it out to their satisfaction. The settlement leadership planned a large cookout this evening to celebrate our safe return. Our friends from all the groups are planning to come over. Some of the newest members do not feel comfortable joining us this evening. Since they did nothing to help gather, prepare, or cook the food they don't feel like they deserve to help eat it. At least it is not too difficult to convince the English speaking friends, but we have to get some help from the Iceland people to talk to the Greenland people for us.

Finally everyone agrees to join us so we can finally go home and get ready for the celebration. Kristi and Jenny and Jill and Tiffani are going to stay with us for a while anyway. Dayna's puppy, who our grandson Jon named Lady, hasn't left her side since we landed. Actually it may have been Timmy who gave him the idea of what to name her. When he hugged his mom the puppy growled at him until he let her go. He looked down at the puppy and said, "It's okay Little Lady, I would never hurt my mom. The puppy started wagging her tail and let him pet her after that. It was shortly after that Little Jon started calling her Lady. Misty, Sara's daughter named their puppy Prince. She said she would call him King, but since he is so small he is only a prince. Either way he seems to love her as much as he does Sara. When Tommy went to hug Misty, Prince bit him on the leg and was pulling on his trouser leg until she told him it was okay.

Biscuit and Cricket along with the other dogs we have in the settlement came over to welcome the new puppies to the family. Even though our dogs are much older and bigger they were playing like pups with the two new additions. The best part of the day is getting to sit down quietly and just talk with our children and other family members about what has been going on. The afternoon flies by and before we know it we have over six hundred people here for the party. It is late fall, but the weather is cooperating perfectly for us. It is cool, but not really cold. A sweater is comfortable, which reminds us of the sweaters we brought back.

Our newest friends are impressed with the number of people in the settlement and with the food. Many of them cannot believe that we have fresh milk and that we can bake rolls as well as several kinds of bread. I was afraid that we would have a lot of trouble communicating with the people from Greenland, but we have several people in our settlement that speak their language. At least close enough to understand each other. The people that understand the language are Matt, Tim, Wyatt, Heber, Joseph, Max, and Junior. They understand enough to tell us that our new friends want to learn English as soon as possible. With that group helping them they should be speaking English very soon.

When the meal is over everyone says they want to hear all about our experiences. I start to stand to tell them that we would prefer to tell everyone in church on Sunday, when most of the people get up and say they really have to be going. Then they all laugh and tell me they are only kidding. When I finish telling them what I started to say, Ryan and Josh ask if Dayna can speak about our experiences. I start to ask them why when they along with most of the group pretend to be falling asleep. I know when I am beat. I laugh along with the others and sit down. Dayna stands up and everybody listens attentively. She tells them that if they would like one, we have some sweaters that we found on a military base in England.

She just happens to be wearing one. Everybody asks where they can get one. We have already distributed the case of sweaters to the different groups so they can get them when they get home. We have more than enough for everybody, but we do not have the small sizes for the young children in this style. We found sweaters for them in the Base Exchange that are even nicer than the adult sweaters. We wish we had enough of the really nice ones, but those are special and we will only wear them on special occasions. We have several family members that ask if we have enough of the Mini Cooper cars for every group.

We make sure everyone knows that like everything else we have, the cars belong to all of us and anyone who can drive is welcome to take one for a spin. This is one of those times that we have to make a list for people to sign up to drive one. Colonel Bob comes over to Dayna and me after supper and tells us that he could swear that he and Marie, his wife have seen cars like those in their travels. We wouldn't mind having a few more so if they can remember where they saw them we will go get a few more. As luck would have it today is Saturday so we get to rest tomorrow. That will be a good time to go around with our children and other extended family members to see how the work has progressed without us. It is so nice to sleep in our own bed for a change.

It was kind of funny because when we left Kathy said that she could use a short vacation from LT, she was only kidding of course. When we got back she came running and told him that he is not allowed to ever go anywhere without her again. Their new found family agreed with her totally even though we did bring home some really great stuff. The golfers in all the groups can't wait to try the golf equipment we brought back. Our scientific people like Mike and Morgan, James and Jenna, and Dave and Kimberly, who are not even in our group, tell me this evening that they would like to talk to me tomorrow after church. I joke and tell them that I will check my calendar and see if we can fit them in.

When they don't laugh and make a joke about it I figure this may be more serious than I first thought. They tell me that they would appreciate it very much. I tell them that nobody has needed an appointment to see any of us since we came here, hopefully that's not going to change now. Dayna and I spend a while trying to figure out what they might want to talk about, but as tired as we are we fall asleep before we can come up with anything that might make sense. In the morning we ask our children if they have any ideas and they think they know, but they don't want to speculate in case they are wrong.

I'm not sure whether I told you or not, our good friends Kristi and Jenny, and Jill and Tiffani are staying with us until they decide if they would like to live in their own house or not. It's so much fun listening to Jenny and Tiffani talk that the entire family has fallen in love with them. When they come downstairs for breakfast this morning they ask if there is any milk left over from the celebration yesterday. Dayna and I have been hungry for oatmeal so we made a big batch this morning. Our new family members remembered having some oatmeal when we first went to England, but that was eaten without milk and sugar. Jenny and Tiffani both agree that they could eat oatmeal this way every day and not get tired of it.

Nickie, our daughter in law, tells them that she was hoping they would like to try some pancakes, eggs and sausage for breakfast tomorrow morning. They say that they are not sure what all that is, but they are willing to try it. So far everything they have tried has been very good. The walk to church this morning is one of the most enjoyable in a while. Our new friends are so excited about everything they see that it is contagious so we are excited as well. I think I told you a while back that we had to add onto the existing church building we have been using. It is beginning to look like we are going to have to think about adding on again.

Ken, who is also our architect, says that he already has the plans drawn up for the new addition. We will get together probably tomorrow to discuss when we will start on the work. The crops are all in so we have some free time now. It is getting colder, but we have the best cold weather clothing that money can buy. Today is Wyatt and Tori, his wife's turn to teach the lessons. I am still not totally up on the jargon that they use in the church. Wyatt just reminded me that they are giving the talks today. The lessons will be taught by the people that have been called to teach. It feels so good to be sitting here with the people we love.

Not that we don't love the people we met in our travels, but it's always nicer to be with family. In our priesthood class and I am sure in the women's class called Relief Society we talked primarily about our travels. Everyone wants to know if we are planning on another trip. When I tell them we have discussed it they tell me that someone named Harry talked to them on the radio and told them that we told him we will come back in a couple years to bring him and his wife Ginny back to the states. I tell them that we did say something to that effect and everyone in the room volunteers to go with us.

When our meetings are over for the day we enjoy the walk home as much as we did the services today even though the temperatures are in the high forties. When we get home and change our clothes we grab a quick sandwich to hold us over until supper, then my sons and daughters take Dayna and me along with our new family members to see the progress that has been made. As soon as we walk out of the house we are joined by LT and Kathy, Sara and Gary, and Ken and Carrie along with their children. Our newest family members are very much impressed with everything they see. They are especially impressed with all the large outbuildings we have and I have to admit that the new hangar, which is completed is very impressive indeed.

Dave and Kimberly, who are visiting our settlement from Missouri, ask if we could possibly help them move some larger buildings to their settlement. They started one project when they got the C-130, but it is simply too big for them to accomplish on their own. We get to see how the cattle herd is doing. When we get close we can see a donkey grazing in with the cattle. I start to ask about it when Trey and Junior come up and tell me that the donkey is to protect the cattle from predators. We have seen wolves or at least large wild dogs in the distance, but they have never come close.

I guess when the wolves saw the heard of young cattle grazing they figured they would be easy pickings. Our family members from out west grew up with cattle and wolves and went looking for a donkey to protect the herd. They got lucky and found four of them. They put one in with the milk cows and gave the others to our neighbors for their herds. The first night the donkeys were in with the cattle they killed a wolf that apparently came looking for a beef dinner. They hung the wolf's hide on a large tree next to the pasture and they haven't seen any wolves since. I will take their word for it because I have no experience with cattle, wolves, or donkeys except that I have eaten a lot of beef.

From everything we are seeing our family did a great job of finishing up and starting some new projects while we were gone. My sons tell me that they made some changes to both of the obstacle courses so any time I feel like getting beat just let them know and they will oblige me. That gets Sara, Jenna, and Carrie's attention. Now Sara won't be happy until she beats me on the new and improved obstacle course. I tell them that I will try to find time tomorrow to at least get used to it and that we might be able to race later in the week. Sara looks at LT and tells him that she has some rooms that need painting in her house if he would like to make a small wager.

He just laughs and says that he still needs to paint the outside of her and Gary's house. He has learned his lesson about betting against ringers. Misty, Sara's daughter and Dayna and my son Thomas's girlfriend tells LT that a bunch of the young people got together and painted it when they had a warm spell for about a week.

LT tells her that he can't thank the young people enough. Just like her mom, she tells him that they will think of some way for him to repay them. We go about three steps when Misty says she has just the project that will make them even and he can even get help from us oldens.

Dayna and I look at our sons and tell them that didn't look too much like they had planned it ahead of time. They tell us that seeing the large hangar that we brought back and set up for the C-130 gave them, the idea. I think I know what it is before they even say anything. Before we can discuss it the wind picks up and it feels like the temperature is dropping so we decide to continue this conversation indoors. We go to the meeting room we have here and we are joined by a large number of our extended family from all the groups.

Our son Teddy starts the conversation. He says that the number of people wanting to play real golf has been growing every year. The major problem is that they don't have anywhere that they can keep their skills at a high level and they take several weeks to get back to where they were at the end of each season. What they are proposing is that we find another large hangar. It doesn't have to be as large as the last one we put up, but is should be good sized so that they can put up a net to drive the ball into and still have room to setup either nine or eighteen holes of miniature golf. Misty adds that it would be nice to have a practice green and maybe a short fairway to practice their short games on.

Knowing our youth, I ask them where the building they have in mind is and where are they planning to erect this building. Our son Timmy says he thought we would never ask. He asks if we mind taking another short walk and they will show us where they are thinking would be a good place. I'm sure if anyone that isn't with us this afternoon looks out their window they will think we have a parade heading toward Ryan and Carols group. We get just about a mile from our group to a very nice place that is roughly between our two groups. When we first came here this would have been open land, but now there are homes that run almost right up to it from both sides.

We can see where someone has marked off a rectangle that looks like the outline of a building. The outline is not much smaller than the large hangar at all. The young people have a sketch of what the building will look like outside and inside. They tell us that if we will help put up the building they will do the work inside during the winter. They realize that it will probably not be done for this winter, but should be available for many years to come. I ask them what the committee says about this project. I know that Teddy is on the committee, he and some of the others tell us that they wanted to get our input before a final decision is made.

I tell them that as long as I am still here I will be happy to help with the project. Our son Tommy says that the building has been found and they have started taking it down, just in case. I turn to the group that asked to talk to me today and ask them if this is what they wanted to discuss. They tell me no, although they all think it is a great idea. It is getting colder so I invite them to our house while most of the others head to their homes. The group tells us that they have to get some paperwork for what they want to propose so they will meet us at our house in about ten minutes. Sara tells me to make sure we have plenty of food to feed them all because this could take a while. If Sara is in our house for more than five minutes she expects to be invited for whatever meal is next.

14

Our sons tell us that they know what the others want to talk about, but they will let them tell us. Dayna and I are no closer to figuring out what they want to talk about than we were earlier. Mike and Morgan are the last to arrive. I only mention this because they are the ones making the presentation. Morgan starts the presentation by telling us how far we as a people have come since winding up here. She starts to name the more memorable achievements that we have had and it comes to me what they want to do. I tell her before she goes any farther that if they would like to start our own museum to highlight our achievements for generations to come, I will do whatever is necessary to help make it happen.

Morgan just puts her hands on her hips and tells me that the least I could do is listen to her presentation instead of ruining it by agreeing so easily. Mike is smiling and so is their son Mike Jr. He tells his mom that he told her all she had to do is mention it and everyone would be on board. Morgan tells me that I shouldn't speak so soon because they may want to put some of my prized possessions on display. I ask her which ones she is talking about. She points to the Sharps Buffalo gun that is setting on the side table in the dining room. I tell her to go ahead and take it. I agree that we should have items on display from the history of this world before we came here.

Mike and Mike Jr. go over and picking the gun up ask if they can shoot it before we put it up. I tell them that will be no problem since we brought back a couple cases of them as well as several other guns that would be great additions to the display. Dave and Kimberly ask if they could possibly get a few of the guns that we have more than one of. They would also like some of the golf equipment we brought back with us. They also add that since we are being benevolent, they noticed that we had several cases of those great looking sweaters left.

The comment about the sweaters reminds Dayna that we have some of the extra special ones for some of the people. Actually we have enough for about half of the people in our groups. We already know that the sizes won't fit everybody so it shouldn't be too bad. Billy and Ramona come over while we are talking and are more than happy to get a sweater. I found one that is large enough even for Billy. He is as happy as a kid at Christmas because none of the other style fit him. We continue the discussion of setting up a display that can be added onto whenever something important happens. They already have a building picked out that we can take apart and bring it to the settlement.

Now that everything is settled everyone asks me what we are going to feed them after keeping them busy all afternoon. Our newest family members get a kick out of how I get picked on by all of our friends. When food is mentioned both Jenny and Tiffany come over and tell me they could use a snack as well. The way they put it is that they are proper hungry. Dayna and the other women start to go to the kitchen to fix something when our sons tell us they already have this covered. As soon as they open the back door we can smell the pork roast and the ribs that have been slow cooking for the past several hours. There are baked potatoes and even some corn that has been taken off the cobs and frozen.

The two littlest ones say that they have no idea what this is, but they are sure going to find out if it tastes as good as it smells. I feel a little guilty eating this great meal if our other friends and family are not having any. Tim tells me not to worry. Everyone that wants this for dinner has it. They used the group grills and smokers to prepare the meal. Having all of our closest friends over for dinner makes us feel like we never went away. Izzie and Lillie make sure we all know that they shot the pig that this meal came from. Sara asks them how they can be sure and they tell her and all of us that they have shot the last five or six hogs that have been gotten. Apparently a couple of the young ladies living with LT and Kathy have been going along on the hunts as well.

While we are talking and enjoying our meal I notice that Jill and Kristi keep looking toward the door. I am not the least bit surprised when we have a knock on the door and I answer it to find Junior and Trey standing there with their hats in their hands. I can tell they are nervous, but they ask if Jill and Kristi would like to go for a walk around the settlement to see everything they haven't seen yet. When I look back into the room the girls already have their coats on along with their daughters. I tell the guys that I am not sure these young ladies should be going out without chaperones.

I hear a cough from the sidewalk in front of the house and look to see Wyatt and Tori as well as their children Ariel and Ephraim. I have to laugh and tell them to have a good time. Tori yells up to ask me if they can use one of the vans so they can go to the other groups as well. She says it is just a little colder than she is comfortable for the children to be out for any length of time. I tell them the vans belong to them as much as they do to me, just make sure they put gas in when they are through with it. Wyatt is patting his pants pockets and yells up that he forgot his credit card, but he will fill it next time for sure.

Finally I have had enough fun at their expense so I start to move out of the way and get pushed aside by Jill and Kristi. My little girl friends stop to give me a hug and Jenny even whispers in my ear that her mommy really likes Junior. They are right about it being too cold for walking any distance comfortably. Heber and his wife are going by taking a walk when the couples run to get to the van. He looks up at me and tells me that if he was single and twenty years younger he would give those two a run for their money with those cute young ladies. His wife smacks him and tells him that if he was twenty years younger he would still be old enough to be their grandfather.

We all laugh including both of them. He tells her that he guesses she is stuck with him then and calls her grandma. They kiss and he tells her they should go home and make out. She smacks him and tells him they have a houseful of children there. How are they going to make out. He gestures that he is relieved and tells her that he is glad to hear that, he isn't sure anymore how to make out. She laughs and smacks his behind telling him he is hopeless. He winks at us on the porch and tells her that if she keeps that up he may just remember one of these days.

We all get a kick out of hearing them bicker like that. Actually I have never seen any couple closer than they are. I swear that if one of them gets hurt they both feel the pain. Dayna and I are trying very hard to have a relationship like theirs. When we think about it Joseph and his wife are just about as close as they are. Our friends all tell us since they can't get into any arguments here they may as well go home. They all say it is beginning to look like we may get a snow storm tonight. It is November so it wouldn't be out of the realm of possibility.

We spend a quiet Sunday evening just talking to the children and catching up on what has been going on in our absence. When the others get home from their date the older teen age and somewhat older single ladies in the house tease them and ask them all about their date. Jenny and Tiffany both tell them that it wasn't much of a date. Junior and Trey didn't even kiss their moms. Then they ask if we have any more of that brilliant meat we had for dinner. The moms agree that it might be better to stuff the two younger ladies mouths with food so they can tell the girls about their date. The little ones fill up on warmed up spare ribs and then a large bowl of ice cream to wash them down while the girls in the family hang on every word that they are being told.

When the others go to other parts of the house or over to a friends, Kristi and Jill ask Dayna and me what kind of men are Junior and Trey. I start to answer, but Dayna tells them that they are real gentleman and they are very religious. They ask us if we would allow our daughters to date them or possibly marry them. Again I start to answer when we hear Lillie say that she has her eye on Tyler, he's Doc Betty and Joshes son. Then Izzie yells into the room that she likes Mike Jr. that's Mike and Morgan's son. Dayna tells them that she would have no trouble letting any of our daughters date or marry Junior or Trey if they loved them.

The day goes by while we play some games that just about the entire family enjoys. It feels just as good tonight to climb into our own bed as it did last night. Dayna and I agree that if any traveling comes up in the near future, someone else can go. Unfortunately when I get to sleep I have a dream where I am talking to my mom and dad and Gunny and Ma Horton. At first they were congratulating us on our successful trip to England then all of a sudden they are warning me that there is trouble coming and some of my friends and extended family are going to need all my skills to survive.

What I hate about news like that is that they are always right and they always leave as soon as they give me the message. I was going to ask them if they could at least tell me how long I have to get ready and possibly where this trouble may come from. I wake up and Dayna is staring at me. She tells me I was so restless that it woke her up. She asks me if I had another dream where my parents came to see me. I tell her yes they did and as usual they drop a bomb on me then leave. She smiles and tells me to look at the bright side. We shouldn't get bored anytime soon. She had the same dream and although she is worried she knows that these things happen.

In the morning we are telling the children about the dream Dayna and I both had. Jill and Kristi are coming into the kitchen and hear the last part of the discussion. They ask if they heard correctly, that we had a dream where my deceased parents came to us and told us about something that is going to happen. My daughters Tina and Tammy tell them that it happens all the time. They even tell them about the time when they were only four or five they got lost in the woods and Gramma and Grampa carried them until they heard their mom and dad coming. They continue saying that day was just about like today as far as weather.

Kristi and Jill have tears in their eyes when they tell us that they had dreams kind of like ours last night except their moms told them how proud they are of them for the choices they are making in their lives. Jenny and Tiffany say they had a dream about some people that said they are their grammas and grampas. They never saw them before so they will take their word for it. Then they ask if they can have some of that meat that smells so good. Dayna asks them if they would like some waffles and eggs as well and they both say, throw in a glass of milk and we have a deal. The older young people in the family almost choke on their milk. Their moms ask them where they heard that and they say that they heard Little Jon say that to his mom at the celebration.

They are worried that they might be in trouble, but we have all heard him say something to that effect so we just laugh along with them. Dayna fixes them a plate of bacon, waffles, and eggs and gives them each a big glass of milk. Both of the little girls tell their moms that they should have moved here a long time ago. Their moms tell them that they agree totally. The trouble is that they didn't know we were here and they had no way to get to America if they did. Teddy, Nickie, and Little Jon come over for breakfast. We tell Nickie and Teddy what our friends from England picked up from their son.

Teddy says that Little Jon was in a hurry this morning to come over because he was afraid that his Gramma and Grampa might be gone again along with his new friends that talk funny. When Little Jon has his plate full of food he climbs up to sit between the two girls. Nickie laughs and says we will have to watch him close. He's a real ladies man just like his Grampa and his daddy. Teddy makes a sandwich out of some bacon and an egg and tells me this is a good time to find somewhere else to be. I agree and finish my breakfast quickly. As we go out the door our wives yell at us calling us cowards. We have no problems with that.

It did snow last night and it is a brisk clear morning that makes you glad to be alive. We must be on our way to an agreed upon place because as we get closer we can see at least a dozen men here. Teddy tells me that if I don't mind we can go do some work on the new building. Some of the guys and girls will stay here today and get the ground ready for the cement slab. It's a good thing we have the proper equipment to do the job correctly and efficiently. The rest of us are going to where the building is and continue taking it down. The building is just about an hour away. When we get there I can see that there has already been quite a bit of work done. There are four large flatbed trucks waiting to be loaded. One of them already has some of the roof stacked neatly on it.

I love being able to get up high on the walls or the roof of a building like this and take the panels down to be rebuilt back at the settlement. Not everyone enjoys being forty or fifty feet in the air while they work, but heights have never bothered me. I always remember what Gunny told me about working high up. He said that most people are afraid of falling. He said that he never could understand that because the fall doesn't hurt, it's the sudden stop when you hit the ground. To him that always meant he should fear the ground more than the height. I tell that to some of our newer friends and they just look at me like I have just grown another head.

Teddy tells them they can think I am crazy if they want to. Those who know me better are sure of it. When we all laugh they must feel like we are joking with them because they laugh as well. The younger men on the crew are teasing Junior and Trey this morning about asking Kristi and Jill out so quickly. They know that the others are as happy for them as they are, so they joke right back, which makes the day go much more quickly. We brought some homemade trail mix bars for lunch so we don't have to lose so much time going for lunch, besides all of the restaurants near here are closed on Mondays. Just checking to see if you are paying attention.

We pretty much work right through lunch and by the time we knock off for the day we have about the equivalent of an entire side taken down along with the entire roof. The roof is loaded on the truck and that's about as much as we dare put on one truck so we are going to drive it back to the settlement, actually to the construction site. I always enjoy driving the big trucks so I get to drive this one home. When we get there we can see that our crew here was at least as busy as we were today. They have the entire rectangle dug out about a foot down and the outside edges are down just about three feet so that the foundation doesn't move after it is poured.

Tomorrow they will put about six inches of gravel and then put rebar in to give the floor more strength and durability. The people planning this project want to leave some of the ground inside the building as dirt and grass along with a couple of sand traps. Tomorrow this crew will go into town to get the gravel and the topsoil needed to do what they are planning. I am really proud of the young people in our family for having the vision of such a large project. We figure it will take just about another week to get the rest of the building down and marked so that we can put it back together.

I no sooner get in the house, wash up, and sit down to eat when Sara, Lindsay, Jenna, and Morgan, come over to challenge me to a run on the upgraded obstacle course. I knew this was coming, for one thing Nickie, my daughter in law, told me that these women practiced the obstacle course at least three times today. Second, they always want to prove to me and everyone else that they are my equal in every way. I tell them that as soon as I have a chance to practice as much as they have we can run the course for competition. They want to know when they can expect to beat my butt as usual. I tell them we will knock off a little early the next couple of days and I will practice then. We can race on Saturday morning, that way everyone can see me smoke them.

That gets them wound up. After that the only thing that can quiet them down is the spaghetti that Dayna and our new family members cooked for supper. Jenny and Tiffany made sure that I know they helped. They were the official taste testers along with Little Jon. Naturally I make a fuss over that information and tell them that is probably the most important job of all. They also got to play outside with the puppies and a bunch of young people close to their age. Dayna assures me that Biscuit and Cricket were never more than a few yards away and made sure no one wandered off even though there was always a couple of parents with them.

Dinner is great even if the company is a little suspect. Their husbands all came looking for them and it was just a little too coincidental to be an accident. That's okay Dayna and the others made plenty. Before everyone leaves, the competitive ladies in this group have invited Kristi and Jill to run the obstacle course tomorrow. That's all I need, two more women in this family that want to kick my butt at everything. We end our evening by having a lesson on eternal families for Family Home Evening. Our new family members have some questions that I can't answer so we assure them we will ask Wyatt or they could ask Junior and Trey. I am sure they will know the answers.

15

On Tuesday we have another good day, but there is still a lot to do. We are not worried about it because the concrete is going to have to set for a while before we can build on it. The weather seems to have become milder which helps doing the kind of work we are doing now. When we get home I change my clothes and head over to the obstacle course with Dayna. When we get to the obstacle course there must be half the settlement here today. I have to tell them that all Dayna and I are planning to do this evening is run the course leisurely to get used to the changes. There will not be any competition between me and anyone else at least until Saturday.

Some of our friends say that they want to do the same thing we are doing and get our opinion on the new changes. We have a lot of the newer people here this evening that want to do exactly what Dayna and I are doing. We agree to start out just about a minute apart with Dayna and me leading off. We say we are going to take it easy, but there are areas in the course where you have to go pretty fast or you will not get over the obstacle. We really like the changes that have been made, but we also have some suggestions to make it just a tad more challenging.

While we are talking about some new changes Heber and Joseph come running out of the course exit. They ask what changes we are discussing and say they agree that it needs to be a little more challenging. We are waiting at the end to see what the others think when Junior, Trey, Kristi, and Jill come running out. Heber and Joseph tell Junior and Trey that they can remember what it was like chasing pretty girls, but they don't recall ever chasing them through an obstacle course. The guys let the girls go first so they could be there if anyone got injured or had trouble. Heber tells the guys like he is whispering, but we can all hear, that it is more fun if you actually catch the girls you are chasing.

We all laugh and all four of them say they are glad we reminded them of that. It's been so long since they have dated they forgot the most important stuff. It's been another good evening and we are sure tomorrow will bring more of the same. Dayna and I are beginning to wonder if possibly my parents are not correct this time. We are not betting on it though because we have both seen how quickly things can go from great to pretty darn bad. We are just going to enjoy the good times and handle the more difficult ones as they come up.

On Wednesday we are still taking down the building and marking the sections. After work for the day Dayna and I decide to run the obstacle course again. Dayna told me when I got home that there was a crew working on it today so the changes we recommended may have already been done. This evening there are not as many people to run it as last evening. We start out running and we notice some changes right way. Someone not only made the changes we suggested, they made some of the other obstacles more difficult as well.

It's not bad, but before some of the people who are not into the challenge of the obstacle course as much as they are in just doing it to stay in shape would come and go through this one. Now I think they will think twice, at least until they get used to it. Dayna and I get all the way through with no incidents or accidents and I have to say we are impressed. I personally have never been on a tougher obstacle course. It is definitely a challenge and if you are not carful there are even more places where the course can grab you and you wind up in one of the water hazards. I want to run it at least once more before I try to do it for time.

On Thursday morning the wind is blowing pretty strongly and it looks like it could either rain or snow, depending on what the temperature is at the time. Those of us working on the building are glad that we are not working at the top anymore. We are also glad that we have scissor lifts to work in and we are now at a level that we can use an excavator to lift the large panels when they are loose. The wind does cause some problems and a couple of scary moments, but we manage to get through the day without any accidents. It starts raining when we are on our way home. It sure does feel like it is going to change to snow before too long.

When we get home it is kind of a mix between rain and snow. That makes running the obstacle course just a little too dangerous so we are going to relax for a change. Lillie and Izzie went hunting today with Matt, Max, and Tommy. They invite me down to the barn to see the two deer, one extra large hog, and a very large steer. They have also started hunting turkeys to get ready for Thanksgiving, which is in about two weeks. They didn't shoot any, they just went looking so that they know where to go when it is time.

Our newest family members ask the girls if they ever see pheasants or grouse when they are hunting. They tell them they see them all the time, but it takes so many to feed even one group that it is hardly worth hunting them. Some of our people hunt them for a personal meal or two from time to time. If they would like some, the girls will be more than happy to get some for them. Dayna says that she would enjoy some fresh pheasant once in a while. She really enjoyed it when we were in England. Some of our people really like rabbit as well. Those are things that they usually hunt themselves, but again the girls will be happy to get some for those that want them.

After supper Dayna and I take a walk with Lillie and Izzie to see how successful they were today. They are right that the hog and the steer are very big and the deer are not exactly small either. We have some family members that prefer venison over any other kind of meat. As plentiful as they are it is never a problem to bring some home. The butchers have the animals skinned and quartered, and now they are letting them hang to give them better flavor.

Friday morning gets here with an overcast day. It did not snow enough last night to leave more than a dusting on the ground. We are hoping to finish taking down the wall panels on the building and start trucking it home either this afternoon or Monday. We do not have enough trucks to bring it all home at once so we are going to load the bottom panels onto the last empty truck we have and unload them as we set them in place. We were going to bring them home as we take them down, but when we discovered our lack of vehicles we decided not to handle them twice and just bring them home as they are needed.

It actually turns out to be a nice day and we get the rest of the walls taken down. We even have enough time to hunt a few pheasants. It seems that word got out that someone would like some pheasant for a change of diet and now about half the settlement would like some. That will take quite a few birds and since the area we are in seems to be loaded with them we figure we may as well try our luck. None of us have any trouble shooting a moving target with a rifle, but using a shotgun is totally different. We are using a strategy where some of us walk ahead of the others who are on the front groups flanks. It has been our experience when we have hunted pheasants that they often fly behind you. This way the group behind has a chance to get them.

Our strategy sounds good, but nobody told this group of birds how they are supposed to react so we are splitting up in groups of two and just hunting them. Most of these birds have probably never seen a human being except at a distance so they don't fly up as quickly as some birds. The birds we are getting are larger than the ones Gunny and I used to hunt. That's not a bad thing because it will take less of them to feed the group that wants them. LT and I are hunting together and have gotten six birds between us. That's not bad when we have seen probably fifteen or sixteen. We saw some birds fly up and we missed them, but we saw them land again near a rundown building about fifty yards ahead of us.

We get close and see two of the largest turkeys either of us has ever seen. Thanksgiving is next Thursday so if we get a turkey today it will still be very good by then. We brought some slugs and buckshot with us today along with the birdshot. We load our guns with buckshot and plan to aim for the head so that we don't mess up the meat. We work our way as close as we dare then we say that we will shoot on three. I count to two then we both see an arrow hit the bigger of the two, go through him and hit the second bird in the chest.

We are looking for who shot that arrow when Lillie and Izzie yell over to us that they are sorry for messing up our shot. We do not care about who shoots the turkeys, but I remind them that they should have let us know that they are within shooting range. Someone could get hurt that way. While the girl's field dress the turkeys, LT, Matt, and I continue looking for pheasants. Matt tells us that they have had pretty good luck so far today. They have knocked down twenty-two birds so far. He also says that this is the second area they have hunted today and they also got two more deer and another hog for Doc Betty's group. They already took the hog, the two deer, and fifteen of the pheasant's home. They knew we were working in this area and also knew that there is a lot of very good game here.

While we are walking through the tall grass we kick up a group of five, LT and I each get one, but Matt knocks down the other three. They were fairly close together, but he still had to shoot one, aim at another, and then do that all over again. He says that since joining our family he has had the opportunity to do a lot of hunting and has gotten to be pretty good at shooting birds. His wife Sandy and their children enjoy eating the grouse, and the pheasants, as well as some rabbit from time to time. He asks if he has been doing anything wrong by hunting those things. He adds that he always gets enough for his neighbors if they say they would like some. He adds that this is the first time we have asked the hunters to specifically hunt the pheasants.

We tell him he is welcome to hunt anything he wants to, but we would appreciate it if he maybe lets the group know what he is going after. There may be more people than he realizes that would enjoy some as well. He promises to do that and we bag four more birds on the way back to the girls. When we get back to the building site we find out that the rest of our party had some very good hunting as well. With the twenty-two that we have the total for our hunting groups is thirty-six birds. Lillie says that there are other hunters out today as well so there should be plenty.

When we get home the others did have good luck as well so we have to set up an assembly line to get the birds cleaned for eating. In this case though, the correct word might be disassembly line, because we are not assembling anything. With the crew we have it doesn't take long at all and the birds are ready to cook. We have the large cooking drums that we use when we have a big get together. Today some of our more industrious people rigged up some rotisseries to cook just about all the birds at once, if that is what everyone wants. That sounds good to everyone so we sprinkle the birds with some seasonings that we grow ourselves and let them cook. Some people ask if they can put some barbeque sauce on the bird for their family. I don't really want any so I couldn't care less how they cook them.

This is one of those nights when everybody seems to be hungry for something different. That's okay because we very seldom eat our meals in common now. Everybody gets their share of the food we get and it's up to them how they cook it. Some of our family wants the birds, but some of us want some good beef for supper tonight. Since we have the grills going anyway we bake a bunch of potatoes to go with whatever else we are having. The birds smell great and they are big enough that one will feed a family easily. While we are eating Sara comes over and reminds me that we are racing tomorrow morning.

After she says that she hands me a couple pieces of the last batch of chocolate.

I tell her I will wait until after I beat them tomorrow morning to eat the candy. Actually my favorite little people come over and ask me if that chocolate candy belongs to anybody. Little Jon must be picking up some of the English jargon that Jenny and Tiffani use because he tells me that he would be proud to help me eat it. There is enough candy for all of the little ones that came over to see us anyway. Lindsay saw me give it to the children and comes over to tell me that they will beat me even without filling me with chocolate. I am just glad that we are not running the course this evening. I am so full of beef and baked potato that all I want to do now is go to bed. I think the travel and working in the cold all week is starting to take its toll.

When we finally get back to the house and get settled in I start to fall asleep almost as soon as I get comfortable in my chair. I must fall asleep because when I answer a question that was asked of me everyone laughs and says they asked me that question twenty minutes ago. Even I have to laugh and excuse myself so I can go to bed. My dreams tonight do not make any sense. I keep finding myself tracking people through the jungle like when I was in Cuba, only this time I am in Mexico. I am working my way through a jungle when I hear voices yelling at what appear to be prisoners. The problem is the prisoners are our friends Heber, Joseph, and Wyatt along with some people I never saw before.

I have this same dream over and over and what scares me the most is that I wake up at the same place in the dream every time. What is most disturbing about that is that when I wake up it is just as I am being shot. I have no idea where or how badly I get hurt. Finally it is morning and we can get up. I don't say a word when Dayna asks me what I think the dreams mean. She thinks that they have something to do with what my parents said. I have to admit I am thinking the same thing right now. We eat a light breakfast and head over to the obstacle course. There are already a bunch of people here. Some have run the course and some are waiting until after our race.

Sara and the others get here and have to harass me or it wouldn't be the same. We agree that we will run against the clock starting a minute after each other. I prefer to run first mainly because they have blocked me from being able to run while the others win the race. I feel good today as I am going over the obstacles in my mind. When the time comes to start, Heber and Joseph are the official starters. Their wives along with three others will be the official time keepers. They shoot the starter gun and I am off running at what I consider a good pace.

I am having a great time completing the obstacles one after the other and when I complete the course there is no one even close behind me. When I cross the finish line all four of my adversaries are waiting for me. I ask them why they didn't run and they tell me they did. They just took a short cut to the finish line. They all tell me I lost miserably and not to call them cheaters because no one said they had to run the complete course. My first impression is one of anger, but then I really don't care whether I win or not so I bow to them and congratulate them on another victory. As it turns out that is the best thing I could do.

They all ask me what my time was, they are going to beat me running the entire course. They line up and leave only thirty seconds apart. The course is longer than it was and it takes a while to complete it, but they all do, only today my time is seven seconds faster than any of them. I just smile at them and head back home for some breakfast. My sons tell me I am getting closer to their times. All I have to do is take about thirty seconds off my time today and we will be close. We are not home for more than five minutes before Sara, Morgan, Jenna, and Lindsay are coming in and demanding a rematch next week.

The course is a lot of fun, so I tell them that I will be happy to give them a rematch. I also tell them that will give me another week to practice so I may even have a better time then. We finish eating breakfast while we discuss what we are going to do today. It's Saturday and we had some fun this morning, but the only day we don't work around here is on Sunday and some people have to work then to make sure the animals get fed, the cows get milked, and the milk gets pasteurized. There are people who do these jobs every day and enjoy doing it, but on Sundays we take turns relieving them so they get a day of rest as well.

I find out this morning that tomorrow is Dayna and my turn to feed the chickens and gather the eggs. Before the day is over we will go check in with the ladies who run that part of the farm. Jessie and her daughter Jenny are still in charge there, but they have a full crew that keeps track of the chickens that we use for laying eggs, for increasing the flock, and for food. It still bothers them a little that we have to kill some of them for food, but at least this way they are serving two purposes for us. Chickens can only produce eggs for a certain amount of time, when they are no longer useful for this purpose we use them for food.

It is not as easy gathering eggs as it was when we only had a hundred chickens or so. I have no idea how many we have now, but I do know that we have built two very large structures to keep them in, along with fencing in some very large areas for them to run around outside. Enough about the chickens, today we are going to help with the indoor golf range. Actually we are going to work on the area of the building that will be like playing outdoors. We have a couple of books on the subject of designing and building our own practice greens, as well as how to make fairways, sand traps, and even how to make rough for practicing.

I have not seen the base in a couple of days so when we get to the work site we see that not very much of this building will have a concrete floor in it. The foundation goes all the way around the building, but it is there only to support the building. The ground has been marked off for the different areas that people can practice so we break into groups and get busy building our part of it. The foundation is dry enough for us to start putting down the sill plate all the way around it. I love this kind of work. When I get to do this I always find out that I am not in as good of shape as I think I should be. This week has shown me that I need to get back into a workout regimen to get back into shape.

16

We had so much fun working on the new building today that we never even stopped for lunch. The guys I was working with wanted to get as much done as possible today. I was working with Wyatt, Max, Trey, and Junior. Those guys could work a young man into the ground and I am not as young as I used to be. When we quit for the day we have the base plate in place and bolted in all the way around the building. When we started I didn't think we would get much over half of it done today. On the way home Wyatt tells me that he, Heber, and Joseph have something they would like to talk to Dayna and me about either this evening or tomorrow before church.

Right now Dayna and I have to get our instructions from our chicken experts, but after that we are pretty much free. Naturally Sara and Lindsay are coming up behind us when I tell him that. Sara pats me on the behind as she goes by and says that I am finally getting paid what I am worth. Wyatt tells her that's not true, he has worked with me many times and I am worth every cent of a buck and a quarter an hour. By now there are at least twenty other people within hearing range and some say they agree with Sara and some agree with Wyatt. Can't you feel the love here? Dayna and I excuse ourselves to go and get our instructions for tomorrow morning.

When we get to chicken coop number 1, which is the one we are assigned to, we meet one of the newer members of our family working here. Apparently she knows what she is doing because she is running the show here today. She is happy to see us. We haven't seen each other since we brought her and her sisters back with us from one of our adventures before we went to England. She starts explaining that they want a certain number of eggs to go on to grow the flock and the rest of them to be gathered to be eaten. Both large coops are doing the same thing tomorrow. She looks like she is not sure if she can trust us to do this correctly or not.

I think it's funny because when she is thinking hard her nose twitches up, she folds her arms across her chest, and she looks either to the side or at the ground. Finally she must come to a decision that she can live with because she smiles and says that she will meet us here at six tomorrow morning and will help us get the correct amount of eggs for both purposes. We have no problem with that except we feel bad that she has to work tomorrow. She says that she really doesn't mind, when she gets married it will probably be a different story, but for now she doesn't mind at all.

On the way out of the coop we run into the other team working tomorrow and they tell us that Tammy, one of the other regulars on this job is coming in tomorrow as well. When we get back to the house the children have supper ready for us just about the time we get washed up. It is so nice to be able to sit down to a table surrounded by the people you love and share in the things that are bringing them joy or that are causing them to be unhappy. Tonight we are having spaghetti and Italian sausage for supper along with some great French bread that Nickie baked this afternoon. I know I shouldn't, especially since I have to race the ladies again next week, but I eat a second helping of everything.

Just as we are through eating, Wyatt, along with his family, and Heber, and Joseph along with their wives, knock on the door. We just yell telling them to come in. Actually Dayna tells them to come in. I tell them that there is no one home. Naturally they ignore me and come right in. Wyatt's children, Ariel and Ephraim love to play with Little Jon, Jenny, and Tiffany. When they see that there is food left on the table they ask if they can have some. Tori, Wyatt's wife, tells them that they just ate dinner, how can they still be hungry. They tell her they didn't have spaghetti, and they are hungry for some. Actually they pronounce it basketti, but we all know what they mean. Wyatt, Heber, and Joseph reach across the table and grab a piece of Italian sausage and some French bread and make a quick sandwich. They ask if we can go somewhere to talk. Dayna asks if she should come now or wait so there will be no witnesses.

They tell her that she might want to wait because this could get ugly fast. Sara and Gary walk in right then and she tells Wyatt that anything that involves me starts out ugly. Then she starts to sit on my lap while I am getting up to join the others. She complains to Gary that I am trying to get her to sit on my lap, but he is busy making a sandwich as well so he couldn't care less. Tori always laughs whenever she is around and Sara and I are having one of our little discussions. She says it reminds her of the way her mom and dad got along.

We men have to go outside to talk. We will not find anywhere in the house that is not taken by someone. It's a great night anyway so we don't mind at all. When we sit down they ask if we can start our meeting with a word of prayer. Personally I don't remember to do that enough. Heber starts the discussion by saying that he is the one who this is mainly about so he will explain why they wanted to talk to me. He continues by saying that he and his wife have two sons that were on their missions in South America when the war hit. They have always assumed that they didn't make it and that they would have to wait until the next life to see them.

I ask him how that has changed, if it has changed. He takes off his hat and rubs his hand over his head whenever he is not sure of what to say or what to do. He does that now and looks me straight in the eye and tells me he really doesn't know. He and his wife have had dreams for the past several nights where his sons come to them and tell them they went to Mexico to try to find them, but they had left before they got there. He continues saying that they also tell them that they have people with them that cannot go much farther so if he can hear them to please come back to Mexico for them.

Joseph tells me that he and his wife have had the same dreams lately. They knew the boys when they were young and just before they left on their missions. He says they are the type to move heaven and earth to get back to their parents if they could. Wyatt tells me that he and Tori have had the same dreams and they have never met Heber's sons. In fact they didn't even know he had sons until they started having the dreams. I ask them what they would like me to do. Wyatt says that they know it is asking a lot, but they are wondering if they could use one of the airplanes we have to go back to Mexico to look for them.

I tell them that I can't just turn over one of our planes without asking the council. I will be happy to plead their case for them, but do they think they can do this adventure alone or do they think they will need help. They say they are hoping that I could go with them in case there is something that might prevent them from being able to come back. Now it is beginning to make sense. I ask them what makes them think that someone or something may be stopping them from coming to them. Heber looks kind of sheepishly and says that in the dreams his sons tell him that they are being followed by some bad men so we should come as quickly as possible.

I tell them that they should have said that in the first place. We go inside and I ask Teddy if he can call an emergency meeting of the council to discuss going on a possible rescue mission. Now we have everybody's attention. My son's Timmy and Tommy tell me that they have not had the chance to go on a mission to help anyone yet. They both say they can shoot as well as anyone, except maybe me, and they are both in excellent physical condition. Personally I think they can both shoot as good as I can. The thought of taking them anywhere that we may run into danger scares me. I know it does Dayna as well, but she tells me that it might be good experience for them. That opens the door for Allen who is my son with Robin and Jon and Kevin, who are Tim and Charity's sons. Both are the same age as Tommy.

They may feel like men because they have been doing a man's job since they were about ten or eleven, but they are still in their early teens. I draw the line when Izzie and Lillie ask if they can go. I use the excuse that we have no idea how many people we will be picking up and we don't want to take the C-130 down there. That's the biggest problem with projects like this one. We have no idea how many people we will have to bring back, if any. Wyatt and the others tell us that they know for sure where we can get fuel for the plane when we get there. Plus it is not that far away by plane. We can get there and back in the same day.

Tim tries to raise someone on the radio from there and we have no luck. We are waiting for Teddy to come back from talking to the council to know whether or not we can even go. Sara comes in and tells us to go ahead and plan for the trip. We all know the council will not refuse anything I ask for. Teddy comes back and tells us that he has some good news and some bad news. When we don't answer he asks which we would like first. Nickie, his wife smacks him and tells him to tell us the good news first. He acts like he is hurt, but he won't get any sympathy from this group.

He tells us that the council says that we should go if there is any chance of helping other people in need. The bad news is that they feel that Wyatt, Heber, Joseph, and I be the only ones going in case they have more people coming back than we think. The young men are disappointed, but they know we are always going on what they call adventures so they will get to go soon. I am relieved and so is Dayna and Charity. We start planning to leave tomorrow morning even if it is Sunday. They feel that time may be running out on those people. Wyatt is going to pilot the plane, but Heber and Joseph both know how to fly planes.

There is not much to plan, we are going to fly there, land, and look for Heber's sons. We will take some provisions with us in case we need them primarily for the people we are going to get. I am taking an AK-47 along with my usual two or three hand guns and my fifty caliber in case we need to do some long range shooting. I am also bringing one of my Special Forces bows with at least fifty arrows. When Wyatt sees what I am bringing he smiles and says that he would hate to see how I prepare for a mission when we are expecting trouble. I smile, but I tell him truthfully that I always expect trouble, no matter where we are going. That way I am pleasantly surprised if we don't run into any.

We want to leave before sunup so we are going to bed early. For the first time since we started talking about this trip Dayna tells me that she is worried about me and doesn't have a good feeling about this at all. She reminds me about the dream we had, it really wasn't necessary because I was already thinking about it. Contrary to popular belief I do not enjoy fighting for my life or taking others lives. Sometimes we simply have to do what is necessary to protect the ones we love and our way of life. I do not sleep well. I keep having the same dream over and over again until I decide to just get up and wait for the time for us to leave.

Dayna and I go downstairs to sit in the kitchen, it can't be more than five minutes before all my traveling companions are knocking at the door asking if we would like to get an early start. Why not, there is no sense sitting around waiting for the dial on a clock to tell us it is time to leave. The area where the planes are kept is a ways from our homes, so Dayna and Timmy give us a ride there. The plane was checked out last evening, but just to be safe we do another preflight inspection. Everything is fine so we climb aboard and get ready to take off. I tell Dayna not to worry. We will be home in time for supper this evening. She kisses me and says she is going to hold me to that promise.

Wyatt is a good pilot, he takes off and we can barely tell when we leave the ground. I yell up to the front telling him that and he yells back that we haven't left the ground. All he knows how to do is taxi the plane so we are driving it to Mexico. I tell him that it sounds good to me, wake me up when we get there. I must fall asleep somewhere during the flight because it is dark out one minute and the next the sun is shining brightly. Wyatt calls back that he has turned on the no smoking sign and that we should prepare to land. I really enjoy working with these guys. They told me that Junior, Trey, and Max were pretty upset when they found out we were going without them.

Wyatt asked them to please hold the church services this morning and we will be back to tell them how boring this trip was a little later. Wyatt sets the plane down on what appears to be a small runway that is just about long enough for the plane we are using today. He taxi's it right up beside a fuel truck to see if it has enough fuel to fill our tanks. He even points the plane in the direction that we will be taking off just in case we have to leave in a hurry. These guys know what they are doing. Heber says that he could swear he saw some smoke coming from an area just about a quarter mile away so while they head off in search of people I stay behind to fill the tanks on the plane.

There is a good chance we could make it home with the fuel we have, but why take chances when the fuel is readily available. I finish topping off the tanks, grab my guns, and head off in the direction my friends took. I am being wary just in case. For one thing there are plenty of animals, insects, snakes, and spiders that can kill a man as quickly as any bullet and will probably be more painful as well. While I am thinking all these pleasant thoughts I am listening for any sound out of the ordinary. I can see what appears to be a clearing up ahead and start to hurry to see if that is where the others are. When I get close I hear a voice that is not familiar telling someone that they should forget fighting. The men they see are trained killers that will do just that if they resist.

I hate it when I am right. Now we have to see what I can do to get the others out of this predicament. Luckily the ground is hard enough that I am making almost no sound and apparently the bad guys think they have everybody. That will give me the element of surprise. I also know that at least Wyatt, Heber, and Joseph have hand guns and knives hidden on them. Hopefully if I can get the bad guys attention they will be able to get them into play. I get close enough to look into the clearing and I can see a pretty large group of people being held by what appears to be eight bad guys all carrying guns.

I count the good guys and including Wyatt, Heber, and Joseph there are twenty two people, but there are at least six of them that are children and none of the people look to be very large so weight should not be an issue for the plane. Heber looks directly at me and nods just the tiniest bit. He whistles a bird impression that he does quite well and one of his captors threatens to shoot him if he is trying to warn someone. He asks the guy who he could be warning. Then he tells the guy that he caught him red handed. He is telling the larger birds in the jungle to fly overhead and take a dump right on the bad guy's heads.

The guy he is talking to tells the man in charge what Heber just told him. At least he knows that Heber is just being sarcastic. He walks over to Heber and asks him who he is signaling. Heber looks him straight in the eyes and tells him that he is just showing his grand children, that he has never seen before, how well he can do bird impersonations. One young lady who appears to be sixteen or seventeen tells Heber that she is very much impressed with his bird calls. One of the bad guys tells her that she will be impressed with what they are going to do to her as well.

The look Heber gives that guy makes my blood run cold. He tells the guy if they touch her he will kill every one of them even if it means that he dies. They just laugh, but Joseph tells them they have no idea what they are messing with. He continues telling them that Heber is a high priest and can call down the powers of heaven against them. I am taking that statement as a cue for me to start something. I am trying to figure out what I can do that would look like the wrath of heaven raining down on one of them.

I am looking all around then I see that there are some very large trees hanging over the clearing where they are being held. There is a large limb that had broken off some time in the past hanging precariously close to where one of the bad guys is standing. I start to climb the tree to see if I can dislodge the branch. I brought another fairly long stick with me that has no branches except at the end, so if I reach with it, the stick should look like another branch. I am in position to poke at the larger unstable branch, now I am just waiting for a signal.

Heber can't see me, but I make the noise of a bird as well, only mine is not as good as his. The guy closest to the large branch starts to say something when Heber says in a loud voice that he is commanding the spirits to show these animals what kind of power they are messing with. I figure that is about as good a signal as I have ever heard, so I reach forward with that stick and that large branch acts just like we want it too. The only trouble is that when it dislodges it breaks a couple of small branches and that sound causes everybody to look up.

The branch falls to the ground just missing the man standing under it. It seems like everyone is moving at once when that limb hits the ground. The bad guys seem pretty shaken and are not sure if Heber brought that down on them or not. Their leader is telling them that it is only a coincidence, but these men are superstitious enough to believe Heber, at least partway.

17

The good thing is that it has caused the bad guys to take their eyes off Heber, Joseph, and Wyatt long enough for them to get their guns out and start shooting. I open fire from the tree I am in, but I realize that I better get to a better defensible position. I jump to the ground and take a position behind a tree where I have a clear field of fire at the attackers. I see Heber, Wyatt, and Joseph telling the others to run for the plane. Heber has his knife out and throws it at the one who made the comment about his granddaughter. It takes him in the shoulder, it is just a glancing blow, but it causes the guy to jump behind a tree for safety.

The bad guys are all trying to find places to hide and shoot from, but there is no one left to shoot at. The people being held are through that opening and are running as fast as they can for the plane. Some of them are being carried by those that can so I am giving them some cover fire to keep the bad guys pinned down. The leader yells at his men to go after them and one brave, but foolish soul jumps out from behind the tree and now he can tell some of his ancestors where he went wrong in this fight. One more starts to jump out and changes his mind when my next shot kicks bark off the tree next to him.

They must be starting to key in on where I am because their return fire is getting pretty close to me. I start to fall back to make sure that everyone gets to the plane when I hear the engines start. Wyatt is coming back to tell me that the plane is full, but they think there is room for me to squeeze in. I tell him that my weight will put the plane over its load capacity so they should get out of here, but they should call home when they are safe and tell someone that I could use some help here. He says that he will stay with me and I tell him to get back home to those beautiful children and wife of his. I tell him that I will be fine. I may even have time to catch a nap before my rescuers get here.

I no sooner finish talking when bullets start hitting the tree branches around us. I tell Wyatt to get out of here before I shoot him myself. He heads for the plane and I go to the side to draw the gunfire at me. I don't think they saw Wyatt, but to be sure I fire some rounds to keep them honest. I hear the roar of the plane as it flies away from us and any gunfire that may be pointed in their direction. Now I am alone and I better do something to even the odds against me soon or there may not be anyone for my rescuers to find. I decide to go on the offensive to whittle the opposition down some.

I drop back to regroup and to decide the best way to do what needs to be done. This reminds me of a mission the team was on in Central America. I try to forget thinking about that one because it didn't end as well as we would have liked. While I am thinking about all this I hear a noise like someone sneaking up on me through the jungle. I turn just as whoever is coming steps into the very small clearing I am in and have my gun ready to fire. When I see it is two teenagers who have their hands chained together I realize that they are not a threat to me. Although they are not a threat, I keep my gun trained on them when I ask them who they are and what they are doing here.

They speak very little English, but they know enough to tell me they are not my enemies. I speak to them in Spanish next and they tell me that they were taken from their home this morning when those men came through looking for the group that must have left in that flying machine. I tell them they are correct about that and ask them who they are. Apparently they are brother and sister. They were living about an hour south of here with a small group of their friends. Their friends were able to hide this morning, but they were not as fortunate as that. They also say that when the gunfire started they decided to try to get away and here they are.

I help them get their chains off and tell them they should go to a safer place until my help comes. Then if they would like they can either come back to our settlement in the United States, or they can return to their friends. They ask if their friends could go with us as well. I tell them they are all more than welcome. I add to that if I can convince the bad guys that I am not worth all the trouble they will have trying to catch me. The young lady points at my bow and tells me that she can use that to help me eliminate the opposition.

I would love to see her do that, but that's the tool I am planning to use so that my position is not given away every time I shoot the gun. I explain this to them and she asks for one of the knives I am carrying in case they are found. That way they will have a way to defend themselves. That I can do. In situations like this I have never been the type to hide and hope that I don't get found. Besides these guys may decide to come north and cause trouble there. That could cause some of our friends to lose their lives needlessly so I am taking the offensive and see how many of them I can take out.

I know that sounds barbaric, but when there is no organized law we have to take action on our own. People like this would probably be just as bad if there was law here. There is plenty of good land near here for farming and plenty of animals for food, but these guys choose to take advantage of hard working people who want nothing more than to survive. I figure I have about three hours before I can expect any help. That should give me plenty of time to whittle down their numbers. I am heading back to where this all started when I hear a couple of voices coming my way.

At least these guys are smart enough to travel in pairs. I am not looking to take prisoners and I am sure they will kill me as soon as they see me, if they see me. I hunker down to listen to their conversation. They are speaking Spanish, but I understand that almost as good as I do English. I am thinking that Sara, Morgan, Jenna, and Lindsay would say that they hope the bad guys speak slow and only use single syllable words. That way I may understand part of what they say. The bad guys are complaining that their captives got away. They were planning a big celebration after taking the women from the other group as well.

They are talking about what they will do if they catch them. Apparently they have forgotten about me or they think I was able to get on the plane before it left. One of them says they better be on the lookout for whoever helped those people. The other one says that whoever that was is long gone by now. Only an idiot would stick around when there are so many tough fighting men after them. Now Sara and the others would definitely agree with that statement. Oh well I guess it's time to show them that they are not the only ones hunting around here.

They are past me now and it goes against the grain to shoot someone in the back so I whistle softly. I can see their backs stiffen and I know they are wondering if that was a human whistle or a bird. Right now I bet they are hoping it's a bird. I am counting in my mind as they start to turn ready to fire at whatever made that sound. I have the arrow already to shoot as soon as they turn. The bow has a pull of about a hundred pounds and the arrows I am using will go through a Kevlar vest. It looks like they are counting to three or something before they turn.

They must hit their number because they both turn at once and fire in my direction. They must have miscalculated where I would be because they are not even close. That could also be because after I whistled I moved about ten feet to the left to get a better shot at them. At the angle I am shooting from my arrow takes the first one high in the chest and goes straight through him and hits the second one in the chest as well, only this one does not look like a killing shot. It doesn't go through so it must have hit bone or something solid.

The first one is just standing there looking at me, then he falls face down in the deep grass. The second man is trying to bring his gun to bear on me, but he doesn't seem to have the strength to lift it. I am about to shoot again when the young lady jumps out of the brush behind him and stabs him in the back. He goes down instantly. She grabs my arrow and pulls it out. She brings it over and tells me she could have killed them both with one arrow. I ask her if she is related to Lillie and Izzie. She just looks at me and says she knows an Isabella and a Lillianne, but they are back at their settlement.

The others will have heard that gunfire so we better get out of here. Her brother comes out of the brush and we head off toward the sounds we are hearing. I ask them if they know how many men there are. They tell me that they counted ten. I only counted eight, but I could easily have missed a couple of them. We no sooner get back in the brush when we hear what sounds like a stampede coming our way. We get as close to the ground as we can and wait for the men to go past us. Unfortunately for them, three of them get right up even with us and stop to discuss what may have happened.

They are calling the names of the other two and do not like the fact that they are not answering. I signal to the two with me that I am going to get their attention then shoot them with the bow. The young lady tells me using signs that there are too many for the bow. She and her brother show me the guns that they took off the first two. I was hoping to do this quietly, but they do have a point. I was planning to shoot one, then disappear in the brush until I could get another shot. I point to one of the bad guys and signal that I will take him. They should choose one each and when I give the signal we will fire.

I start to show them my hand counting to three using my fingers, but as soon as I hold up the one she stands up, calls them pigs, and opens fire with her gun. Her brother is doing the same thing. I do get a shot off with the bow, but I think the guy was falling already anyway. The young people run to get the guns and we go looking for the others. With all the gunfire and no one calling out to the others they are now very much on edge. The five of them that are left are debating their options. Some of them want to run for it and the others want to kill whoever it is killing their comrades.

I figure it is now time to really scare them. I signal to the young people what I am planning. They promise to let me do this my way, at least for now. I climb a tree that looks like it was made for climbing. I get about fifteen feet up and I have a clear field of vision into the predators camp. I take the fifty that I brought with me and sight in on the leader. Just as I pull the trigger he moves and I hit the guy right behind him. Odds are I would have gotten them both if I had hit the one I was aiming for. Those guys don't waste any time getting out of there. They disappear into the brush, but I take another shot into where I can see the brush moving.

We hear someone let out a scream then there is silence except for the sounds of men running. I am contemplating just letting them go when the leader calls out that he will kill all of us before this is over. Then he asks me if I would like to join forces, together we would be unstoppable. He promises me all the women I want. The young lady with me swears at him and starts shooting in the direction of the voice. I grab her and her brother and pull them as far away as we can get before the bullets start hitting the leaves around where we were standing.

I tell her that he did that to get us to fire at him so they could get a fix on our position. She looks kind of sheepish and says she will wait until I tell her to shoot again. I doubt it, but maybe she will. I get an idea so I explain to her and her brother what I want them to do. Oh, I want them to shoot at where the sound of the guns came from every thirty seconds or so, then move so that they don't get pinned down. I am going to try to flank them so that I can get a shot and maybe end this nightmare.

Before I move, I have them move twenty or thirty yards to the right, then I shoot toward where the gunshots came from. I am moving as soon as I fire because I know they will return fire. They are smart, the sound is nowhere near where it was just a few minutes ago. I head off through the jungle following the sounds of gunfire. From the sound of the return fire at least one of them is working their way toward me. I hear a shot fired from quite a distance away and I am starting to think that I may have been outsmarted.

I am moving quickly, but as quietly as possible. There is a clearing ahead of me so I stop and look the situation over carefully before proceeding. Just as I think it might be safe I hear something coming through the jungle on the other side of the clearing. As I am watching I can see one of the predators step into the clearing and hesitate waiting to hear where the gun fire comes from. I take aim with the AK I am carrying and he sees me just before I pull the trigger. He fires back, but my bullets take him square in the chest. One more down and now two or three to go.

I am thinking what a close call that could have been. I am also thinking about my dream where I am being shot at. I hear the gunfire coming from the predators, but none being returned. Now I am scared, I forgot that the two young people may run out of ammunition. I am heading straight for the last location I heard the gunfire. It is only a couple hundred yards, but through this brush it seems like miles. I hear the voices before I get to the small clearing they are in. I stop to determine what course of action I should take. I wouldn't want to bust in there with guns blazing and get us all killed. Something like that could ruin your whole day.

I can see into the clearing, all I see are two predators and the two young people. The young lady has the knife I gave her and she looks like she knows how to use it well. These guys want her alive so they will not shoot unless they absolutely have to. I am thinking that they don't care about the brother when the leader tells her to put the knife down or they will kill her brother right now. The other predator has a nasty grin on his face as he raises his gun and points it at her brother. Oh well at least I know what course of action to take.

I shoot the guy that is aiming at her brother and step into the clearing. The leader can't believe his eyes. He says he thought his other man would take care of me easily. I tell him he thought wrong. He can bury his men if he wants to. He looks confused and asks me where I learned to fight. I tell him he wouldn't believe me if I told him. He asks me if I came here from another world. The young people don't know what to think of this situation. To be honest I am not sure myself. I tell him that he is correct. I was a Navy Seal in that world. He smiles and says it would be just his luck. He tells me he is from that same world. He has been here for about a year.

I ask him why he didn't use his knowledge to help others instead of attacking them. He shrugs and says it just isn't his way. In the other world he was a drug dealer and made his living off the suffering of others. There is something in his tone of voice that warns me he is going to try something. He looks away for a split second, probably hoping to get me to look where he is, then he swings around and fires his gun at me. He has an automatic weapon and it fires several rounds before mine takes him in the chest and knocks him down.

It is like reliving that dream I had almost exactly. I make sure he is not getting up, then take a step toward the young people to make sure they are okay. The young lady is by my side almost instantly and asks me if I am hurt badly. I start to tell her I am not hurt when I notice the blood stain spreading on my side. It doesn't hurt much so I open my shirt to see how badly I am hurt. It appears that the bullet just grazed my side cutting a furrow about two inches long. It is bleeding pretty good, but is not life threatening.

I look at my watch to see how much longer we should have to wait for help. I look around and notice that we are only a couple hundred yards from where all this started. We are heading toward there when we hear the sound of a small airplane flying overhead. We hurry to the clearing and start waving to get their attention. The plane tips its wings and circles for a landing. We run to the landing strip and get there just in time to see LT and Tim coming out of the plane. Sara is right behind them and they are all heavily armed.

My new friends ask if we are going to where we live in that flying machine. Sara tells them that is unless they want to walk. They ask if we can still take the rest of their friends with us. We assure them we will go down and find their friends. We fill the tanks on the plane and head south. An hour of walking can be covered in a few minutes on an airplane. They point out where they live and Sara finds a road to land on not far from there. It only takes a few minutes for them to gather their meager belongings and tell their friends what we are doing and we are on our way home.

18

I would like nothing more than to sleep at least part of the way back, but our new friends keep asking questions about our settlement and what it's like where we live. Luckily we have LT and Tim to answer most of the questions. Sometimes I wonder why they even bother asking because half the time they don't believe us anyway. It does make the trip go by faster. It's a good thing there were not more of our new friends to bring back or I may have been hitch-hiking. The young lady and her brother that were with me back there ask if we have any Spanish speaking people other than the three of us.

I tell them about Wyatt, Heber, Joseph, and the rest of the group that came from Mexico. Then I tell them about the families that live with us from Cuba and especially about Lillie and Izzie. They say that they cannot wait to meet them all. By the way the young ladies name is Carmen and her brother's name is Tomas. He and the other young men ask what kind of work they will do. Tim explains that we all do a variety of jobs and goes into more detail explaining the kind of work that has to be done every day. The more they hear the more excited they become.

Finally we land at the settlement and it looks like they are disappointed at first. The runway for our planes and the hangar we keep them in is almost a mile from the actual settlement so they are seeing primarily fields that have been prepared for planting in the spring. As soon as we taxi up to the doors of the hangar Dayna and most of our children are here to greet us. Naturally Izzie and Lillie are here along with several of the people that came back with the other group earlier. A very pretty lady that I don't recall seeing before comes up and gives me a big hug. Dayna smiles and tells her that is the only hug she gets, I am a very happily married man, at least I better be.

Everyone laughs and I see a couple of gentlemen that were with the group this morning. They come over to me then start to shake my hand, but wind up hugging me. Heber is right behind them. He introduces them as his long lost children. He pushes them out of the way and gives me a hug that I am afraid will break my ribs. It does start the bullet graze bleeding again, which causes Dayna and my daughters to just about throw me on the ground to check out my side.

My daughters, Tina and Tammy, who are twins if you remember, have worked with Doc Betty learning medicine for the past ten years or so.

They tell me we better get home so they can take a look at that wound. We have enough vehicles to carry everyone back to the settlement. LT and Tim are going to stay back and put the plane back into the hangar. Kathy, Charity, and several of their children are here to help them. It sure is good to be back home, I mention that we have to find homes for our newest members and I am told that it is already taken care of. When we go in the house the worries of the morning just melt away. That's the way I always thought home should be.

Tina and Tammy make me take my shirt off so that they can wash out the wound. Getting shot didn't hurt as much as cleaning it. Kristi and Jill must have been out somewhere because when they come in Jenny and Tiffany look at me and say that Gramma said she was going to shoot me herself. Then my Grandson Little Jon comes up and tells me that Gramma says I am hopeless. Then he shakes his head to affirm what he said. The little ones see the wound and have to poke it and ask if it hurts.

Dayna is laughing and so is most everyone else including me. The twins are trying to decide whether or not the wound needs stitches. While they are discussing it Doc McEvoy stops by to make sure I am okay. Now he is involved in the discussion about the stitches. While they are talking, I take a large piece of gauze, put some anti-biotic cream on it and tape it to my side. Dayna yells at me for not taking a shower first. I peel the bandage off carefully and head upstairs to take a shower.

I feel much better after that so I can go downstairs to talk to our friends and family again. When most of our family goes back to their houses, Heber, his wife, his sons, and their wives come over to talk for a few minutes. I find out that the very attractive lady that hugged me earlier is one of Heber's son's wife. They thank me for helping them get away even at the possible expense of my own life. I try to make light of it, but Heber's son Mike tells me that those men are as bad as they get. They personally know of several people that were killed by them and what they did before killing them is even worse.

I tell them that they won't get to do that anymore. Mike's wife asks if I killed them all. I feel kind of like joking a little so I tell them that I gave them a stern lecture and made them promise not to do bad things anymore. The look on Heber's son's faces is priceless. Heber looks at me and tells his kids that means I read to them from the good book. Heber and his son's have read the same books that Gunny used to where the main character used to say that if he had to hurt or kill someone. We all say it is unfortunate that is the only way some people will ever leave others alone.

Since Doc McEvoy and his wife are here Dayna asks if anybody would like a hot dog or a nice Italian Sausage sandwich for a snack. Mike and his wife say that they hope she isn't just being mean and they can't really have those things. My daughters come in carrying a platter almost full of both sausage and hot dogs. I thought I smelled something good. Everyone digs in and it is plain to see that our newest guests are savoring every bite. Tiffany and Jenny come into the family room drinking milk. The children ask if they can have some as well. Their moms tell them that you don't ask for something as precious as milk.

Dayna looks at Heber and tells him she should smack him for not telling his children and grandchildren all about our home here. He just smiles and says that he wanted some things to be a surprise. His son's ask what else he wants to be a surprise. He shrugs and says what we are having for supper. They all ask what they are having and he tells them that Tori, Wyatt's wife, is cooking a large pot roast with potatoes and carrots and they have peach cobbler for dessert. They all say they never dreamed that anyone would be living like this. Mike's little girl, who is about the same age as Tiffany, Jenny, and Little Jon, asks her mom again if she can have a small glass of milk now.

Her mom explains that the children have only had milk once and that was goat's milk. She is not even sure if they will like it. Dayna tells her there is no better way to find out than to try it. She had nothing to worry about because when they try their first sip they drink it down like all of our children do. The adults are so impressed that they would like a glass as well. As with the sandwiches they drink it like some people drink wine. We ask Heber how long it will be until their dinner is ready. He says just about enough time to show his family around the settlement. I would volunteer to help him show them around, but I am sure they would prefer to be alone.

They start to leave when Heber asks me if I am sick or something. He tells them that all this started because of me so it should be me showing them around. I tell them that it was a group effort, Tim and I may have given them a little leadership to get started, but it has been a family affair since then. I will be happy to show them around though. Dayna comes with us and we run into Lillie and Izzie showing the other new members of our family. The rest of the group that was with Heber's family in Mexico meets us for the tour as well.

All of them tell us that they have been thanking Heavenly Father since they boarded that plane this morning. Many of them tell me and Dayna that they prayed with all their strength that I would be okay until help could come back for me. Heber tells us that he was worried about my safety as well until several of the long time members here told him about some of the adventures I have had. He says that according to our son Teddy, if Satan himself came after us with his legions, they wouldn't stand a chance against me. I laugh and tell them you can't believe everything you hear.

Heber's other son, Patrick, says he isn't so sure of that. I went up against ten very mean, vicious men and I am still alive, they are not. He says that sounds pretty tough to me. I tell them that I was very lucky and that I pray every time something like this happens that it's the last time. Mike's wife says that it's time to forget the past and look forward to a bright future. When we get to the chicken coops many of our new friends say they can't wait to have fresh eggs again. They also ask what kinds of jobs they might be able to do here. Many of them say that they wouldn't mind working with the chickens or with the milk cows.

The group being shown around by Lillie, Izzie, Amy, Nickie, and Teddy all want to get started helping so they can earn their keep. One of the children complains that their shoes have holes in the bottom and it hurts when they step on stones. Dayna looks at Heber and tells him he better straighten up. She leads off toward the warehouses mumbling under her breath something about clothing and shoes being far more important than any tour. When our new friends see the racks of clothing and the shelves full of shoes they say they were going to ask if there is a city nearby where they could get some of the things they need.

Dayna tells them it won't be necessary because we have everything they need right here. She takes the women to the next warehouse and shows them the furniture and other things that they are more than welcome to. It's kind of chilly out so we show them where they can get all the cold weather gear they need. Everyone gets what they need so now they are at least more comfortable than they were. We decide to continue the tour tomorrow so they can go eat their meal. When we get to Wyatt's house he comes out and apologizes for leaving me behind. I tell him that he didn't leave me behind. I stayed behind to clean up a mess.

I tell them all that we will see them in the morning and see what they may want to do here. My little buddy Ephraim comes running out of the house and tells us to tell Little Jon that he and Ariel will come over tomorrow morning to play with him, Jenny, and Tiffany. He asks if Prince and Lady are still here, he likes to play with them too. He always gives me a hug when we have to part. Actually just about all the little children in all the groups give both Dayna and me hugs and most of them call us Gramma and Grampa. We are not even forty yet, but neither of us mind at all.

We eat a much simpler meal for supper, then spend the remainder of the evening talking with our family. My side is starting to hurt, but no worse than it has many other times. I tell Dayna that I am just happy I am not injured as badly as I was back in Rochester that time. The worst part is that it is the side that I sleep on. I try to sleep on the other side, then I give up and lay on the hurt side until I get used to the pain. By morning my side either doesn't hurt as much as it did or I am just so used to the pain it doesn't bother me anymore. Either way I have work to do so I am not going to let it bother me.

We eat a great breakfast of oatmeal with milk and honey on it. This has to be one of our favorite meals. When we are done and I go out on to the porch to see what needs done first I am met by pretty much all of our scientific people plus David and Kimberly. They say they wanted to talk to me after church yesterday, but they heard that I was busy elsewhere. Kimberly says that they heard I got shot saving those people from a horrible gang. I tell them it was just a graze. It won't even slow me down. James tells me that's good because they have a mission that they feel we really need to go on. I tell them I'm sorry, but I can't go right now. I got shot and can barely walk.

They all laugh and tell me that's what they thought I would say. I am waiting for them to tell me what they have in mind, but apparently I am going to have to ask. I tell them I was only kidding about being too injured to help them, what can I do for them. Jenna reminds me about the great double-decker busses that we had back in England. I tell her I remember them well. I think I know where this is going so I ask if they want to go to Florida to look for some of those busses at the theme parks they have there. That opens the lines of communication because now they are all talking.

To make matters even more confusing Sara comes over and tells me that I promised to take them to look for the busses when we got back and I haven't done that yet. I tell them to put together a plan and we can discuss when we can go. Then I start walking toward the new building we are putting up for the golf. My sons and some of the other people working on this project meet me before I get to the jobsite. We get our assignments and get started. Today I am working with the people moving the top soil so that we can setup the practice greens and the short fairways we are planning.

The greens will have a layer of gravel, covered by a layer of top soil, then covered with a layer of sand mixed with the top soil. The people who planned this actually went to a golf course that is totally overgrown and dug up a green to learn how they were made back when those were made. It may not be perfect, but we are sure it will be good enough for us. They also have a book that said basically the same thing. They got the top layer directly from that golf course so it should be authentic. They also salvaged some sand for the sand traps as well. These people are serious about this game.

It's a nice day for this time of year. With all that has happened the past couple of days I totally forgot that Thursday is Thanksgiving. We decide to work through lunch so when I do not come home, Dayna brings me a sandwich. Mike and Morgan and David and Kimberly come with her to ask me if I think it would be okay to leave on Friday to go to Florida. They say that Sara said she could fly us down in the large helicopter and we could see what kinds of new technology they were using in those places. They say they are planning on Friday and Saturday to check everything out and then come home to plan how best to use the technology they find there.

Actually I never thought about the technology used in those places. There has to be something there that will make our lives better, easier, or maybe just more fun. I ask them who they are planning to go down with. They say that they are hoping that I will go with them. I start to tell them that there are several very good fighting men and women in our group. They interrupt and say they know that and everyone of them will tell anybody that asks that I can smell out danger quicker than anybody they ever saw. LT and Tim are working right next to us. LT looks at me and says he is one of those that says that all the time.

He also says that he wants to be part of this project or adventure, whatever we call it. Kathy and Dayna both say that if their husbands are going, they are going. I tell them I will go, but I want to think about it for a while. Several of us working on the project discuss the upcoming adventure while we work. Matt, the gentleman we met up in Michigan thinks it would be better to bring back any technology that we want, rather than have to make two trips. Wyatt agrees with him and thinks that we should take the C-130 so that we have plenty of room to bring it back.

Billy, who very seldom gets involved in projects like this one, says that we should take some drivers along in case we can get even one bus running. It won't fit in the plane so it will have to be driven back here. If we find more than one, we will need more drivers. I ask him if he and Ramona would be interested in coming along. He says he wouldn't have wasted his energy talking if he wasn't interested. Then he laughs that big laugh of his that is so infectious. In case you don't remember Billy is a little over seven feet tall.

19

By the time we quit for the day we have some suggestions for this project. The scientific group is waiting at our house when some of us get there. I am not sure if I told you or not, but we have made several additions to this house since we first moved in. One of those is a huge family room that is often filled with friends and family just for discussions like this evening. All of our suggestions are accepted without an argument and several people are added to the list of those going. Maybe now we can eat supper. Lillie and Izzie come in after our discussions are over and ask if they can take Carmen hunting with them tomorrow.

Nickie tells them that Ruth wants to go with them as well and so do Amy and Misty. Tim, Tommy, Allen, and Jon all say that they were planning to go hunting tomorrow as well. Dayna tells them that's a good thing. They can make sure the girls don't get into any trouble. Lillie tells her that the girls are going to keep the boys out of trouble. She looks at me and asks me if I remember giving her a beautiful hunting bow and many arrows. I tell I do remember that. She smiles and says that Carmen and Ruth can really use one now as well. She shows me the K-Bar I gave her and says they can use one of these as well.

I feel like I have failed at doing my job here lately. I tell them to call Carmen and Ruth and anybody else that needs hunting equipment. We go to the warehouse where that equipment is kept and we distribute guns, bows and arrows, and knives to those that want them. Some just got guns and some got both guns and a bow with arrows. With all the new people we have the need for fresh meat is growing almost daily. Heber's sons and their wives all say they have done quite a bit of hunting and they are proficient with butchering and preserving meats and vegetables.

They add though that after seeing how we are doing they think they may need some lessons from us rather than the other way around. I tell them that I am sure they have much to teach us and we can maybe show them a thing or two. That's what makes our group so strong. We all do whatever is needed when it is needed and we are all more than willing to share anything we have. I add as long as it is morally clean and acceptable to Heavenly Father. They agree that is the best way to go. Now that everybody that wants or needs a gun has one, we can go back and have supper. Some of our newer members have not been trained for using guns or bows and arrows safely, but that will come soon. Then they will receive them as well.

I am a little concerned with how much game as many people that are going hunting can bring home in a day. It's a good thing we now have three meat freezers on the property in different barns. They were there all along, but we didn't get them all functional until we started getting more and more group members. The other groups all have at least two freezers and the capability to use more if need be. Dayna made enough supper for the company that she invited over this evening, which includes Heber and pretty much the whole family.

While we are eating, Ruth says that she would really like to get a pig tomorrow. She says that she has shot some in Central America where they lived that must have weighed a good hundred pounds. She says she heard that the domesticated pigs around here used to get to be two hundred and even up to three or four hundred. She says she imagines though that if they got to be that big the fat to meat ratio would be significantly higher. I tell her that we have shot a couple of pigs that were in the upper range and the fat ratio wasn't bad at all. Heber says he bets it's because the pigs here run wild like the ones in Mexico and Central America and run the fat off.

Ruth and Esther say they are looking forward to hunting tomorrow, they hope they can see one of those larger pigs we are talking about. My son Timmy says he is pretty sure he knows a spot where there should be plenty of game. He says he is hoping to get a good sized steer and Lillie says that she, Izzie, and Carmen are looking for venison tomorrow. They are all going to be on the lookout for six or seven turkeys as well. Our new friends ask if the other groups hunt together with us or if we all go our separate ways. We explain that we all work together in pretty much every project we do. Timmy explains that they got the orders of what the other groups need as far as meat is concerned.

There will probably be a couple representatives going with them tomorrow as well. Tommy tells them that they usually separate into groups separated by a couple of miles so they don't endanger anyone else. Lillie continues saying that you can hear a gunshot from the distance they are apart and if there is trouble they have a code they use. Nickie laughs and says the code is they call the others on their walkie-talkies. The ones we have are good military quality and we have used them for quite a while. Mike and Patrick tell us that they never dreamed that anyone could live as well as we do.

We tell them that we are just trying to make life as enjoyable as possible. All this technology exists already so why not take advantage of it. They say that they are afraid that they have lived in a part of the world where there was not much technology before the war and now there is almost nothing. We get into a discussion about that very subject. We tell them that we have some friends in Cuba and the outlying islands there that thought pretty much the same thing until we went down and showed them how to take advantage of what they do have.

As if to prove us right, Sara, Morgan, Lindsay, and Jenna come in along with their husbands. Sara has samples of their latest batch of chocolate candy for everyone. Our new guests are surprised to find out that we are starting to manufacture our own chocolate candy. I joke and tell them that we are having a hard time getting the word out so marketing may go a little slow for a couple of decades. They start to disagree, but then they think about it and say it may take even longer than that. We spend the rest of the evening telling them about the other settlements that are doing well around the country.

Ruth and Esther say that we should be writing down a record of everything that we have done since Tim and I came to this world. Dayna tells them that she, Becky, Melissa, and Robin along with some of the younger people are doing exactly that. She tells them they are more than welcome to help. They could write down their history and we can put them all together when we have enough for a volume. They catch that word volume right away. They ask if we have already done one volume. Jenna and Morgan tell Dayna they will get them so she can remain seated.

They come back with the five volumes that the girls have already filled and we went to an old book publishing factory and between James and Jenna and Mike and Morgan they were able to print enough copies of each volume for whoever wants them. The ladies ask if we would happen to have an extra typewriter they could use. Dayna smiles and goes over to one of the large closets we added when we added this room. She opens the door and tells them to choose one and if they don't see one they like we will get some different kinds next time we go through a city.

They are laughing as they go through the large number of machines already here. They do find a couple that they like and ask if they can take a couple more for the other members of their group that would love to do something like this. I think Ruth is a lot like Sara because she tells me that if I can find a certain brand of typewriter, she would prefer one of those. I write down the name because we are going to be going to a place that we may just find several different kinds. I take this time to ask Morgan and Mike if they have started taking that building down that they want to use for a museum. That gets the new peoples interest. They ask if they can help do whatever is necessary to get it started.

Morgan smiles and tells me that they are kind of planning to take the building down when we come back from Florida, probably next week. Dayna tells us that she was talking with some of the wives in the group and they were saying that with the crops all in and not much happening other than putting up the building for the golf, we have several ready, willing, and able men and women that would love to do that project as soon as possible. I knew that many of our people are helping with some projects on the other groups, but apparently we have the manpower so we may as well get it started.

We will take care of that little detail first thing in the morning. The evening ends and our new friends tell us that it has been a very interesting, eye opening evening for them. They say that they will thank Heavenly Father every day for the rest of their lives for bringing us together. We tell them we will do the same. In the morning we call a quick meeting to tell anyone that needs something to do that they are needed on this new project. Some of our people ask if they can be relieved of the project they are on to do this one. We tell them as always, if they can find someone that would rather trade projects it is perfectly okay with the council.

We wish our hunting party good luck as they load the trucks to go to their favorite hunting spots. Actually today Timmy told me he wants to hunt an area that he doesn't ever remember ever hunting before. It's about twenty miles north-west of here and I am sure it has not been hunted there in several years. The rest of us get busy doing our jobs for today. Today I am helping put up the walls on the new building. We saw the other group pull out of the yard around nine o'clock this morning to get started on the building that will be our museum.

Today while we work the topic of conversation is about the upcoming trip to Florida. I am working with Trey, Junior, and Max. They have been helping at the chocolate factory, but they enjoy working with their hands and they enjoy being up in the lifts working as much as I do. Today we are not very high, but it is still a lot of fun having to man-handle the pieces of steel that make up the walls, into place and fasten them in place. They have been asking me about our adventure down in Mexico. At first I thought they were kidding me, but then they told me they had heard of that group that I fought with. From everything they heard those guys were very tough, totally vicious and without conscience.

They want to know how I was able to take all of them on at once. I tell them that I didn't, my strategy was to divide them and pick them off one or two at a time. They seem to be impressed and it's like they are seeing me differently than they did before. They want to know if I could teach them how to fight like that. They tell me that they have had several fights, but those were mostly fist fights where no one really gets hurt badly. They are sure that they could shoot a man if their lives depended on it or the life of someone they love. I tell them that I hope for their sake they never have to, but I will teach them all I can.

The day goes by very quickly as it has a tendency to do when you are busy. We are thinking about knocking off for the day anyway, but seeing our hunters returning makes it easier. We all go down to meet the hunters as they get out of the trucks. We can see that they had a very successful hunt as usual. I don't remember the last time that our hunters didn't have a good day. I don't think that has ever happened yet. Ruth and Esther come running over and yell at me for not telling them how big the pigs get around here. I remind them that I told them they will probably see some in the two or three hundred range. I just didn't mention that they would also see some in the nine hundred to a thousand pound range.

Their husbands were working on the same project we were today and they are standing close enough to hear our conversation. They are smiling because Heber and Joseph told them how large the animals have gotten around here. Ruth and Esther can at least laugh about it. They say that when they saw that hog come out of the woods toward them they were thinking that it looked like a small car. They say that they shot it in the head from the front and it just kept coming. Timmy told them that they have to shoot it from the side to penetrate the thick skull. He was ready to shoot when the ladies stepped to the side and fired at it again. This time it went down, it still took it a few minutes before they would go near it.

We get to see the hog and it is quite impressive as is the large steer they shot and the three large white tailed deer. That is all on the largest truck with the hoist on it. The other two trucks also have a hog, a steer, and at least two deer in them. I ask them if they think maybe they got a little too much meat for a single trip. They tell me that all the other groups need meat as well, otherwise they wouldn't have killed this many animals. The other trucks are going to deliver the meat to the other groups now. They just wanted us to see what a great day they had. Our new friends from Iceland and Greenland are impressed with the game that was brought in.

Sven, one of them that can speak English very well comes over and asks Timmy if they ever see wild goats or sheep when they hunt. Timmy smiles and tells him that actually today is the first time he has ever seen wild goats when he has been hunting. Sven asks him why he is smiling about seeing wild goats. Timmy calls over to Lillie, Izzie, and Carmen and asks them if they kept that goat they shot. Lillie tells him of course they kept it. They don't kill anything unless they intend to eat it. It is right next to the steer and the three deer. I didn't look close enough the first time, but there are also seven or eight large turkeys in the truck as well.

Sven and some of the others are excited about the goat. They say if we need any help preparing the meat to please let them know and they will show us how to prepare it to be fit for a king. Rod, one of our best butchers is here looking at the work that has to be done. He tells Sven and the others that they are more than welcome to come down to the preparation room and help all they want. With this many animals to be processed there will be several of us helping to get them skinned and quartered so that they can be hung for aging. With as many hands as we have working the job is almost done by the time the others get back from taking the other meat to the groups that need it.

Lillie and Izzie are interested in learning how to butcher a goat. They used to eat quite a bit of it when they lived in Cuba and it seems that our new members of the group are used to eating goat and lamb as well. I never acquired a taste for that kind of meat. The turkeys always take quite a while to dress for the freezer. Heber's son Mike is helping with that job. He said the same dumb thing I did one of the first times we got turkeys. Our butchers told us they needed to be dressed to go in the refrigerator and I suggested we put coats on them and maybe even a small hat. Everybody threw things at me when I said it and they do now when he says it. That just makes him feel more like part of the family.

Our new members that haven't seen this part of our settlement yet are very much impressed. We show them the smoke house where a large portion of the hog that was shot today will go. We also have some large industrial dehydrators where we make several hundred pounds of beef and venison jerky every year. Some of the group members have been asking when we are going to make another batch of breakfast sausage and Italian sausage. The meat from the last hog that the girls brought in has aged just about perfectly to make some of it into different kinds of sausage. It doesn't take long to mix the pork and the beef or the pork and the venison depending on which the people like the best.

Personally I can't tell the difference except that the venison is a little leaner, but the beef has run wild all its life so there is not much fat on them either. We usually make a couple hundred pounds of each kind of sausage so that everyone that wants some can have it. We also make our own smoked sausage, Polish sausage, pepperoni, hot dogs, and beef sticks. Some are actually venison sticks, but no one has complained yet. Our new members are impressed to say the least. Some of them ask what we do with the hearts, the livers, kidneys, and some other internal parts of the animals we kill. Actually some of our group members like to eat those parts of the animals, but I tell them if they would like some I am sure we can arrange for them to have some.

Our friends from Mexico say that they would like to use some of the stomach lining to make a dish called menudo. Lillie and Izzie both say that they haven't had menudo in several years. They tell us that Marianna, who is in Ryan and Carols group used to make it sometimes back in their village. We tell them that we have not been bringing the cows stomach back when we field dress the animal, but we can start doing that with the next steer we shoot. I mention that to Tim and LT after the job is done and they both say they used to eat tripe soup and tripe cooked in tomato sauce. Tripe I guess is the American word for the cow's stomach lining. If they like it, they can have my share as well as their own.

I brought home some fresh made breakfast sausage and that's what we are having for supper tonight. Our newest members also got some for the first time and they said they will let me know in the morning if it is any good or not. Since this is the first time some of them have ever eaten any I am sure they will like it and Mike, Patrick, and their wives say they haven't had sausage of any kind since the war, so I am fairly certain they will like it.

20

In the morning Mike and Patrick tell me that the sausage isn't too bad, but they have had better. I just figure that everyone's tastes are different and figure that if they don't care for it that could possibly mean more for me. About an hour later their wives come by the job site with their children and tell me that they loved the sausage so much that they can't wait until we make another batch. Mike and Patrick look at me and smile. They tell me that they didn't want me to get a swelled head. I tell them that it is not my recipe, we found those recipes in towns and cities we have been to and there were several very good recipes right here on the farm that we use with some very small modifications.

With Thanksgiving being tomorrow the smell of cooking food fills the air. Today it is mostly pies and other confections that we all like to eat. The meat and potatoes for the meal will be cooked tomorrow. Then we will all meet at the church building to have our meal. Our newer people are not sure what we are celebrating, but anybody that has been here for more than a year can tell them. Wyatt and the others that came from Mexico say that they haven't thought about holidays in so long, they have just about forgotten about them. We have a very good day on the building so we feel justified in knocking off just a little early.

We decide to spend the extra time we now have going over to the church and making sure everything is setup for tomorrow. When we get there several people from all the groups seem to have the same idea at the same time. This is great because it gives me a chance to talk to some of the people we don't get to see near enough. One of those is Doc Betty's husband Josh. I am hoping that he will want to go on the new adventure we are starting on Friday. He and Betty say that they would love to go. Betty says she hasn't been to an amusement park since she was a little girl. Everybody within hearing range tells her that she has them beat, they don't even know what an amusement park is.

She starts to try to explain what it is and they all tell her it doesn't really matter. They will never get to visit one that is working anyway. They are not upset about it, we all just accept the fact that our world will never be like the one that was here before. Again, those of us who know what that world was like hope it never does get back to that state. With the number of people we have to setup it takes almost no time at all. We even take the time to clean the chapel and make sure there are hymnals on all the pews. Mike, Patrick, and their wives and other family members came along as well. When the work is all done they ask if it would be okay if they just sit here in the chapel for a little while.

We know how much having a place to worship that is familiar can be worth to some people. For others it doesn't really mean that much, but as soon as our new friends walked onto the ground of the church we could see a reverence in them that we haven't seen very often. It reminded Dayna and me of the way Wyatt and the rest of the people that were in their group acted the first time they saw this building and still act when they are here. Seeing how they act makes us and our family, want to be more reverent when we are in the Lords house as well.

The evening goes by quickly and morning is here before we know it. We have started having some athletic events on Thanksgiving depending on the weather of course. Today we are having a couple of football games. Touch of course, but since there are both males and females on all the teams we have to be careful where we touch. Believe me the girls are not the least bit shy about smacking the ball carrier and they have been known to tackle rather than touch more than you might think. Some of the young and not so young people like to play soccer and some even want to play softball and maybe even a round or two of golf. Some of our more avid golfers want to try out some of the new clubs we brought back from Scotland and England.

Today I was planning to just relax because my side seems to have gotten infected a little and is still pretty painful. The worst part is that my shirt keeps balling up in that area and rubbing it raw all the time. For the moment I am doing KP duty peeling potatoes for Dayna. We have both red skinned potatoes and sweet potatoes for our dinner today. We will also have to husk about five hundred ears of corn for this meal as well. That's not just for our group, that's total. It would be more if everybody wanted corn with their meal.

The Turkeys are cooking in ovens all over our group and in the other groups as well. There will also be several hams and today for the first time on our table will be goat meat. Please don't ask me how it is being cooked because our friends from Iceland and Greenland are taking care of that. Several others in the different groups though apparently know what it tastes like because they said they would like to have some as well today. Personally I am planning to fill up on ham and turkey. After the food is ready to cook, Dayna and I go to watch our children play the games they enjoy.

We are happy to find out that the teams are not keeping score although both teams in every sport being played claims victory. It always leads to some good natured arguing. Our new friends are impressed that so many people can play sports and not get into an argument. We tell them that it didn't start out this way, but when it became clear that no matter how good of friends the combatants are, there were still fights and arguments at every game. That's when we made the rule that there will be no losers here, we do not keep score so both sides are winners. We have had some people try to change our way of playing, but a large majority of our people enjoy it the way it is.

Finally it is time to eat and all the food and people make our way to the church. After the meal we like to let those who wish to say what they are thankful for have a few minutes to let us all know. This year it seems like we have many more new friends that want to tell us all how much they appreciate being part of our family. Even Heber and Joseph stand up and as far as I know this is the first time any of us have ever seen tears in either of their eyes. Our friends from England, Jill and Kristi, get up shortly after them and say that a few short months ago they were contemplating taking their own lives because of the hopelessness of the way they were living. Now they can't wait to get up in the morning because every day is a new adventure.

It is a very tearful afternoon as usual. When it is over we all pitch in to clean up the cultural hall which is what we were told it was called by the people who built this building. There are a lot of leftovers that get divided up to those that want them. The only leftovers I want are of the cherry and Dutch apple pie that was not eaten and I will settle for one piece of those. In the morning we are going to get ready and leave for Florida to see what may be of use to us there. I have been thinking about something quite a bit lately so I have my own agenda for going. I tried to explain it to Dayna, but she has no idea what I am talking about. That doesn't stop her from being excited about the possibilities though.

Tonight I do not sleep very well considering how tired I am. I keep waking up every couple of hours and in between I seem to be having the same dream over and over. In the dream I am walking up a hill and when I get to the top there is a beautiful building there, but no matter how hard I look I can't find a door to go inside. The last time it seems like I am still awake when I see this guy standing next to my bed telling me that we need to build a temple. I tell him that I have no idea how to build a temple. I wouldn't even know how or where to start so he must have the wrong dream. He just smiles and says that he is sure he is in the right place and that I will be given further instruction on what we are supposed to do.

Whatever was causing those dreams must have worn off because I don't have any more at least for tonight. In the morning Dayna wakes up and tells me that she had the weirdest dream ever, but it was beautiful as well. She goes on to tell me that she had the same dreams that I did except she didn't see anybody in our room. When we go downstairs she shows me a picture that she found in the church building of the Washington, DC temple. She tells me that this is the building that she kept seeing in her dreams. That's the one I was seeing as well. Now I am even more confused, I have no idea how to even start building something as beautiful as that. I sure am glad that it was only a dream.

We already have everything we are taking with us packed and ready to go. Our children are all here to see us off before they start their day. We meet up with everybody that is going and head for the C-130 plane. For this trip I invited my former wives husbands to come along. They are excellent workers and have a great deal of experience driving large trucks with even larger loads on them. Becky, Melissa, and Robin were invited as well, but they prefer to stay home and watch the children. Billy and Ramona are just a bit nervous. I do not think they have ever flown before. Actually that's true of more than half of the people going.

Our scientific people ask me why I am bringing so many people along. They say we will probably not need more than two or three drivers coming back. I tell them that I have some things that I have been thinking about quite a bit lately and I intend to see if I can even do it. Now their interest is peaked, they ask me what that could be. I tell them I don't want to tell anyone until I know for sure whether we can do it or not. They all say they guess that's fair, but they keep trying to guess what my secret is. I just lean back in my harness seat and close my eyes. Finally they quit trying to get any information from me.

It doesn't take very long to get there, but then we didn't think it would. It will probably take a day and a half or two days to get back home driving. When we unload the plane with the equipment we think we may need, Sara asks if she and Gary can go down to Cuba and pick up a load of cocoa beans and maybe even some sea food. Several of our coworkers ask if they could possibly go and then get dropped off here on the way back. We figure what we want to do here will take at least a couple of days so they should be fine. We refill the tanks on the plane so that we are sure they have enough and they are on their way.

On our way to the first theme park LT is telling us all that he wasn't able to get reservations in the better hotels, but since it isn't the busy season we may be able to find an open room or two anyway. Junior, Trey, and Max all say they wish they had known. They would have brought their frequent flyer cards and we could have gotten a discount. Most of the people with us have no idea what we are talking about, but they think it's funny anyway. Dayna, Kathy, and the other ladies with us say that they want to check the hotels and motels here for bedding, towels, and anything else they find that we can use. As we get closer to the park entrance I can already see some of what I am interested in on this trip.

Jenna and James are straining to see one of the double-decker busses, but so far there are none to be seen. I am hoping that we have to look in some of the large warehouse like structures to find them. Out in the open this close to the ocean will not help them at all. The scientific people are seeing pretty much what they hoped to see as far as the technology. Now they have to find where the paperwork is kept and then find what they are looking for. LT and I along with our wives go looking through the warehouses we see. They are pretty fancy, but they are still warehouses. The others break up into groups to check out some of the others.

On the way to the first warehouse that we are going to I look to the right and see a large building that has a sign declaring that building to be the main office. I call over to James and Mike to tell them what we see. That's what they are looking for, so the scientific people head that way while the rest of us continue to check out the warehouses. The ladies say that we should consider taking some of these buildings down and taking them home with us. They are decorated with the characters that made this particular theme park famous. We all agree that the children would get a big kick out of seeing these every day.

They are a nice size so I was planning to check out how difficult it would be to take them down. The first one we come to looks promising because the doorway is definitely high enough to accommodate a large bus. We go inside and sure enough there are two of the double-decker busses that look just like the ones we used in England. Actually they look to be in better shape than the ones over there. LT and I know what we are going to be doing, but for the moment we are going to do a little more exploring. We are keeping in touch with the others with some walkie-talkies that we use. The funny thing is that as soon as we tell them we found two busses they come back and say they saw their two busses first.

They say there are also a bunch of smaller vehicles kind of like golf carts in that warehouse as well. We have pretty much the same thing in this one. Dayna and Kathy are walking slightly ahead of LT and me. They stop in their tracks and tell us that they have found what they want to take back. We catch up to them and right there in front of us is a small version of the double-decker busses. It is similar to the small busses that we have found only it has two levels. Junior comes on the radio then and tells us we will never believe what they just found. We start to answer when Trey says that they are claiming one of them for their fiancées back home.

Dayna and Kathy start to tell them that they saw them first, when they realize that he said fiancées. Then they remember that he said one of them so they ask how many do they have there. Junior comes back and says they can see three of them and there may be more than that. We continue looking and find two more and several more of the smaller golf cart type vehicles. We are getting ready to check out another warehouse, but before we do, LT and I decide to see what kind of engine those small busses have in them. We pop the hood on one of them and are totally surprised at what we find. The first thing we do is call the others and ask them to do the same thing.

They do and they are as surprised as we are. I am calling James and the others when they walk into the warehouse we are in. They say that they will have to take the filing cabinets home and go through them at their leisure. I ask them if they are ready for a pretty pleasant surprise. Naturally they say they could use one about now so I take them over and show them the engine in the small busses. They all say "no way" at the same time. LT is standing on the side of the bus they are looking at and tells them "yes way" and shows them the cord to plug it in with.

They are so excited that they tell him to plug it in so we can see if it will hold a charge. LT looks at them and says that if we had electricity we could find that out, but until we get the generator running plugging it in will do no good. They laugh and ask us what we are doing standing here when we have a generator to get running. Trey and Max from the other group come running in saying that all the golf cart like vehicles are electric as well. They say Junior is trying to get the generator running so that they can see if they will run. They start to say something else when we hear Juniors voice yelling that he needs some help, now.

I am the first one out the door and I have my 9mm in my hand when I get to the other warehouse. I don't see him so I yell asking him where he is. He yells that he is in the back and that I better be careful, but to please hurry. I run to the back watching closely when I see him in a small room that must house the generator. I get close to the door and see what he is talking about. There is the biggest snake I have ever seen between him and the door and it is up like it is getting ready to strike. I tell him to step to the right so I can get a clear shot without having to worry about the bullet hitting him.

He says he is planning to go straight up. I look and see that there is a ladder on the wall directly over his head. I tell him to jump on the count of three. I start to count and that stupid snake lunged at him on two. He jumps and I fire hitting the snake in the head. I'm not sure what I was expecting, but seeing that snake thrashing around and striking out at anything it sees isn't it. I fire three more rounds into its head, okay it takes me six rounds to get three of them into its head, but it finally does stop moving. Have you ever tried to avoid being beaten to death by a snake and shoot it at the same time? By now the rest of our group is here. David and Kimberly are the snake experts apparently. They say that this kind of snake shouldn't even be in this part of the world.

They continue saying that this is an Anaconda and they are usually only found in the jungles of South America and in Africa. They go on to say that in our world they were starting to have problems because people would buy these snakes for pets and when they got too big to keep, they just let them go in the wild. This one is at least thirty feet long and has to be about a foot in diameter. If we wanted to eat this thing we would have plenty of meat for a while. It takes three of us just to drag it outside so it doesn't start stinking up the warehouse, besides with that in here, there was quite a bit less room.

21

While Junior works on the generator some of us go looking around the inside of the warehouse to make sure there are no more surprises here. When we finish checking this one we go back to the one we were in and check that while James and David get the generator running. The rest of the scientific people are going over the electric cars with a fine tooth comb. Not really, it's just an expression to say they are looking them over very carefully. With those two warehouses checked we move on to see what we may find in some of the other ones.

This time some of us look around at what there is to find and the rest of us check it out for anything that might eat us. Aside from some very large spiders and some bugs that I am not sure what they are we don't find anything. This warehouse has a lot of equipment for the rides. There are shelves and racks of parts for several of the rides. When we come out of this warehouse we are met by James and David who are driving one of the smaller busses. Apparently it has a top speed of about thirty-five miles per hour, which would be good for somewhere like this. Actually around the settlement it would be perfect and not endanger young people as much as the regular trucks and cars do.

In the fourth and fifth warehouses we strike gold as far as I am concerned. These are apparently warehouses where they stored some of the rides that must have needed to be portable. They may have stored them here for carnival season in different parts of the eastern states. This is primarily what I came here for. I saw an amusement park from the air when we flew over Texas and I thought how great it would be to have our own merry go round and some other rides especially for the children. I mention this to the guys and they say they would like to see how difficult it would be to disassemble the big ones in the park and transport them home.

In the other world Junior, Trey, Max, and Wyatt worked at an amusement park and their job was to move the rides when they wanted to change things around. We go outside to the merry go round and I would love to take this back with us. The horses and other animal figures are very ornate and are brightly colored. Luckily this particular piece of equipment was indoors since the war. It is a temporary structure that can be taken down and put back up when it is necessary. Max, Trey, and Junior look it over carefully and say they are sure we could take this apart and put it back together again back home.

Now that my idea is out in the open everyone has ideas about what rides we should take back. There are also some games that may be a big hit back home as well. The wives are going around making a list of all the items we want to take back with us. LT and I figure we better get busy trying to get some large trucks ready to go. We find a warehouse on the edge of the grounds that has possibilities. We go in and find exactly what we are looking for. There are six flatbed trucks in here that are made for wide loads. They remind some of us of the ones we used to move the pre-fabricated homes onto the settlement.

Being diesel they are easier to get running and to keep running long enough to smooth out. Naturally the tires are flat, but most of them hold air when we put it in. There are plenty of spare tires in the warehouse so it is not too bad to swap them if it is necessary. We do them one at a time and by the end of the day we have four of them running and our scientific people have two of the double-decker busses running and have plugged in most of the electric busses to charge. We decide to spend the night in what was once the gift shop. It is in the middle of a bunch of buildings all attached that must have been like the head quarters buildings.

One of the buildings had enough cots for all of us to use and we even found a store room that was full of everything you could need to run a park like this. There are enough mattresses that are still wrapped in plastic to cover all the cots that we will need plus many more. The ladies were rummaging around and found several cases of canned chocolate candy. The cans are still sealed so we figure we may as well try it, no sense letting it go bad if it isn't already. We have the food we brought so we are set for the night.

We decide that after what happened this afternoon that we better post a guard, just in case. As usual I get the time that is at the end of the night. Also as usual Dayna gets up with me and we sit and talk quietly while we stand guard. We learn the common night sounds then trust our instincts to warn us if something is different. We are discussing where we should put the amusement park when we set it up back home when we both hear something that is not quite right. Dayna whispers asking if I think it is another snake, I tell her I don't think so. It sounds more like someone walking and kind of sliding one of their feet.

I can tell where the sound is coming from so I signal Dayna to stay here while I go see what or who it is. On the cement floor with a carpet over it I can move almost totally silent. I work my way toward the direction the sound is coming from when I hear voices. The first one I hear is a young girl's voice. She is asking whoever is with them if they think we may have some extra food for them. The answering voice is also a woman's voice saying that they have to be careful about being seen before they know what we are after. The other voice says she doesn't think we are bad people, we have women with us and it looked like we were working most of the day.

I decide to go back and get Dayna before saying anything. If I start talking to them they will probably run and we may never find them again. Dayna is more than happy to meet them so rather than sneak around again she walks right out of the room we are in and turns on the light showing us two ladies eating out of a can of chocolates that were left on the table we were using. They look like they would like to run, but the younger one is using a crutch and looks to be having a lot of trouble walking with it. The older one appears to be a few years older. She tells us that they didn't mean to take our food. They are just so hungry that when they found it here they couldn't resist.

Dayna smiles and walks over to greet them. She tells them it is no problem, however she thinks they may find some of the other food we brought with us more filling. It's kind of cold for the way they are dressed as well, so we get them some coats to put on. We always carry more than we need just in case we run into a situation like this one. By now everybody in our group is up and wondering who our new guests are. The ladies finally feel comfortable enough to sit down, which we can tell is a big relief for the younger one.

Luckily Doc Betty is with us, she tells the young lady that she is a doctor and asks if she might take a look at her foot. The girl tells her that she got bit by an alligator two days ago she thinks it was. They apologize and say they lose track of the days sometimes. I ask them what they were doing when she got bit. She says they were looking for edible plants along the lakeshore and it came out of nowhere and grabbed her foot and ankle. One of the boys with their group beat it with a stick and it let go long enough for her to get away.

We ask where the rest of their group is. The older one tells us that they were on their way north to find a settlement that they heard about on the radio. When they couldn't keep up the group told them they would send someone back for them when they get to the settlement. Max says he would like to meet whoever would leave two ladies like this in this environment alone. It is almost certainly leaving them to die. Doc Betty has a solution that she made and now tells the young lady to soak her foot and ankle in it. At first she says it hurts pretty badly, but shortly after that she says it is starting to feel better.

Some of us men step out to discuss what we should do. I say that we should try to find the rest of their group. Before I finish, Max says that he agrees that we should find them and teach them that you don't desert friends. I tell them that I think we should find them, then take them to the settlement in the Florida pan-handle. Junior and Trey tell Max that they know how he feels, but if we were in their shoes maybe we would have done the same thing. Max says he would never leave a friend, no matter if it cost him his life or anything else he has. We all agree with him, but we remind him it's not up to us to judge anyone. Heavenly Father will take care of that chore better than any of us can do.

We go back in to tell the others what we think we should do. The older young lady says she is happy to hear that we will help her friends. I ask her if they would like to go with us to find them. She says she would like to go with us, but if we don't mind they would like to go with us back to our settlement. She continues saying that the ladies here have been telling her and April about our home and they think it would be like being in heaven to live there. Doc Betty tells me she needs me to help her find some herbs so we go outside. She tells me that we got that wound in the nick of time. She says there is already some blood poison, but she can draw that out now and with rest and good food the young lady will be fine.

James tells us that if we need a vehicle to look for those other people he has a nice electric bus that we are more than welcome to try. According to Summer, that's the older young lady, there are seven more people in that group. One of the small busses will work fine. We decide that Max, Josh, and I will go to look for the others while the rest of our group works on getting the busses running and seeing how to take the rides we want apart. April is sitting on one of the cots with her foot resting on a stack of pillows eating a stack of the left over cookies from our Thanksgiving meal when we tell her we are leaving to find their former group. She tells us to give them her love and to tell them she doesn't blame them for leaving her and Summer.

Summer has some idea what the route they will be taking is so we head that way. The bus rides beautifully even on the broken roads. We do have to move some cars out of the way, but we would have to do that anyway to get the big busses and trucks home. We actually find them quite a ways before we were expecting to. They try to hide when they hear us coming, but we already saw them. This electric bus doesn't make much noise at all. Summer calls to them and tells them we will take them to the settlement up north. They finally get in and we can proceed. We find out that the leader of this group twisted his ankle early yesterday, that's why they haven't made better time.

Max just can't hold it in any longer. He tells the guy that maybe we should leave him behind to die like he did April and Summer. He tells him he is lucky this didn't happen ten years ago when he didn't really believe in God. Then he would probably have broken both of his legs and left him right where he was. I can see that the guy is scared. I tell him and the others that the people where they are going will be able to help them. One of the younger boys asks if April died from her injuries. Josh tells him that we caught the poison in her system in time and she will be fine. They all breathe a sigh of relief , Josh continues saying that if we didn't meet them this morning like we did, she would not have lived another day.

He tells them that although it might not have been the most humane thing to do, leaving her behind saved her life. We drive in silence for quite a while after that statement. One of the women in the group asks us if we know the people in the group we are taking them to. I tell them I do, they are really a nice bunch of people. One of the things that James wanted us to find out is whether or not these electric busses will recharge themselves as we drive. I can't speak for the others, but this one does. We get to the settlement kind of late in the afternoon. It would have taken this group at least two weeks to walk here.

Our friends tell us they could really use one of these busses if we have an extra one. We tell them we will make sure to drop one off on our way home. We tell them where we are staying and several of the women tell us that they could use some bedding, towels, and everything that goes with them from the hotels there. They give me a list before we can leave. It is after midnight when we get back to the amusement park. Summer has been worried about her sister all day. When she sees her walking much better she tells her that she has been praying all day for her. April tells her that she has been praying for her safety all day as well.

It is a very short night for all of us, but we get up early and get back to work. We walk over to the merry go round that the guys are working on and they ask me how big a load do I feel comfortable driving home. They ask because they say we can save a lot of dismantle and reassemble time if we don't break it down like we would for normal traffic conditions. I tell them that from my experience the biggest concern we have is narrow bridges for width and just plain bridges for how high we can go. We decide that we can probably use double the width of the large flatbed trucks we have as a guide.

They say that will save a lot of work, but we will have to have a large fork truck or crane to load it on the truck. LT tells us that is no problem, he knows right where a very large fork lift is. We go to check this out and he is correct, now all we have to do is get it running. Since it has a diesel engine, that should not be too much trouble either. Everyone is busy today which is a good thing. Even our newest members are helping Dayna, Doc Betty, and Kathy go through the hotels and any other place that may have what they are looking for. I asked them earlier what that is and they said they will know when they find it.

We found a small electric scooter like thing that April can get around in easily. Her foot and leg are on the mend, but she is far from being able to walk more than a few steps at a time. The other ladies are riding around in a golf cart. It definitely beats walking everywhere they go. They are all carrying guns today as well. April and Summer had never fired a gun before this morning, but they took to it like soldiers. They can still use some target practice, but I am confident that they will hit what they are shooting at, if it comes to that.

Our scientific people are making sure all the electric busses run properly, then they are parking them in one of the huge warehouses here. Those must have been used quite a bit because we have found ten already and we seem to find them pretty much everywhere we go. The girls called on the radio earlier to tell James and Mike that they found some of them at the hotels they have visited so far. The girls told us that they would put everything they find that they want to take in the lobby where we can pick it up with the truck later. That will save them a bunch of trips back and forth to our headquarters.

We work so hard today that we are actually surprised when the sun starts going down. It was really a pleasant day, we didn't even need our coats or jackets while we were working. The ladies found some canned foods at the hotels today that are still sealed so we are going to try some of them this evening. Some of that is canned beef and another good item is noodles. They are both good as far as we are concerned when we open them so we heat up the beef and cook some of the noodles. When the beef is hot we make a gravy out of some of the flour we brought with us and eat the beef and gravy over the noodles. We eat that back home quite a bit, but there we use fresher beef most of the time.

Our new friends tell us that if we eat like this all the time, they are very happy that we are allowing them to join our family. We tell them that we are very happy that they chose to join us. Tonight we turn in early because we are all tired from not getting much sleep last night. We are confident that where we are sleeping is safe, at least as safe as it can be under these circumstances.

22

I am awakened out of a sound sleep by the sound of someone or something walking and dragging something across the floor in the outer area. I start to move and Dayna is awake as soon as I start to sit up.

I hold my finger up to my mouth signaling her not to make any noise and she listens and hears the same sounds that I do. We both get up and try to look out the window on the door of the office we are sleeping in. We can see nothing and the noise is still continuing like whoever is making it doesn't care if they are caught. I am beginning to think that it is a something, not someone. We have the generator in this building working, but to conserve fuel we turn it off at night and during the day when no one is around.

The sound is coming from the far right so I decide to open the door and see if I can see anything that way. I open it and have my gun ready while Dayna shines her flashlight where the sound is coming from. The light shows an alligator that is all of twelve or thirteen feet long and looks to be as wide as a small boat. When the light shines on it the alligator turns much more quickly that you would expect from something that size. By now Max, Trey, and Junior are standing here with us. Then most of the rest of our friends come out as well. April sees the alligator and says she is very happy the one that grabbed her was about a third the size of this one.

The one we have does not seem to be intimidated at all. It appears to be sizing up the situation before it decides what to do. Junior tells me that alligator tail is very good if you cook it right. Just about all of our scientific people agree with him. I have had alligator and was not impressed, but it wasn't terrible either. I ask if that means they would like me to kill this one and they all say not necessarily. If we do that then we have to dress it tonight and try to keep the meat from spoiling before we eat it. We decide that if our visitor is still here in the morning we will probably have to shoot it. Otherwise we will wait until we are headed home in the plane to get some alligator meat.

We go back to bed and somehow manage to fall back to sleep. I am the first one up so I check to see if our unwanted guest from last night is still around. There is some sign of him, but other than that we cannot find him anywhere around here. We can track it in the fresh dust that has settled on the road from test driving the electric busses. Today we are going to start loading the merry go round onto at least three of the trucks we have. One thing that made us very happy is that the park must have used solar power to run most of the rides here. We found a fenced in section that is located close to at least four different rides. When we checked it out there are dozens of solar panels setup in that fenced in area and wires leading to a generator that appears to control at least those four rides.

That gives us something else to take down and use back home. We are all getting excited about the projects we will have for this winter. We know the rest of the groups will feel the same as we do. Actually just getting everything home that we want to take back is probably going to take at least two and possible three more trips. LT is going to start working on the double-decker busses today. Just as we separate to go to the different projects we hear the plane fly overhead and then turn around and land not far from here.

James and Mike along with the other scientific people think it will be great to pick them up at the plane in a couple of the electric busses. Since they are doing that the rest of us get to work except now LT is going to leave the busses to some of our friends on the plane. It is a noisy and fun reunion with our friends. They bring the love of our friends down in Cuba along with enough seafood for all of the groups back home. Everyone is happy to meet our new friends. We all agree that we better load the plane with anything we can put on it to take back and let them go. That way they can have a celebration with the seafood and they can unload the cocoa beans that they have.

The rest of us will finish loading the trucks that we have and that we can still get running and leave either tomorrow or the next day for home. James tells us that he found a couple of trucks that look like they were made to haul the small busses. They want to try to load one on the plane to take back now. When we see how many cocoa beans and other things from Cuba are already on the plane we decide to wait until next trip. It will fit by the way, but not by a very big margin. The plane will hold all the bedding, towels, pillows, and other treasures that the ladies found yesterday. While everything is being loaded some of us go hunting for a couple of alligators.

When everybody saw the body of the snake we killed the other day they are shocked by the size. I didn't realize it, but Max, Junior, Trey, LT, and Josh skinned that thing and are planning to take the skin home to tan it over the winter and make things with it. It does not take very long to find a couple of very big alligators not far from where we have been working. I never noticed that there is a pretty good sized lake about a quarter mile away. There is so much brush between here and there that it was almost impossible to see it. LT says he is looking for another large snake to skin.

We have to get one of the golf carts to drag the alligators back to the plane. Since so many people like the meat and our hunters seem to want the hides so badly we decide to just field dress the gators and send them back with Sara. We kind of anticipated something like this happening so we got one of the large ice makers working the second day here and now we have enough ice to pack in the alligators to keep them from spoiling. Our newest friends are afraid to fly so Doc Betty and Dayna go back with them. They are planning to come back the day after tomorrow to take back a bunch of things that James and the others found.

We spend the rest of the day loading trucks and getting more trucks running. Once in a while we find one that we simply can't get it to run so we move on to another one. Those larger flatbeds are great for what we want them to do. The bus carriers that James was talking about were really easy to get running. When we would get one running the others would load all the small busses onto it that they can. It seems that they were made to carry five of the busses easily. With the trucks that we found we can take back fifteen of the busses. We are planning to make them available to any of the other groups that might want one or two of them. David and Kimberly already put in their order for two of them.

We spend the next day getting the double-decker busses running and the tires inflated. It is starting to look like a major military operation with all the trucks we have lined up for the trip home and we are adding to it all the time. Sara does not make it back today, but then we really didn't expect her to. We spend part of the evening deciding which other rides we would like to take back home with us. We even visit the other theme parks in the area and we think we have a pretty good idea what we will start with. We already have our teams back home preparing a slab to set the merry go round on.

During the night we are awakened by what sounds like a ferocious fight right outside our door. We cautiously look out through the window and again we can't see anything, but we sure can hear it. LT and Josh have their .44 magnums out and ready to fire if they have to as I swing the door open. Just as I push it open, it gets pushed right back at me by the large alligator and the very large snake it is fighting with. The alligator has a hold on the snakes body while the snake has its fangs buried in the alligators neck and is working to wrap itself around the alligator. It appears as if the snake is going to win this one until both LT and Josh shoot them both.

They are happy because now they have another snake skin to take back with us. We get busy skinning the snake and dressing the alligator to take at least most of it back with us. When we called home this evening on the radio we were told that several of our group members and a bunch of the other groups really like the alligator that was brought back. Now they want us to bring back a couple more if it isn't too much trouble. I almost forgot, I was asked personally to get enough alligator teeth for all the children in all the groups under twenty. I told my son Tommy that I will bring him back the alligator if he wants to pull its teeth.

Well at least we have one to take back. Max, Junior, and Trey tell me that it sure is convenient to have them delivered for us. We found some more of the extra large flatbed trucks again yesterday so the top priority is to get at least three of them running, then load them for the trip. After that we will be out of drivers unless they bring more back with them. All of the trucks we have loaded are open bed trucks, but we do have two trucks with trailers. These are full of solar panels and generators for them as well as a bunch of items that our scientific people can't live without. I know they have all the filing cabinets in them.

While some of us get the trucks running, several of the others scout the other parks to see if there is anything that we may not want to wait until later to get. Everyone is carrying their side arms and some are carrying hunting rifles just in case. The other parks are closer to the water than this one is. Yesterday we saw plenty of sign that there are some very large animals frequenting those areas. At least now we know that if we shoot alligators the meat and hide will be used and not wasted.

LT and I are working on our third big truck when we hear a very loud vehicle coming toward us. LT looks at me and says that either the gators are becoming motorized or we have company. We go out the open large door just in time to see some of our friends from the settlement up north of here. After greeting each other they tell us they didn't see us go by on our way home so they figured we must still be here and might need a hand. We ask them who their mechanic is because he is not doing a very good job fixing the muffler on that car. I said that because I know their best mechanic and he is standing right here next to me.

He tells me he represents that remark. We all laugh and he tells us that the muffler was fine when they left home. They hit something in the road in the dark and broke the pipe from the manifold to the muffler. He sees that there are a couple of lifts in this building so he figures he will fix it while they are right here. One of the leaders of that group is named Barbara. She asks me if we remembered that they can use a bunch of bedding, towels, and anything else along those lines that they can find. I tell them I know we loaded a truck with a bunch of boxes of all that stuff and we were planning to drop it off on the way home, but they are welcome to either take the truck and we will pick up any items they don't need on our way by. Or they can find a truck of their own and we will help them get it running and load it.

It just so happens that there is a really nice twenty-six foot box truck right here in this building. It has a diesel engine and we have it running in about an hour or so. While some of us worked on the engine, a couple others worked on the tires, so when we have it running they can just pull it out and go to the other warehouses. Barb and Dominic, her husband went looking in the warehouses and to a couple of the hotels right in the park and found enough supplies to fill the truck full. They ask us if we mind if they come back to get more of the things they can use.

Naturally we tell them to leave our find alone, not really, we tell them like always, if there is something you need or simply would like, feel free to take it. If we need it as well, there will more than likely be somewhere else we can get it. I tell them about our idea to setup a small amusement park in the settlement back home. They think that's a great idea, I tell them which rides we are thinking about taking, but we also show them the smaller carnival rides that are pretty much ready to travel and be setup. They say that they will definitely be back and if we don't mind they will take some of those rides.

Actually the same rides are available in all the parks down here that we have visited. We already have a couple of those rides lined up ready to go back with us. They see our alligator and the snake. They ask if we have seen many of these here. They also tell us that they have not seen any snakes or alligators this large up north. Just knowing that they get this big is enough to make them watch closer to make sure they don't get careless. They seem to be ready to go, but they also seem to be waiting around for something. Finally Barb tells us that they are waiting for their electric bus.

I thought that was probably it. We were going to take one to them, but since they are here we go to the warehouse and let them pick out a couple of them. James, Mike, and David are happy to show them all about the busses. They figure since they have more room that they can take more treasures home with them. We load them full and promise to stop by on our way home. They leave and we get back to work on the trucks. We have more running now than we have drivers for, but we are going to load them anyway. One of the rides I really want is a Ferris wheel and we already have one taken apart enough to load it onto trucks. It's not a huge one, but we are all sure it will bring many hours of enjoyment to our groups.

We no sooner get it loaded when we hear the C-130 fly directly overhead. It lands and we go to meet them in a couple of busses. They did bring more drivers back so we have plenty to drive all the trucks back. We are not planning to waste a lot of time today. We load the plane with what it will hold easily. We are able to get two of the small busses in along with a large amount of the other items that the scientific team wants to take back. We also have a total of four more alligators to take back.

The guys that went looking in those other parks said they didn't even have to go looking for them. It actually seemed like they were going to attack them. I can believe it, the smallest of the four is the one we shot early this morning in the building and that one is an inch shy of being thirteen feet long. The largest one is over fourteen feet long, Luckily it is only about forty degrees out so the meat will stay fresh, especially with the bodies packed with ice. Those will also go on the plane. When the plane is loaded and we have all the trucks assigned drivers, those that don't really drive big trucks are welcome to go back on the plane. Heber and Joseph along with their wives and Heber's sons came along to drive back. When Heber and Joseph see the alligators they say they will go back on the plane to make sure the meat is taken care of properly.

His son Mike laughs and tells him that Ruth and Esther are there to take care of it so he can drive back with the rest of us. We tell him that we will be home sometime tomorrow or the next day so he can prepare the meat any way he wants to then. All the trucks are fueled to capacity so after the plane takes off we head out to make the long trek home. We have driven most of the way we have to go so most of the cars and trucks that would block our progress are already out of the way. We do have to move some because our loads are much bigger than they were when we came this way last.

We are making good time when we stop by the settlement and make sure they got home safely. They are planning another trip probably next week to go back down. They invite us to spend the night, but we can get another couple of hours in before dark so we want to do that. Besides I tell them we have reservations at a five star hotel up the road a ways. Actually we stop at an outdoor supply store that surprisingly we have never seen before. There is some sign that someone spent some time here in the past, but the sign is old so they have probably moved on.

We simply cannot find one of these stores and not try to take most of it home with us. There is some room in the trucks for items that we can jam in, so we fill the double-decker busses and the electric ones on the truck. We also call our friends at the settlement we were at earlier and tell them about the find. They will come up tomorrow to check it out. It's just a little over two hours away from them. In the morning we leave while it is still dark out so we can make it home today. We are now on roads that we haven't been on before, but there are very few cars on them so we are making good time.

It is early afternoon when we find another outdoors store. This one we are just going to stop at to see if it is worth coming back for. We find that it is definitely worth coming back and we also find sign that someone has been here recently. We spend a little while waiting and looking around then decide that they may not want to be found. We go about five miles down the road when we see a man, a woman and three children walking on the side of the road. When they hear us they run into the woods beside the road. We pull up and Dayna along with Jenna, Morgan, and Kimberly talk them into joining us. It didn't take a lot of convincing. They were looking for a settlement in Virginia they heard about on the radio.

23

We make it home today, or perhaps I should say this evening. It is a little after seven when we pull into the parking area in the settlement. Our new friends are surprised at the size of the settlement and with how happy everyone is to meet them. We decide to wait until morning to unload the trucks rather than do it in the dark. We do unload the alligators and the snake skin though. Everyone is impressed with the size of those beasts. We called ahead using the radio so our newest friends have a place to stay tonight. Not that they wouldn't have if we hadn't called ahead. It's just that this way they have a house of their own to stay in.

We get to go along while Teddy shows them where they will be living, at least for now. They keep telling us how appreciative they are for everything we are doing for them. We tell them we will see them in the morning as they go into the house. We are walking away when the father comes running out and says we must have made a mistake, there is already someone living in this house. Teddy stops and says he moved the things in himself this afternoon so there is not supposed to be anyone else living here.

We go into the house and they show us that there is milk and a bunch of other food in the refrigerator as well as food and pretty much everything a family will need to live comfortably. We smile and tell him we hope they will be comfortable living here. Nickie and Dayna tell the wife that they will come by in the morning and take her shopping so that she can pick out the furnishings that she will be more comfortable with. She says she has never had a real house to live in so everything that is here will be fine. They tell her they will come over anyway to show her what is available and to explain how we all have jobs to do, but we all also receive what we need and sometimes even more than we need.

As we are leaving we hear the children asking their mom and dad what milk is. The dad tells them after they thank the Lord for blessing them this way, they can all find out. I tell Dayna and the others with us that I never get tired of seeing how people's lives can change so drastically in a few short hours. I tell them that another thing I never get tired of is coming home to the people I love and to our comfortable home. When we get to our home I find out that April and

Summer are staying with us so that the twins can help her take care of her foot. It is healing much better, but it still has a ways to go.

After Dayna and I get our hugs from the entire family including the newest members, the twins tell me to take off my shirt, they want to see how the wound on my side is doing. I have to admit it has been bothering me more the past few days and it really doesn't look too good. When they look at my side they ask me how it got so badly bruised. Dayna looks at me and smacks me for telling her that it was nothing when that first snake hit me in the side when it was in its death throes. I tell her at the time it didn't hurt too badly, but the day after I started to feel it. The twins tell me that they are going to tell the committee that I am on limited duty until my side heals.

They look at their brother Teddy and ask him if he got that. He is the leader of the committee at this time. I tell them that I have to help with the equipment we brought home with us. Our sons tell me that I can supervise. A man of my advanced years has to take it easy sometimes. They are running and laughing when they say it. If I could catch them I would show them who is getting old. Dayna asks the twins if maybe I should be put on bed rest for a week or so. That way we could catch up for some lost time. All of children and our new friends tell her that is way more than they wanted to know about. Besides if I was on bed rest and she was with me, I wouldn't get much rest.

We get to talk about the latest adventure much later than I was planning to turn in. I am so tired lately and I have been looking forward to sleeping in our own bed all week. When we finally do turn in I seem to be having trouble getting to sleep. When I finally do get to sleep, at least I think I am asleep, I dream that I am awake and I am talking to the same guy that visited me in my dreams before. He tells me he knows that I have seen the Washington temple at least in a picture. He also tells me that we don't have to build a temple like that one, but we will have to use some of the materials that were used in that one to build ours.

He also tells me that Wyatt will draw the plans for the temple we are to build. He continues saying that everyone in the settlement must be allowed to participate in the building of our temple. I ask him what our time frame is for this project and he just smiles and tells me that the Lord has his own schedule and it will be made known to us when it is time. I start to ask another question and again he smiles and says when it is time we will learn what we need to know. I must wake up because I look over and Dayna is staring at me. She says she was worried because I was tossing and turning in my sleep, then I was almost totally still and started talking in my sleep like I was carrying on a conversation with someone.

I tell her that I was visiting with our friend about building a temple. She tells me that she was talking to Ruth about the dream we both had and she said that people have to have a temple recommend to even go into a temple once it has been dedicated. I tell her what my dream visitor said and she says we will just have to wait until it is time. In the morning I am planning to go to the new construction site to see where they decided to put the merry go round and the other rides we brought back. As usual I am impressed with the amount of progress that has been made in such a short time.

We brought back the instructions on how to install the rides down to how to prepare the base that the rides will be resting on. Today we have two different opinions on how we should go about setting up the rides we brought back. Two of them are obvious, but the merry go round leaves some room for discussion. Some of our team thinks that we should setup the portable building that we brought back first. That way if the weather turns bad we can work inside setting up the merry go round itself. The other option is get the merry go round in place, then setup the building.

After a short discussion we decide to put up half the building mainly in the direction to block the wind that usually comes with the cold weather. That way we will not be limited in how we get the large parts of this ride into place. With that out of the way we start unloading all the pieces. We tried to load them so that we could just unload them and put them in place, but the large base pieces had to be put on first to keep the load balanced. That's not a bad thing, it will just take a little more planning this way.

I am ready to go back to work on the other building we were working on before we left, but Dayna and the twins find me and tell the guys on the work crew that if they come back and I am doing more than supervising they will tell their wives on them. I tell them that there are a lot of things I can do that do not require lifting heavy objects. I fully intend to do those chores and if my side starts to hurt, I will rest until the pain goes away. I get smacked for adding that is unless it is like some of my daughters that never go away. We get to work and unfortunately everything that needs done now is extremely heavy lifting until we get the base in and locked in place. I don't know where they got it from, but my sons bring me over a rocking chair and tell me they will get me a blanket to put over my knees if I need it. Again I try to chase them down, but they are just too fast. Finally I tell them they have to come home sometime, I will get them then.

For unloading the large base pieces we have to use a backhoe with a chain to lift them. Before we start to put them in place though we mark the spot on the concrete base where each part goes. While some of the crew is working on that the rest of the crew is using an excavator to lift the heavy wall sections into place then bolt them down. I am always impressed with how well our teams work together no matter who is on them for that particular project.

Today even though we have several of our newest family members and it is going as smoothly as if we have all worked together for years, which some of us have. Even those that do not speak much English are doing very well. We have enough people on the crew that speak both English and Spanish that they can communicate very well. Actually Dayna and the twins have very little to worry about, all the heavy lifting is being done using tools to make it easier and safer. Actually the way this project is going I am not really needed at this time so I am going to check out the other projects that are going on.

The museum building is going well. It takes time putting up the large sheet metal panels that are the outside walls and roofs of these buildings. Once those are complete we insulate the inside of the building, then finish it off in whatever way we decide is best. Luckily we found the spray type of insulation, before that we used to put up the fiberglass sheet and that is awfully dirty and time consuming. I am able to help a little while a couple of people take a break, then I am free to go over to the golf building we are working on. That's the one I was working on before we went down to Florida.

The work is going much better than we thought it would since this is the first project of its kind for us. The outside shell of the building is almost complete and they have some side panels in place. The other crew on this project is busy getting the short fairways completed and the greens for practicing putting. This is the project that Mike and Patrick are working on. Apparently they were avid golfers when they were young. Every time I see them or their wives they tell me they must have passed over to the other side because living here is the closest they have ever been to heaven.

I get involved with the crew smoothing out the ground that will be one of the putting greens. I admit that I have very little interest in playing golf, but I may come in here once in a while during the winter to putt on these greens. It's a good thing we have the people we do to tell people like me how the greens should be designed to challenge golfers at every level. That means they will have breaks from every direction on some of the hole placements and some will be straight or almost straight putts on other areas of the same green. The basic shape is done using a small bull dozer, now we are fine tuning so to speak using rakes and sometimes shovels.

They tell us that when it is pretty much where we want it we will roll it to help it maintain the contours and to help set the grass seed that will be used. Even that is a special blend that was developed primarily for golf courses. Even the fairways will be planted with a special blend of grass. I asked a question that I guess may have been dumb even for me. I asked why we don't use the same grass that is on the fairways they play on most of the year. It seems to me if you get used to hitting the ball off a different type of grass it may make it more difficult to adjust. Again it doesn't really matter to me.

The day passes by quickly like they have a tendency to do when we are busy. Dayna meets me on my walk home and asks me what I would like for supper this evening. She gives me a couple of choices then tells me that everybody else would like sausage sandwiches if that is okay with me. That is always okay with me. My side feels much better this evening after taking it kind of easy today. I tell Dayna that I will try to do pretty much tomorrow what I did today and she tells me if I do I will be working alone because tomorrows Sunday.

That's even better. I can rest and not feel guilty about it. After supper we have several young men come over to take several young ladies out for the evening. At least there is a lot to do here. They can go bowling, play miniature golf, watch a movie, or go to the library and read good books together. That's what Dayna and I are doing this evening. It seems like forever since we have had a quiet evening to just sit and read a good book. Our quiet evening only lasts for a little over an hour when our scientific people come over to talk about some of the great things they found in Florida and to ask when we are going back.

Apparently some of the important papers that were in those filing cabinets included the plans for the electric motors in the small vans. James tells me that the engineer they had working there before the war was a genius and was way ahead of his time. They found some of his or her notes. Jenna, Morgan, and Kimberly remind us that the engineer was not necessarily a man. The name on the notes could be either a man or a woman. The twins, Tammy and Tina come in and say it must have been a woman because all men think about is going as fast as they possibly can and obviously this person cared about the environment, not how fast they could make cars go.

Kimberly tells them they and Dayna have always been her favorite members of our family. I tell them I do not really care if they refer to the engineer as he or she. I just want to get back to my reading. Tina whispers loud enough for everybody to hear that is another reason it must be a woman. Men have no patience. We can all laugh at that remark. Jenna continues this time, she says that they found some notes that indicate they were working on building an electric motor to power even the larger busses. Naturally that gets a discussion going on if you had an electric motor for the large busses you would still need the right transmission and rear end to move it efficiently.

While we are talking, Junior and Trey come in with Kristi and Jill, and Max comes in with Summer. Now they are all involved in the discussion. I tell Tina to tell them that we can go back any time they would like to, but not to wait too long. Christmas will be here before we know it. With that Dayna and I go upstairs to finish reading and to go to bed. Everything is fine for about a half hour, then we hear someone coming up the stairs and just opening our bedroom door. Sara looks disappointed that we are sitting in chairs reading. She makes a comment that I really am getting old and tells me they want to go back to Florida sometime around Wednesday or Thursday next week.

Dayna smiles and tells them we will check our calendar and let them know tomorrow after church if we can fit it in. She walks over to the door and kind of pushes Sara out into the hall and tells her that if she doesn't leave we may have to prove to her that we are not even close to being too old. Sara gets a big grin on her face and starts to say something when Dayna closes the door and locks it. We both start laughing when we hear Sara telling the others what just happened. Actually we both fall asleep reading our scriptures, but our friends don't know that. We wake up in the middle of the night and climb in bed. Dayna looks at me when we get in bed and says that maybe we are getting old. I give her a kiss, then she shakes her head and says no we're not, but we turn over and go to sleep anyway.

In the morning I get up and start to fix a great breakfast when I get reminded that today is Fast Sunday. We are supposed to fast for two meals usually starting on Saturday evening. Since we can't eat breakfast we decide to walk slow to church and visit with some of our friends that we haven't seen in a while. When we get to church we are talking to our friends from the other groups and they ask if we have had any corn missing. I am not sure what they mean, they tell me that they have found that they somehow lost several bags of the feed corn we all keep for our livestock. I haven't heard anything, but then I haven't exactly been available to find out what is going on.

When we go into the church I run into Tom and Frank who oversee the farming equipment and in the winter they work closely with the livestock. They tell me that they have noticed that the corn is disappearing faster than usual. If it was very cold that could explain most of it, but it has been pretty warm for this time of year. Other people tell me that they have smelled something out of the ordinary over where the people from Iceland and Greenland are living. They all say that they think it is the sheep. I make a mental note to check this out after church today.

Teddy and Nickie sit in the same row we do along with Little Jon and about half the group that are all our children. I make it a point to see who is in church and who isn't. Usually just about everybody in all the groups are here, but today I notice several people from the group we brought back from our trip to England. The ladies and the children are here, but there are at least four of the men that are not here today. I work my way over to talk to the women after church today and ask if the men are okay.

I asked if their husbands are okay and two of the women tell me that they are not married to any of those worthless bums. The ladies are quick to tell me that those men stay in a house of their own. This is all news to me. Nickie tells me that she has talked with these women before when they come to the bakery to get bread and rolls. She was told that none of the women in this group want anything to do with the four men who were not in church today. Teddy tells me he doesn't remember the last time he saw them in church. I tell Teddy that we need to have a council meeting to discuss when the council needs to get involved in what might otherwise appear to be private matters.

We no sooner get home when Tom comes over and says he knows for sure someone has taken some of our feed corn. He counted it this morning when he fed the dairy cows and when he just went back to the barn we are short four bags. I go over and ask LT and Tim to accompany me to the settlement we talked about earlier. By the time we get out of our settlement we have at least ten good men along for support.

24

I try to get some of them to stay home, but they tell me they have a bad feeling about some of the men in that group. Junior, Trey, and Max are along and so is Wyatt. They tell me they just don't like the way some of those guys look at the girls when they are around. They also say that isn't very often because they seldom show up for their work assignments. They say they haven't said anything because they would rather they don't come around. I tell them this is exactly the sort of thing that could possibly escalate into real trouble. If we put a stop to behaviors that we won't tolerate as soon as they start it is much easier and there is less chance of violence.

I came over here expecting to set some people straight about what is expected in our groups and now I am not sure what to expect. This could easily become real nasty and that's the last thing I want. We get to the group of houses that the people from Iceland and Greenland are living in. I can see right away which one the guys in question are living in. It's the only one that looks worse now than it did before we fixed it up for people to live in. I can smell what the others were talking about and it is not the sheep. I also know where the corn that has been being taken is. We walk around back and sure enough these guys have a still working, making moonshine whiskey.

Two of them are outside tending the still and two others join them when they see us come into the yard. One of the women from church this morning tells me quietly that there are two more men inside the house. She says she has never seen them before. Now I know this is going to get ugly. Oh well, we are not exactly strangers when it comes to violence even though we would prefer to handle situations peacefully. One of the guys outside is one of those from either Iceland or Greenland that likes to hug and talk right into your face. He is smiling telling me he was going to surprise us with his first batch of good shine, but that is no longer possible.

He is walking toward me and I notice he is holding his right hand in a strange position. When he is close he raises both arms to hug me and I catch the faintest glint of sunlight on steel. I react by blocking his right hand, grabbing it and bending it back behind him. I was right. He has a hideaway knife in his right hand, if he would have hugged me, this would have been sticking in either my neck or the back of my head. I push him away and he falls trying to catch his balance. He tells his friends to take us, but with several guns pointed straight at them they decide to drop their guns. He thinks he still has an ace with his friends in the house. Unfortunately for him LT and Wyatt snuck in the front door while they were watching what was going on back here.

They march those two out here with the others. I ask them how they thought they could get away with breaking almost every law we have and still live here. No one is talking so one of the women tells us that they have been bragging that they were going to kill me and then take over the entire settlement. I ask them if they think killing me would have stopped these men from coming after them. I tell them that we have fought more threats than any of us care to think about and we are still here and so are our laws. This settlement is much bigger than any one person no matter who that person is.

There are several members of our committee here with me so I ask them what we should do with these guys. William, who if you remember joined our group earlier this year with several of his friends, says that if we kill them now it would be murder. Killing someone in battle is one thing, shooting them when they are unarmed is another. I tell him I agree with him one hundred percent. Now what do we do with them besides killing them. There is a perceptible sigh of relief in all of them. Two of the guys say that they didn't agree with the leader, but they were afraid to go against him. He told them he would kill them if they did. Another of the women says that she doesn't know how true it is, but he did tell her that the other day.

It looks like no one wants to be the one to start the conversation about what we should do with them. I tell them and the others that if they are willing to abide by our rules and carry their share of the load they are welcome to stay. They will be on probation and the first major infraction and they are gone. Actually that will depend on the offense, if it is as serious as the one today, I will make sure it never happens again. The two that said they were forced say they would like to be given a second chance. The one still on the ground and the other three ask what if they don't want a second chance. I tell them we will give them a car, food for a few days, and they are on their own. If we ever see them back here to cause trouble it will not end this peacefully.

One of them asks if they can take their guns. I tell them they are lucky to be getting the car and the food. They can use their ingenuity to get some guns and whatever else they need. They ask which car they can take, they want to load their still into it, but Billy is already dismantling it and he just dumped the liquor in it on the ground. One of our guys goes into the house and comes back out with a bag of food. The car we are giving them is one that we have not driven in a while, but it starts right up. When they drive away we all hope it's the last time we will see them, but we do not really believe that it will be. LT comes up beside me and tells me I should have killed him when I had the chance. Now he may kill someone else before we kill them.

Tim goes directly to the radio to warn the other groups about them. Two of our younger men say they will move into that group to make sure the two that stayed don't cause any trouble. I tell them to be extra careful, we do not know if we can trust them or not. Until we know for sure, we will keep an eye on them. At least the rest of our Sunday goes peacefully. We almost always have company and today is no exception. One item of business that we finalize is that we will go back to Florida on Tuesday. That way we should have plenty of time to get what we want and be back on Saturday at the latest.

We spend part of the afternoon making a list of the things we want to bring back this time. We also have several lists of items that our friends would like to be able to get so that they can use them for Christmas presents. If we can't get them at the amusement parks we know where there are some outdoor stores on the way back where we can get the rest. Just before it is time to call it a day we get a visit from some of our friends that are going to Florida with us. LT and Kathy, along with James and Jenna, and Mike and Morgan tell me they want to run something by me to get my opinion on it.

I tell them I am open to just about anything that isn't illegal or immoral. Gunny used to say that all the time. Speaking of Gunny, I haven't seen them in a while. Back to what our friends want to talk to me about. LT asks me if I remember how many hours we spent getting trucks running, then filling or finding new tires so that we could drive them. I tell him he is right, we should drive the trucks we brought back and save all that time on this trip. I tell them we can even take an enclosed trailer to haul anything that the weather could create problems for.

Our friends ask me how I knew what they want to talk about. They barely finished talking it over themselves. I tell them I didn't know for sure, but I have been having the same thoughts for most of the day now. Now that we have the road cleared and know the best route to take, we may even be able to make it back down there in a long day or at least a full day and a short second day. With that out of the way, James and Mike ask if we could possibly make a side trip to the manufacturing plant that made those smaller electric busses. I tell them that it shouldn't take all of us to go to that factory, so Dayna and I are willing to take the side trip along with them of course.

Some of the others say they would like to see the factory as well so those that would like to come back as soon as they are loaded can, and those that want to see the factory can do that. After they leave we can finally get some sleep. My side is healing nicely now and there is very little pain. In fact I don't even notice it most of the time. Tonight Gunny, Ma Horton, and my real parents visit me again in my dreams. They tell me that they heard through the grapevine that I have an important mission to fulfill early next year. They go on to say that it is without a doubt the most important mission I have ever been on.

I ask them what it is and they tell me that they can't say any more than they already have. I am telling them how frustrating it is to have them constantly telling me things and never finishing what they start. Gunny just laughs and tells me that I will find out soon. I ask them if it has anything to do with that other guy that has come to talk to me. Again they just tell me I will learn what my mission will be when it is time. They tell me they have to go now and that they love me, Dayna and all the children. They are no sooner gone when I wake up and it is already time to get up.

Dayna asks me how I slept and I tell her about the visit from my parents. She says she had the same dream and she is sure that it's related to the other dreams we have had recently. We also agree that we will forget it for now and concentrate on what has to be done right now. First on the agenda is to go over and see if they need any help cleaning up after we had to ask those guys to leave yesterday. When we get there Zach, Sam, and Chuck who came over to help clean the place up ask if we can tear it down and build a new one. They take me inside and it is obvious that they butchered some animal in here. There is blood all over the walls and the carpeting is disgusting.

The house inside smells as bad as our chicken coops so we discuss it with some of the other group members and decide that since this is one of the smaller houses anyway and it still needs a lot of work even after we get the inside cleaned up we will take it down. The guys tell us that they know where there are some Quonset huts in very good shape and they are sure they could have one in here and setup in less than two weeks. We all laugh and tell them we were pretty sure they had an ulterior motive for wanting to tear it down. They act all innocent and tell us they are just the contractors, the cost will come out of our budget.

Those guys are always saying that. They are really some of our very best workers so when they ask for a small favor we are more than happy to let them do what they want. It is never anything that is contrary to our way of life. I ask them if there is anything else they would like to do and they tell me since I mentioned it they would really like to go to Florida on this next trip. They tell me that they heard through the grapevine that some of those that went last time don't want to go back. I tell them they are more than welcome, but if they leave who is going to put the Quonset hut here. Just as I ask it William, Noe, and Brandon come over and ask if this is where the next hut is going. They go inside the house and say that this thing will be down by the end of the week.

The biggest question is whether or not we want a basement under the hut. None of us are sure if there is a basement under the house or not. Brandon tells us he will be able to answer that question in about fifteen minutes. He takes off running toward another group of homes not far away. In a few minutes he returns driving a bulldozer. He asks if we want anything out of the house. We decide to take the woodstove, the refrigerator, and the stove out before we demolish it. Brandon looks around and decides to drive right through the front door, kind of. It doesn't take more than five minutes to determine there is no basement.

William disappeared for a few minutes, but he comes back driving a backhoe to help Brandon. The entire house will be down before the end of the day, but then they have to clean up the wood and the furniture in the big pile. Something tells me this was planned because just about the time the house is down Steve comes driving up in a very big dump truck to load the mess into. These houses were built pretty solidly so there is still some decent wood in that pile that can be used for firewood if nothing else. The good wood is dragged out of the pile and the rest will be loaded into the big truck.

Actually some of us left just about the time Brandon showed up and we saw Steve driving the truck toward there and asked him where he was going. This is not the first building we have torn down so we all know exactly what it takes. It will probably be Wednesday before everything is out of the way. Naturally it is not quite as easy as I described it. The water has to be shut off and capped. The electricity has to be disconnected and the batteries that are charged by the windmill have to be gotten out, all that was done before the bull dozer broke through the wall.

I make my rounds checking on the status of each of the large projects that we have going. Some of the guys and girls that were with us for the last Florida trip tell me that they would prefer to stay home this time, if we can get replacements for them. I tell them not to worry and thank them for all their help on that first trip. A crew was assigned to fill all the trucks with diesel fuel and make sure they are all empty. I head there last and get a surprise that I was not expecting. Jerry, Tyler, and Jarrod show me some stowaways from the first trip. They found three snakes in the tool area under the flat bed of the truck.

These are snakes that are part of the constrictor family, but they have been part of the ecological system pretty much forever. That's according to our specialists. We decide to put them in a box and take them back. Some of our people want to keep them until Jenna tells them that these snakes can reach lengths of twenty feet or more. Right now they are only about two feet long. We go back over the trucks to make sure we didn't overlook anything. There doesn't seem to be anything that shouldn't be there.

We were thinking about leaving this afternoon, but decide that we don't really have to be in any big hurry. Even leaving tomorrow we should be home easily by Saturday. This gives us a chance to spend the evening with our families and get a good night's sleep. We get up early in the morning and head out for Florida. Some of the people going were wondering if we may run into the guys that we asked to leave the settlement. I really have no idea where they went and as long as they don't bother any of the people in our groups, I don't care. I care about them as people, but everyone has to make their own choices and they made theirs. On the way down we pass at least two of the outdoor stores and we see signs for at least two more that are not right on our way.

Sara is flying down to the lower end of Florida to pick up another load of cocoa beans. According to our chocolate experts we are starting to get enough beans in the process that we can make batches although not all the time, at least several times a year. They are going to stop at the amusement parks on their way back. That should put them there on Wednesday morning, which is about the same time we expect to get there. With two drivers in every vehicle we make very good time, but we are still a couple hours away when it starts getting dark, so we decide to stop for the night.

We have a campfire for a while and sit around to tell stories. Unfortunately it usually winds up with our friends wanting to hear some of the stories from when Tim, LT, and I were Navy Seals. Tonight is no exception. Our friends want to hear about the worst mission we were ever on. It takes me a moment to think about which story I want them to know about. We had some missions that I wish I could forget. Zach asks me if I have told them about all the missions already. LT doesn't help. He tells them that a Navy Seal never runs out of mission stories to tell. If they do they will just make up some more.

Everybody laughs including me. I ask LT if he would like to tell them about a mission we had in the Middle East. He asks if I mean the one where the senator's kid was involved. I tell him that's the one. LT is a good story teller, he doesn't even have to embellish the story and he has everyone hanging on every word. When he is through Chuck says no wonder we are not afraid of anything or anybody. LT and I both tell him and everyone that we are afraid quite often. The difference between us and many of them is that we have been tested so many times we know what we can do and we usually do it when it is required.

I tell them that I am impressed with each and every one of them as well as our family members back at the settlement. I was trained to do what I did before we came here. Zach and Chuck interrupt me and say that they were trained by the best fighting man any of them have ever seen, me. I have nothing to say to that. Actually I couldn't if I wanted to because my eyes are watering too badly. It must be from the fire. LT doesn't help. He tells them that he agrees totally when they say I am the best fighting man they have seen. I try to lighten the mood by saying that I always thought I was more of a lover than a fighter. Kathy has to stick her two cents in when she says when she sees all the children in the settlement calling me Daddy or Grampa she has to agree with me.

Dayna agrees with her and starts to yawn. She says that reminds her it is past our bedtime. Everyone laughs and says if they hear me talking in my sleep they will mind their own business. All of the trucks we are driving have sleepers so everyone will get a good night's sleep. See you in the morning.

25

In the morning I wake up just as it is getting light out. Dayna tells me to get the fire going and to make some of the grain beverage we drink hot. She will be out when it is ready. I climb down out of the truck and I see a couple of people sitting at the fire. I assume it is some of our people so I yell over asking them to throw another couple logs on that fire so we can make some breakfast. I am gathering more wood from around the area we are camped in when I glance over at the fire and see someone putting a log on the fire, only this person has long blond hair and there is no one with us that has long blond hair.

I walk over to the fire and say good morning to our guests. I can see they are not very comfortable. There are three girls or young women and one young man. The young man is holding a revolver in his hand when he answers me. He tells me that they hope this is going to be a good morning. I ask him what would make it a good morning for them. The blond young lady says that it will be the best day of all if we don't try to hurt them and if we are from a settlement that has room for them to join it. Another of the young ladies says that if we have enough breakfast to share with them it will be an even better day.

I hear Dayna's voice behind me telling them that it should be a great day for us all then because they are more than welcome to join our settlement and to share our breakfast with us. I tell the young man that he really doesn't need the gun, but if it makes him more comfortable to go ahead and keep it within reach. I ask him if he would like to help me get breakfast started. He says he would be happy to and all three young ladies volunteer as well. Dayna tells me that I should get them some warmer coats to wear.

The ones they are wearing do not seem to be doing the job. We always carry a bunch of clothing with us because situations like this happen all the time and we just want to be ready for them. By now we have several members of our team up and about. They all welcome our new friends, especially Zach, Chuck, and Sam. They ask them if they like bacon and eggs for breakfast. One of the young ladies looks embarrassed and tells them they don't know what that is. They tell them they are in for a treat then. Kathy asks Chuck if he is going to make some pancakes to go with the bacon and eggs.

They can actually start cooking now that the young man, whose name is Shawn, and I have setup the portable propane cook stove we always carry with us. Shawn is acting kind of strange so I ask him if everything is okay. He says that they haven't been totally honest with us. We are waiting to hear more, but he seems to be reluctant to tell us. The girl with the long blond hair says that their parents and another brother and a sister are about a half hour from here. She continues that they heard the trucks last evening and thought about asking us for help then, but they were afraid that we might hurt them.

Early this morning their father seemed to get sicker and their mother told them to see if we would be willing to help them. Shawn says that they were afraid to tell us because we might not be willing to take on seven people. Dayna scolds them a little asking them if they were just going to go off and leave their family here. They say they are not sure what they were going to do, they were just so afraid. As always we have a van loaded on one of the trucks that was used to bring the small busses back last time. We get it unloaded and Dayna, LT, and I take two of them to go get the rest of the family.

It's a good thing our van is four wheel drive because they are staying in an old farm house that sets back in the woods. When we get there we can see that their father is in pretty rough shape. I was a medic in the seals and have learned a lot more since being here. We always carry some common medicines with us when we go anywhere. Most of what we use is natural remedies and herbs that are good for you. Personally I think he is more rundown from lack of good food than anything else, not that he isn't very ill. Malnutrition can kill someone as easily as pneumonia.

We get them loaded into the van and head back to where we are camped. On the way back the young lady that came with us tells the rest of the family that we are having something called bacon, eggs, and pancakes for breakfast. The mother says there must be some mistake, where would we get those foods in this world. Dayna tells her that we smoke the pork to make bacon, we have several hundred chickens for the eggs, and we grow our own wheat to make the pancake flour. She says she thinks there may even be enough milk for them each to have a big glass. I think the sound of that breakfast is helping the father feel better already.

Everyone is excited to meet our newest friends and to help them feel comfortable. I could smell the bacon a half mile away and I am really looking forward to eating this morning. We make sure our guests have enough to eat before we quit cooking. The young ladies in the family all say that they could eat this for breakfast three or four times a day. Their brother tells them that it wouldn't be breakfast if you eat it for lunch. Dayna tells him that we eat breakfast foods often for lunch and dinner. She tells them that when they get settled into a home in our settlement they will get all the food they need and how they eat it is up to them.

The youngest member of the family, who is about four or five, asks if they will get some milk with the food. Dayna picks her up and tells her that she can have all the milk that she and her whole family can drink. They will also have ice cream to eat. She says oh boy, then asks her mom what ice cream is. Even her dad smiles at that comment. Her mom tells her that it is like frozen milk with fruit or different flavors in it. Now the entire family can't wait until they get to try some. While they were eating and discussing the future we called the settlement in northern Florida and the one in Georgia to ask if they have had any new people join them lately.

I didn't mention it yet, but they told us that they were living with three other families in those houses until three or four days ago when the others left to try to find a settlement. They promised to send help back when they did find one. We just want to make sure they made it. If not we will send out a search party to look for them. We found out that their friends did make it to the settlement yesterday. They told the people there about these people and they were going to go looking for them today. We ask the family if they would prefer to go where their friends are or go back to our settlement.

They say that they would prefer to live with the people in our group especially if they are all as friendly as we are. The mother gets to talk to one of their friends and wishes them all the luck in the world. We have to be going, but we don't want to make this family go all the way down to the amusement parks with us and then have to wait until we go back. Zach volunteers to drive them back in the van, then join us afterward if we need him. We tell him that we would appreciate it if he would drive them to the settlement and stay there to help them get settled in.

We make sure they have enough food for the trip back, then when they leave we head out to finish our trip. The young man insisted on coming with us to show that they are willing to carry their share of the work. The rest of the trip goes by without any more surprises. Shawn, our newest family member wants to learn how to drive the big trucks that we are driving. We promise to teach him and let him practice in the large parking lots here. We know exactly what we came here to get so we go to work loading the trucks. Everything is just as we left it so it makes our job that much easier.

There is very little that we can load by hand, but we already had the equipment we need running so it is ready to go. Luckily we have enough people to divide into groups to get everything done. Dayna, Kathy, and Ruth supervise loading the warehouse full of supplies that are always needed in the settlements. That's the linens like sheets, pillow cases, pillows, curtains, towels, I think you get the idea and can see where there is a need for all that stuff. We are even stacking the cases of these items neatly on pallets so that they can be loaded using a fork lift. Several of the guys keep joking around asking who their union steward is because they have a grievance.

I have to go over and tell Mike and Patrick to quit giving the guys any ideas. They didn't even know there was such a thing as a union before they told them about it. Everyone is just joking anyway. We are all used to working until the job is done. We all work well together which makes it that much easier. Luckily we have the box trailer for the items that we don't want getting wet or exposed to the weather because it starts raining shortly after we get here. Not heavy, but a consistent drizzle that will soak you to the skin in no time. Luckily we found a room where the crew must have kept their rain gear last trip. It is coming in handy right now.

Last trip we got the merry go round, a ride called a Tilt A Whirl and one that is like a small roller coaster for the children. They will sit in seats that are made in the caricature of little animals. This trip I tell the guys to get any rides they think our family will enjoy. The first thing they see is what I consider a smaller Ferris wheel, but it should be okay at least to start with. They are checking to see how difficult it will be to take it down when I tell them that there are several rides that are already dismantled and on trucks to be used at carnivals before the war. That makes it a lot easier, now all we have to do is get those trucks running for the trip back.

One machine Dayna, Kathy, and Ruth want is one that makes cotton candy. Kathy says she worked in an amusement park one summer and sometimes her job was to make cotton candy. They also find a taffy pulling machine that they simply have got to take back with us. One thing I see that I want to take back is one of those huge popcorn popping machines. We have a couple of smaller ones similar to these, but the ones they have here will make about a bushel of popcorn at a time. The great thing is they keep popping as long as you have corn in them. We load the trucks with the small busses and even some of the great electric golf carts they have here.

As usual on a project like this one I have the list of what we came to get and I am going from group to group making sure we are getting the right items. Everything is going great until I get to the group with LT, Chuck, and Sam in it. They have their truck almost fully loaded, but they got distracted by a waterslide that has to be a couple hundred feet long. When I get to their area they are checking the slide out to see how difficult it would be to take it apart to transport. I tell them that I already looked at one of these in the other park last time. We feel we can have it down in less than a day and since we are not planning to put it together in its entirety we won't need all the support beams.

While they are working on that, Dayna and some of the other women come looking for me. They want to show me something that they know the children at home would love to have. We have to go to one of the other parks for this one. What they want to take back is a miniature train. It's big enough for small and not so small people to ride on. At first I thought it was a steam engine, but upon looking closer I can see that it was solar powered electric. At first glance there are only a couple of cars actually on the tracks, but in the building these cars were apparently stored in there are at least fifteen or twenty cars and a bunch of extra track.

While we are investigating the easiest way to take up the track, some of our other groups come looking for us. They stopped by the gift shop and found several cases of good canned chocolate candy. They are using one of the golf carts so they brought a couple cases with them to pass out to us. They toss a can to Shawn and he asks if it is okay if he saves it for his family. We tell him it's okay to eat some of it, we have plenty for our families as well. He smiles and tells us that if he doesn't eat any of it there will be that much more for his family. That makes the rest of us feel a little guilty so we put the candy away until we get home.

We take a vote to see how many members of our team think this is something worth taking back. The vote is unanimous. We all think that the children will love it. The women are envisioning a track running from our group to the other groups. Some of the people in our group say that they remember seeing track like this running around and through the other parks as well. Now that we have a proposed project we break up into groups to look for more train cars and track. It takes some looking, but we do find where the cars are kept in each park and we also find what used to be known as round houses for the trains.

They could pull the engine and a couple of cars into the round house and turn it around so it would be going the opposite direction. None of it looks too difficult to take apart, unfortunately we only have so much time to get it done in. While looking for the trains LT and Kathy found a big trailer that looks like it was made especially for hauling the train cars. It has partitions that look like they were made to hold them to prevent damage in transit. LT and Sam are working on the truck to see if they can get it running. If they can't we can always swap one of our trailers for that one. By the time we call it quits for the day we have all but three of our trucks loaded more than half full.

We have a good meal from the provisions we brought with us and some of the food items that we found here in cans or sealed jars. We get a call on the radio telling us that our newest friends got there late this afternoon and everyone is doing well. They asked to be able to tell Shawn that it is like heaven there. They already have a house. Doc McEvoy gave the father a checkup and said that plenty of rest and a good diet should have him back to normal in no time. The little one, whose name is Chad, tells them to let me know that he likes ice cream just fine.

After the radio conversation is over Shawn tells all of us that he will never be able to repay us for all the kindness that we have shown to him and his family. We spend the evening talking and getting to know each other a little better, then we turn in because we know tomorrow will be at least as busy as today was. Nights down here are more stressful than they are back home. I cannot recall a night here when we couldn't hear the life and death struggle of at least two animals and it is often many more than that. Just like last time we hear that struggle taking place in very close proximity to where we are. When we check it out I can't believe that it is a huge alligator and an equally huge snake.

This time we just shoot them both. We have quite a few orders for both alligator and snake meat. Personally I have eaten several different kinds of snake meat and although it's not bad tasting, it's nothing I would actually look for unless I really needed food. The alligator, again I have tasted it and would prefer to eat most anything other than that. Some of our people back home canned some of the alligator we brought back last time and they want to do more of that when we get back this time.

Doc Betty is flying out with the others primarily because she found several plants in the wetlands here that are excellent remedies for some of the everyday ailments that we get. She wasn't sure which ones to pick so she waited until she got home and looked it up on her computer. Actually she said she wished she had her computer to look things up on. It was much quicker than digging through books looking up what information we need. Personally I think it's a small price to pay for living in this world versus the other one.

By the time we get the two animals field dressed it is time to get up anyway. We have breakfast then break into teams to finish the work we came here to do. When that is done we will tackle the project of bringing that train back with us. We spent a little time yesterday afternoon taking the track up and found out it will not be as difficult as we first thought it would be. We are all hard at work when we hear the airplane fly overhead. Poor Shawn has no idea what is going on. He has seen airplanes in books, but never dreamed he would actually see one flying.

When we all run to meet our friends I guess he figures it must be safe so he comes along. All of our friends are happy to meet him. They are also happy to hear that we have accomplished so much in the short time we have been here. Our scientific people are some of those that really seem to enjoy the alligator meat and the skin for making things with. With the extra hands we get the last of the trucks loaded in no time. That's when we show them the train and tell them we would like to take it apart and take it home with us.

They all agree that it could be very entertaining as well as useful for moving goods and people between our groups. They also tell us that they saw some other amusement parks farther south as well as a military base that they took a little time to check out. Apparently there is much the same things there as there are here so if we need more for ourselves or for our friends in the other groups it is available. There are some items that we are planning to take back in the airplane, but we don't want to fill it up before we visit the manufacturing plant.

26

While our scientific people take care of that, some of us start loading the train cars onto the truck that was built for that purpose. LT was able to get the truck running so we can use that to pull the trailer. The trailer was built very well for this purpose. When we load the individual cars they lock right in place in the sections. The train cars are not very big so the trailer was designed to get two across and five rows back on the first level and one row less on the other two rows. We are able to fill it from just the cars in this park, plus there are at least as many in the other parks. The team taking up the track is doing a great job as well.

After the truck is loaded with the cars we all get to work taking up the track and the heavy vinyl like plates that the track is setting on. They are acting like the railroad ties did on the larger railroads. It appears that they dug a large groove the length of where they wanted the train to run. Then put down gravel to level it, then they put down the vinyl pads to fasten the track to and help absorb the shock of the ride. Our scientific people are excited to see that the train is powered by electricity and that it was charged using solar power. The motors and solar generators were manufactured by the same company that made the small busses.

We are able to take up more than a mile of track and get it loaded before nightfall. We were going to leave, but now we are going to wait until tomorrow afternoon to leave. We want to get as much track as we can before going back home. With all the projects we have, we are not sure when we may be able to get back here this year. To satisfy our alligator enthusiasts we decide to go hunting before it gets dark. We go out in groups of four for safety. We have seen plenty of the large beasts during the day, but they have stayed far enough away that they were no threat.

It is still raining lightly off and on as we go out of the parks to the marshland not far away to look for our prey. Our group doesn't have to go far before we are confronted by the largest alligator I have ever seen. This one looks to be as large as a good sized row boat, both long and wide. We have been informed that the most effective way to kill one is to hit the spot on their head where their brain is. The trouble is that spot is not much bigger than a quarter. At least that's what we have been told. The one in front of us now is not cooperating one little bit in letting us get a clear shot at its head.

This is one time when I wish I had a spot above this thing to be able to shoot down at it. I am trying to get a shot at it, but it seems that everywhere I go trying to get around or at least beside it the beast turns with me. I am hunting with Chuck and Sam. They keep telling each other that one of them should get close and draw it after them so that the rest of us can get a shot. Naturally they are just kidding, but they must see something because as soon as I move again the gator follows me and they run to either side of it. They must have a good shot at it because they both fire at once and the animal swings its tail and rolls to one side. After that it is just lying there not moving.

We move in and poke it with a long stick to make sure it is no longer alive, then we field dress it. When that is done we try to drag it back to where we are staying and there is no way we can move this thing without help. Luckily we have our walkie-talkies and can call for help. James and David come to help us drag it back with a golf cart. It is all the cart can do to drag the alligator up the small hill and into the park even though it is mostly wet grass that we are on. When we get back to our camp we hear some of the other teams calling for help as well. The group with LT and Kathy in it sounds like they need more than help getting their animal back to camp.

We run to get to where they said they are in their call. We get here just in time to see that they not only have a very large alligator in front of them, they have another alligator on each side of where they are standing. All of the alligators appear to be over twelve feet. The angle we have coming in allows us to shoot the gator on their left. That gives them the room they need for one member of their team to get a good shot at the one in front of them. Mike and Morgan are coming up on the scene near the other alligator that we thought would go away when we shot the other two, but it is actually getting more aggressive.

It is starting to move toward LT and Kathy when Morgan shoots the beast stopping it in its tracks. We are in the process of field dressing the tree alligators when we get a frantic call from Shawn that Steve is hurt. They are about a quarter mile away from us, but I bet I cover that distance faster than I ever have before. We get to the clearing they are in and Steve is sitting on the ground trying to catch his breath. Not far from him is another snake at least as big as the Anaconda we killed on the last trip. Steve looks up at me and tells me now he knows how it felt to get hit by that snake last trip.

Shawn is starting to get to where he can breathe again and tell us what happened. Apparently they saw a large alligator in this area and came after it. Unfortunately when they got close they saw the alligator disappearing into the water over there. What they didn't see is the biggest snake either of them has ever seen coming out of the woods or jungle over there. He points to a trail coming out of the woods. They know that we were asked to bring back some snake meat as well so they got close enough to shoot it. The trouble is when they shot, they didn't anticipate the snake writhing and thrashing around quite as much as it did.

Steve was standing too close and got hit in the ribs by the snake's body and knocked about ten feet in the air. The worst part about that is that put him closer to the snake's head where the mouth was opening and biting against the snake's unseen foe. Shawn tried to get another shot at the snakes head, but he is not sure enough with a gun to take a chance on hitting Steve. Luckily the snake quit moving before it found Steve. Now we have to field dress that beast. When we cut the stomach of the snake open there is what appears to be a half digested alligator in there. Naturally it was crushed by the snake before it ate it, but it shows us just how powerful these things can be.

We get the snake field dressed and throw it on the golf cart we brought along. That thing has to weigh a couple hundred pounds. I bet the alligators are closer to eight or nine hundred pounds each. We go back to help field dress the three that group got, then haul them back to where we are staying. Luckily the temperature is in the forties so the meat will stay fresher. There is a huge cooler here that we were able to get running so there should not be any trouble at all. When we get all the meat in the cooler we have six alligators and three snakes. I'm not sure which group got the other snake, but it is a large one.

One of our teams shot a deer while they were hunting and we are all glad to have the fresh meat for supper. We discuss what else we may want to take back this trip and we decide that we definitely want the round houses for the trains. Actually we don't care about the buildings, what we want are the mechanisms that turn the trains around. Some of the guys want to go and check them out tonight so we know what to expect tomorrow. That's an excellent idea, but I just ask James, Mike, and David and they tell us exactly what we will need to do. Actually they already disconnected one of them so all we have to do in the morning is lift it off and disconnect the equipment underneath it.

In fact they volunteer to do that if they can have a team to help with the heavy work. Not that they can't use the heavy equipment we use for jobs like this, they just want to make sure everything comes out the way it should and it's easier to do that when you are at the same level. Steve volunteers to run the excavator that we have been using to lift the heavy objects that we can't get a fork truck under. We ask him if he can do that with his ribs being like they are. Doc Betty says that they seem to more bruised than broken, but if he takes it easy he should be able to run the equipment. Josh volunteers to help out as well.

Doc Betty has already recruited the women to help her look for the herbs and other plants that are brilliant for curing ailments naturally. I think I am spending too much time around our family members from England. They are always using the word brilliant to describe something they think is good. It doesn't matter how you describe it, they are very good to have. We all agree that the women will need someone to watch that they do not become food for the snakes and alligators as well as several other types of animals and other things that can kill you down here. David volunteers, he says that James and Mike can disassemble those roundhouses without him.

I sleep better tonight than I have in a couple of weeks. I do not even recall dreaming until just before I wake up when Gunny comes to me and tells me that we might want to go to that manufacturing plant taking the longer route there at least. I don't even have time to ask him why and I am awake. Dayna thinks I'm losing it when I tell her he wouldn't have told me why anyway. She just laughs and asks if I talked to Gunny last night. I tell her that I didn't say a word. He did all the talking as usual. We discuss what he said and decide we should probably do what he recommended.

Today we eat a quick breakfast and hit the projects that we are working on. With as much help as we have, we get all but a few hundred yards of the track in this particular park. We are able to store quite a bit of the track in compartments under and between the train cars on that truck. The rest of it we are able to put on the other vehicle carriers that hold the small busses. The women were very successful in gathering the plants that Doc Betty wanted. They picked a bunch of the leaves and dug up even more of the plants to be transplanted in the green house when we get home. Josh says he was afraid we would have another alligator to take back, but it decided to go back the way he came.

We have all the trucks lined up to head back home. Dayna and I are going to drive a partially empty trailer to the manufacturing facility, then we will stop by one of the outdoors stores to pick up a bunch of Christmas presents. When Shawn hears about the outdoor stores he asks if they could possibly stop at one on the way home. The guys all tell him no, but their wives tell them if they don't stop they will be sleeping in the old singles barracks in the barn. LT acts like stopping will be the worst thing that could happen, but we know they are all looking forward to stopping.

When I tell the others what Gunny said, they all say that I can go the long way and they will go the most direct route. That will give them time to do what they want to before we get there. I tell them again that I have no idea why he said that only up to this point in time he has never steered us wrong. Sara is taking the plane home with Gary. We loaded everything that is going that way and told them we will see them probably tomorrow sometime. Just before we are ready to go the others tell me to lead the way. It's always better to stay together anyway and the route we are going to take should add less than a half hour.

We figure it should only take us a little over an hour to get there. We have a total of four trucks going to the facility. Some of the others wanted to see the factory that we are going to. We are only about twenty minutes short of our destination when we see smoke coming from a building not far off the road. We decide that one truck will pull into the parking lot and see if this is a group of people who may need our help. Doc Betty and Josh are driving the truck that pulls in, but the rest of us are ready to come running if we are needed. Dayna and I decide to work our way around back just in case they are so frightened they run.

We can see what is going on out front and watch the back door at the same time. I can see that Josh has his hand gun in his hand, but hidden beside his leg. I know that may sound like we don't trust whoever is in that building, and until we get to know them, we don't trust them. Sorry, but sometimes being cautious can mean the difference between staying alive and not staying alive. We can't see the front door, but we can guess at what is happening by Josh and Betty's mannerisms. Apparently nobody is answering the door because we hear Josh knocking again and asking if there is anyone home.

He assures them that we do not mean them any harm, all we want to do is talk to them and see if they can use some help. Now we see the back door open and we can see six people come out. Two are adults, two appear to be children between nine and twelve and two are young children, probably three to five. Where we are positioned they will have to walk right past us unless they want to climb over a pile of old furniture. When the lady who is leading gets to within ten feet, Dayna steps out into their path and tells them we really do not mean them any harm. The lady looks scared, but I am betting that she is more afraid for the little girl she is holding than for herself.

The rest of the family is close behind and now has to stop because she has. The man tells us that they have nothing for us to take, so please leave them alone. By this time Doc Betty and Josh have walked around the building and are coming up behind them. Josh stops in his tracks and tells me I might want to turn around, but to do it slowly. I turn slowly and I am surprised to say the least. This is a first for us. Oh yeah, you can't see what I am looking at. There are approximately ten men standing behind me holding clubs, knives, and one of them is holding a shotgun trained on me.

I raise my hands and tell them that we really do not mean them any harm. I continue telling them that we have a settlement up in Virginia with approximately six hundred people in it and we are always looking for people who may wish to join our groups. The one holding the shotgun asks me why they should believe me. I start to answer when I hear Sam's voice saying because they have ten men standing behind them and they are all carrying guns. Sam continues telling them that we mean them no harm. Everything I told them is the truth and if they are not interested in hearing what we have to offer we will back on out of here and they will never see us again. He also tells the man that although we mean them no harm, if that gun that is pointed at me goes off, it will be the last thing that man ever does. Whether it is an accident or on purpose, he will die.

The man lowers the gun and says what kind of people come on a peaceful mission carrying guns. I tell them all that we have no reason to assume that everyone we meet will want to be friends. We have a pretty full graveyard from those that came trying to steal our women or to take away our way of life. I also tell them I am not offended in the least for them to be cautious. In this case everything we have said is the truth and they are more than welcome to join us if they would like. Obviously they have their own settlement right here and from the looks of it from back here they must plow a couple of acres for crops.

Everyone comes down to where we are and we can talk to them as individuals. The man that we saw first asks me what we have in the trucks. I tell him we have been over to the amusement parks and we are taking back some of the rides to make our settlement a little more fun for the children and the adults. We show them so that they know we are telling the truth. The man who had the shotgun is old enough to be around since the war. He asks me if that airplane they saw belongs to us. I tell him that it does. I also tell him we go down to Cuba, and to other settlements here in Florida, Georgia, Missouri, California, Arizona, and New York.

One of the other men asks how many acres of food does it take to feed a settlement the size of ours. I tell him truthfully that I really don't know how many acres we use now, but at last count it was somewhere around a hundred and fifty. I tell them that almost all of us have our own gardens where we grow some of the things that we might especially like. There are several women here now asking questions as well. We answer questions for a good fifteen minutes then we tell them we really have to be going if we are going to get to the factory we are looking for this evening.

They ask if we can wait a few minutes for them to talk it over. I tell them that if they decide to join us and find out that they don't like our settlement for any reason, we will bring them back here. While we are waiting some of the ladies continue to talk to the women in our group. One of those is the lady that came out of the house. Dayna tells the lady that she has beautiful children and asks her how old they are, for some reason that helps them relax. We go back into the building they are staying in. Actually it is pretty cozy and is very clean compared to most of the places we have seen people staying in.

It only takes a few minutes for the leaders of this group to convince them that they should come with us. They said that they are running out of food anyway. They had a garden, but some men stopped by and took just about all their food when they hid from them. We are thinking it may have been the people that left our group, but the timing isn't right for that. Now we have to be on the lookout for some pretty low life predators. These people are lucky those men didn't find them. No telling what they would have done.

27

We ask them if they would like to come with us to the factory we are going to, or wait until we come back for them. Some of the people say that they will wait for us here, but some of them don't want to take the chance that those men may come back. Some of our men agree to stay here at least until we find the factory and see if it is what we are hoping it will be. The man that had the shotgun knows right where the factory we are looking for is. He tells us that his mother and father worked in this factory when he was a young man before the war. The factory looks like it was a really nice, neat place to work at one time. When we go inside we can tell that it was well kept and that it was made to do the precision work that they did here. There are still some of the busses in various stages of assembly. Actually the busses are fully assembled except where the electric motor goes into them. Some have motors in them, but there are five or six that are still on the assembly line.

The man tells us that his father was an engineer for this company and he always told him that he made sure the technology could continue if the right people find his records. He seems to know exactly where to look because he walks right into an office and shows us which file cabinet everything we could want to know about the busses is located. James says that he would love to meet the engineer that took the time to do such a complete job. The man tells him thank you, I'm sure my dad would be happy to hear that as well. James asks him if he was an engineer here and the man smiles and shakes his head in the affirmative.

We go out to the busses and we ask the man, whose name is Harmon, if he knows the process for installing the motors into the busses. He laughs and tells us that he worked here from the time he could turn a wrench until the day the world almost ended. During that time he did pretty much every job there was here. James asks him if he thinks he could teach us how to install the motors and to get more of the busses running. Harmon tells us that he could probably do that blindfolded, but since it has been several years since he did any of that, he will keep the blindfold off, at least for the first couple.

We can see that it is already getting dark outside so we will have to wait until morning to get started. We go back to the small settlement and decide to stay right here and sleep in the trucks. Just about all of them have sleepers anyway and those that don't have very large seats that someone can stretch out on to sleep. Our hosts are embarrassed that they barely have enough food for the women and children. We have plenty to share. The kitchens at the amusement park had literally thousands of cans of different kinds of food and the cans were still sealed. We tried it while we were there and found it to be very good.

Tonight we open some of the large cans of macaroni and beef in sauce. Our new friends seem to enjoy the meal. Just about all of them eat at least two helpings. While we are eating one of the little girls in the group asks Dayna if there are any children her age. Dayna asks her how old she is and she shows us four fingers and says the word four. Dayna tells her that we have a grandson that is four and there are at least six other four years olds just in our group and there are six groups in all. Dayna tells them there are several five and six year olds as well, and we have quite a few dogs and puppies that love to play with the children.

We spend at least another hour answering questions about the settlement. When Kathy mentions the chickens and the milk cows they can hardly believe it. We get talking about how we prepare meat and I think they have some doubts when Steve tells them we make a lot of jerky from beef and venison. He must sense it as well because he gets up from his seat and goes to the truck he is driving. He comes back with a big bag of both kinds of jerky as well as some pepperoni that we make. He passes it around and since the children can't eat the jerky very well Dayna and Jenna go to the trucks and bring back several cans of chocolate candy.

The older people say they haven't had jerky or candy since before the war. The younger ones have never had either. Morgan tells them that if they like these foods, wait until they get some real homemade ice cream with fresh fruit in it. One of the children that is about thirteen asks how long we are going to work at the factory. He says he speaks for the other young people when he says they would like to go to our settlement as soon as possible. Everyone laughs and tells him we can probably take care of all the business we have here tomorrow.

The rest of the evening is spent answering questions about our settlement and how we were able to do so much. We tell them that everything we currently have was already here. We just found a way to use it to our advantage. We tell them the real secret behind our ability to accomplish so much is the willingness of our group family to work together and lose the attitude that almost killed this world. That is the attitude of what's in it for me before anybody would do anything. Our people know that if it is good for the entire community, then it is good for everyone in it.

In the morning we head back to the factory and everybody comes along. We have room for all their belongings and they have one of the small busses that will just about fit everyone from their group. Some of them ask if they could possibly ride with some of us at least part of the way back. Naturally we don't have any problems with that. When we get to the factory we load the filing cabinets into one of the trucks. We also load some of the motors that are ready to be installed so that our people can go over them with the plans. We ask Harmon what he thinks of the idea of moving the entire contents of the factory back to our community.

He tells us that he told his wife last night that he had a feeling we would ask that. He says he thought about it most of the night and can't see any reason why we couldn't. He tells us there is a warehouse not far from here where the company kept most of the supplies needed for building the motors, and the drive trains needed for these vehicles. We are taking a quick inventory of the contents so that we know what we will need when we come back. We also find two of the small trucks that they put the electric motors in as well. Harmon is as excited to see if we can get them running as we are.

We have been given a time limit before we have to leave so we really have to work at this project. Actually with Harmon's help we get both trucks running with ten minutes to spare. We take that ten minutes and load some of the lighter items that we will have to move anyway. The trucks don't go over forty-five miles per hour, but with the condition of the roads and having to move vehicles off the road for the first part of our trip home we can't even go that fast most of the time. Our timing is pretty good because we get to one of the outdoor stores we want to stop at just about an hour before dark.

Harmon and a couple of the others that were here before the war remember stores like these, but they never went looking for them. We tell them we have shopping lists for Christmas if they want to do some shopping themselves. Any room we have left in the trucks, including the two electric ones is no longer empty. In fact LT and I get busy trying to get a really nice diesel truck with a twenty-six foot enclosed box on it. Our new friends are impressed with our mechanical ability and are more than happy to help us fill that truck as well. The nice thing about stores like this one is that there is almost always cots and sleeping bags to sleep right here.

We even find enough dehydrated foods to feed us all for supper and for breakfast. We are all up before dawn and decide to eat our breakfast on the road so that we can get back home before noon. We pull into the yard at ten minutes to twelve. We were able to call ahead on the radio so we have a large welcoming committee here. As usual everybody wants to see what we brought home and to meet our newest family members. We find out quickly that Doc Betty's group already had homes for them. Some of the guys from that group look at the trucks we brought back and say they have to show the new people their new homes so they will see us later.

We know they are just kidding. They like to joke around that way. With all the help we have the unloading doesn't take as long as you might think. Besides quite a bit of it is just being unloaded into the warehouses and we can do a lot of that with fork trucks. Our new friends are curious and amazed at how everyone works together. They all work well together, but it is easier when you have twenty some working together and over six hundred. Naturally not everyone is here right now. We still have jobs to do and some simply can't let their jobs go. Ryan and Carol are here as well as many of their group members. They along with Doc McEvoy say that they saw some items they are getting dangerously low on in the list we made of what we have on the trucks.

When we load our trucks we make a list of everything in it and we also mark which truck the list is for. Most of the time it works very well, but there have been times when we had to add items to a truck that are not on the list and it caused some confusion. This time is kind of like that because we got so much stuff at the outdoor store that we took some items from their original truck and put them in another truck. It only takes a few minutes to get the items they need off the truck and loaded onto the pickup truck they will use to take them to their warehouse.

When the trucks are all unloaded and everything that should be put away is some of us go with our new families to show them where they will be living at least for the time being. If they decide they would prefer to be in a different group they are more than welcome to move. Of course it may take a while to get a house for them where they want to be, but we will do all we can to help them. When we get there they cannot believe that they can just move into the houses they have ready. Actually they have been bringing in the Quonset huts for a while now and the young people moved into them as quickly as they came available. That left several houses empty for when they are needed, which is now.

We explain that for a short time some families or individuals may have to share a house, but we will fix that as quickly as we can. They tell us there are actually more houses than they lived in back in Florida. We tell them that is up to them how they want to share the housing. We tell them we will let them get settled, then later we would like them to come back to our group for a special celebration meal. Doc Betty tells them not to worry, she and Josh will make sure they know where to go. We start walking away and our new members go into the houses. We barely go a few steps when they are calling us back saying that the people that lived here before left the cupboards and the refrigerator full of food, and their furniture is still here as well.

Doc Betty tells us to go ahead, she will handle this. We go back to our home and get to tell our family all about our adventures. Then they get to fill us in on everything that has been going on here. My sons tell me that they got most of the walls up on the golf building, but no one wants to go up that high to put the top panels on and the roof. They say they have been waiting for a couple of old crazy people to do it like me and LT. We can all laugh at that comment. We decide to take the short drive to where the golf building is located. Actually we decide to see how all of the projects have progressed since we were gone.

We are using a couple of the electric golf carts we have to get there. When we get to the first project, which is the museum Dayna and I are impressed with how much work has been done. There is still much to be done, but our workers are doing a great job. We are getting ready to drive away when we see Josh and William showing Harmon and some of the others from our newest members around the groups. We all go to the golf building and they are really impressed and so am I. We take time here to look around and that is even more impressive. I am hanging back with Dayna just enjoying being home again. We have already said that after we get the factory back here, we are not going anywhere for a while.

We are surprised when Harmon and his son drop back to walk with us. Harmon tells us that we may not know it, but we are the answer to a lot of prayers. I tell them that there were a lot of people in the group that found them. He smiles and tells me that they all said that you changed the route you were going to take at the last minute, because of a dream. I start to talk and he interrupts. He smiles again and tells me that I should know it's not polite to interrupt when your elders are talking to you. He tells us that if we had taken the route we had planned on we wouldn't have come within five miles of them.

He shakes my hand and tells me they will never be able to thank me and whoever told me to go that way, enough. Again I start to tell him he is welcome when he tells me I am being rude again. Now he has Dayna telling me I need to be more polite. He tells her that she is not only very pretty, but she is smart too. He says that's a combination you don't see often enough. He continues saying that someone told him that me along with some other members of this beautiful community came from another world. I ask him if I can talk now and he just laughs and says of course.

I tell him how we came to be here, then he actually shocks me when he says that his mother and father came from the same world we did. He says that his father always wanted to do more with sustainable energy, but in the world he came from the government and the big automakers wouldn't allow it. One night they went for a boat ride and wound up where you found us. The government was somewhat better than in the other world, but he didn't do very well until he got the idea of supplying the amusement parks and other niche areas with electric cars, busses, and small trucks.

He got backing from the amusement parks and built that factory. He says that if his father could meet us he would be proud that other people from his world are helping rebuild this world and are doing it the correct way. He asks me where we are planning to build the new factory. I tell him that we haven't decided for sure yet, but we are leaning toward putting it next to the river, which has a strong steady current and using that to generate the electricity we will need. He just smiles and says he is going to love it here.

I ask him if he would be willing to teach some of our young people what he knows about engineering and especially about electric power. He tells us that would be a dream come true as long as he can teach his own son and grandchildren as well. I tell him he has a deal. He leans close like some people do when they want to ask you a question they may not want others to hear and asks me if it's true that we make our own pizza, complete with Italian sausage, pepperoni, and lots of cheese. I figure I will have a little fun with him, so I tell him that may be an exaggeration. We don't always put those ingredients on our pizza. Some of our people really like the pineapple and ham on their pizza.

He smacks me on the arm and tells me not to joke around about food. He hasn't had pizza in over thirty years and he would almost kill to have one. I tell him that we should go over to the bakery and order some dough so we can make some pizza this evening. He looks at me kind of sideways and asks Dayna if I am pulling his leg again. Dayna tells him and his wife that they better jump in the golf cart and we will take them to the bakery. They are very much impressed and say they can't wait for the rest of the group to see this. We go in and our daughter in law Nickie is happy to see us, almost as happy as Little Jon, our grandson.

We introduce our new friends to her and of course Little Jon and ask if it's too late to get some dough for pizza this evening. She asks how much we need and I tell her at least enough to feed twenty hungry people and maybe enough for her favorite mother in law. She tells us that she already had a couple of big orders today, but she thinks there is enough for the twenty people. I tell her it was a good idea, but I can wait until some other time. She tells us that she still has several loaves of very fresh French bread and some rolls that are out of this world. We both take some of those for our families.

When we leave I ask him if he needs any help making the pizzas and he tells me we have done more than enough already today. He used to make them for his parents when they were alive before the war. He thinks he still remembers how it was done. His wife asks about the pans for cooking them and the rest of the stuff they will need for them. Dayna tells her that everything they need should already be in their houses. Check the refrigerator and the cupboards, if it's not there, let Doc know and she will make sure they get it. When we separate we tell them that church service is held at nine o'clock sharp tomorrow morning.

They say they usually hold church services in their homes, but it will be nice to go to church with other people for a change. We tell them all they have to do is follow the crowd in the morning. We go home to our family and on the way I tell Dayna it's a shame we couldn't get dough for pizza tonight. Dayna tells me she could always make some, but it might not have time to rise properly. The settlement must all be inside this evening because we can't see anyone in the streets. We open our door and the aroma of fresh cooking pizza fills the air. Now we know what that large order was for.

28

The pizza and the company is perfect. We decide to call Harmon on the radio and see if they found everything they needed. He answers quickly and tells me to talk fast because he has a pizza almost ready to come out of the oven. We tell him he just answered our question so we will see them in the morning. We are about to hang up when he says, all kidding aside, they want to thank us from the bottom of their hearts. They never dreamed anyone is living like we are in this world. We thank them for allowing us to show them that there is more to life than surviving, even in this world.

Dayna and I are looking forward to sleeping in our own bed tonight. We both fall asleep almost as soon as our heads hit the pillows. I have dreams like any other night, especially when we have been traveling. They are almost always about the trip and I do the same things over and over until I wake up. I wake up and listen to see if anything caused me to wake up. There doesn't seem to be anything so I go back to sleep and this time I am met by the same gentleman that keeps telling me we have to build a temple. At least this time he tells me it will not be long now. I also see my parents and the Horton's right after that.

They tell me that at least I listen to them more now than when I lived with them. They also tell me that we are doing some great things for the generations to come in the world we live in. Ma Horton and my real mom tell me they are proud of the way I handled that situation here and no lives were lost that way. Gunny and my dad seemed to disappear for a short time while I talk to my moms, but when they return there are two people I never saw before with them. They introduce themselves and tell me that they are so happy that their family is going to be living in our groups and that Harmon will get to take the technology another step or two with our help.

We talk for what seems like hours, but I am betting it is only a couple of minutes of sleep time. This is one of the best nights I have had in a long time. When I wake up Dayna is sitting here smiling at me. She tells me she is really happy that we got to meet Harmon's parents and she asks me when we are going to start that temple. I really wish I knew, I am thinking out loud that maybe they are waiting until we finish a couple of the other projects we are currently working on.

Moving that factory here is really going to be a big one, but it is not beyond our ability.

We are excited to see our new friends in church this morning. They say they are somewhat familiar with our beliefs because they found some copies of the Book of Mormon and read it. They are open minded when it comes to religion so they see no problems with coming here. Wyatt is teaching today. We do not hold our services exactly the way we have been told the church did before the war. We discuss the principles of the gospel and talk about how we can incorporate that into our lives even more than we already have. For our new friends we talk about the Plan of Salvation, then Heber and his wife talk about temples and the blessings that come from temple work.

After church we talk about how we can get the Christmas presents to the people that asked us to get them something. Actually that's just about everyone in all the groups. Some of the gifts were brought back by the group that came before us, but we still have almost a full tractor trailer load of them. The problem is that some of the gifts may be for some of the other people that asked us to get the gifts for someone else. If this sounds confusing to you, think how I feel, I have to figure a way to get the right gifts into the right hands before Christmas. Our newest members and some that haven't been here long will be celebrating Christmas for the first time in many of their lives. This is so exciting to us, we really want it to be a special occasion for them all.

The days are going by quickly, probably because we are so busy. Dayna and I have decided to use the lists we were given for Christmas presents and secretly give those gifts to the ones that ordered them. It's not as difficult as it may sound. We simply pull some of the gifts off the trucks and tell whoever ordered them to come and get them. Or sometimes we deliver them if we know that the one the gifts are for is not home. I have to be extra careful that Dayna doesn't see the gift I got her. Our newest members are able to find a bunch of gifts right here in our warehouses and we have taken them into town to find some things as well.

The projects are going great as well. It's like everybody feels a special need to get them done. LT and I are working on the highest parts of the golf building. We were surprised when Harmon's son volunteered to help us up there. Apparently being up high doesn't bother him either. In fact he says that he feels free when he is high off the ground. We work well together, sometimes that extra set of hands comes in handy. We have been discussing the factory that we are planning to bring here. We have gone out to check out the places we have in mind and it seems like any of them will work.

We also discussed what kind of building we should have. Usually we find a steel building that will fit our needs and we take it apart and bring it back here. James, Mike, and David think that the building should be built out of cinderblocks. They are afraid that the steel buildings will not give us a stable temperature and that is important with the technology we will be working with. Naturally we are getting Harmon involved as much as possible in these discussions. We were talking about how the equipment should be laid out in the building. Harmon told us politely that the equipment is setup the way it is for a reason. His father put many days and weeks trying different configurations and the way it is now is the best.

I think he was afraid that we would argue with him, but when he told us that we told him we will put it in the new building the same way. He agrees with using a cinderblock building as well if there is any way we can do that. We say that we should have measured the building so we would know what the footprint will have to be for the base. Harmon tells us he will have that information for us tomorrow. He has the blueprints of the building, but he has to find the most up to date one. We have been back from Florida for two weeks now and Christmas is the end of next week. We are all looking forward to then to share our bounty with each other.

We have church again on Sunday and afterward Harmon comes over to show us the blueprints of the building. This is where Ken is great to have around. If you recall he was in the Army Corps of Engineers in the other world. Gary, Sara's husband, has had a great deal of experience in the building profession as well. We figure with them leading and us to do the work we can't go wrong. We can see from the prints that the building was powered by solar energy, windmills, actually a wind turbine, and some assistance from the local electric company when absolutely necessary.

We are planning to use the river as well as the solar and windmill as sources of power. Harmon thinks that it will work fine. So do we or we wouldn't even try it. The museum building is complete, at least the building is. Now we have to furnish it with display cases and other means to showcase the items we feel deserve to be remembered. Luckily we have so many places to look for what we need. Several of the ladies have been going over to the candy factory with Sara and they look for the display items we need while her and some of the others help her make chocolate candy.

Sara told me the other day that her goal is to have a small box of fresh made chocolate candy for every family in all of our groups. That's definitely something to look forward to. With three of us working on the high parts of the golf building we may even have it completed by Christmas. We marked off the spot for the factory and we now officially have a team working on putting in the foundation. I enjoy working with the concrete and would love to be part of the team, but the building we are working on is important too. We don't usually work so late on Saturdays, but today is an exception. We really want to get this building done.

It is getting on toward late afternoon and we have had a really good day. We are thinking that we should finish this building by Christmas or very shortly afterward. We currently have all the walls up and most of the roof joists to fasten the sheet metal panels to. The view from up here is excellent, we can actually see all the way to Ryan and Carol's group and the other direction at least a couple miles up the road. We are looking that way when we see a van coming our direction. We start speculating who it could be when we decide we probably better get down there to find out. It's not like we get a lot of cars on these roads.

By the time we get down the van is pulling into the parking lot where we park the vehicles rather than have people driving through the home area where there are children and pets playing most of the time during the day. That means that it is someone who knows us or at least who knows our rules. The van looks kind of familiar, but I can't recall where I might know it from. The driver and their passenger do not seem to be in any hurry to get out, so I guess we will go meet them at the van. We are getting close when the van door opens and we see our old friend Karl stick his head out.

He is smiling and so is his wife, she is the passenger. They meet us as we get closer to them and Karl throws his arms around me. He always was a hugger, when he is done I go over and hug his wife. This is much better than hugging Karl. Dayna comes up and tells me I better not get used to hugging her, she doesn't care if I hug Karl. We ask them what they are doing here. Karl tells us that there is currently about four feet of snow up in New York where their settlement is. He says that he asked if they could come back and we told them it is no problem.

We tell them it still isn't, but if they would have let us know they were coming we could have a house ready for them. They still have a lot of friends here who come running when they hear that they are back. They have several invitations for places to stay in just a few minutes. We get to spend some time talking and it appears that the settlement up there is doing well. The biggest problem they run into is the weather up there. The people up there have gotten used to it and have even taken one of the things we did here.

They have built a series of tunnels under their settlement so that they can move around even when the temperatures are very low and there is a lot of snow on the ground. They want to meet Matt, Sandy, and their children. They have Christmas presents from their friends that joined the New York settlement. They say that they miss their friends very much, but not quite enough to live in that climate again. It's time for Karl and his wife to get settled in so we invite them over for dinner tomorrow after church. Karl laughs and says that we may be cleaning up the debris from when the roof caves in when he walks through the door of the church.

We have a good evening, our new family members from England, Jill and Kristi come home from a date with Junior and Trey and ask if I would be willing to perform a marriage ceremony for them on Christmas day. I tell them I would be honored too, but I do not know for sure if I can do that now that we are part of a church. Junior and Trey tell me that they asked Heber, Joseph, and Wyatt and they all told them that since we have no bishop here, I am the recognized leader of these people so I should be acting bishop. I still don't know why they consider me their leader, but since they do I will be happy to perform the weddings.

We spend the evening decorating the house even more than it is. We had to make a run into town to get more Christmas decorations because we have a bunch of new people this year. LT and Kathy are as excited as the young people they have living with them. Kathy is as great a mom as Dayna is. They always seem to know exactly what to get the children for holidays. I had a close call the other day about Christmas presents. Dayna asked me what I was getting for Little Jon. I told her that I thought she was taking care of that detail. She yelled at me and told me it's about time I learn how to give the right present to our children and grandchildren.

Actually I got him and all of the children in our groups some really nice stuffed animals from the amusement park. They have been packed away in plastic bags so they are in brand new condition, but I don't want her to know that. So I tell her that he really likes his dad's K-Bar knife, I could give him one of those. She smacks me for that answer and yells at me that you don't give a four year old a large knife even if they do like them. She tells me I'm hopeless and that she will make sure our grandchildren have appropriate gifts. That way they may actually be around next year at this time.

Being close to Christmas our hunters ask if they can go hunting on Monday to get the meat that we are running low on. They have lists from all the other groups and they tell me that they have some volunteers from the new people that would like to help with the hunting. It's a pretty big list, but we do have a lot of people to feed as well. The hams we are smoking should be done before Christmas, but we will want to get more in their place very soon. Lillie, Izzie, and Carmen tell me that they have a bunch of people asking when they are going to make more menudo. Junior and Trey say that they really like the tripe cooked in tomato sauce. I tell them I will take their word for it. They are welcome to use any part of the cattle that they kill in any way they like.

I must be getting old because I really look forward to going to bed at night. We all know that we are working longer hours now than usual because of the projects that we have, but soon we will be able to get some much needed rest. Tonight I am having some strange dreams. In them, me and several other members of our group are trying to move some huge pieces of Granite from one place and take them to another place to be used. It doesn't mention it, but I am thinking that it has something to do with the temple.

I am glad that today is Sunday and we get to rest, at least more than we do the rest of the week. It's a little chilly on our walk to church today. It looks like it may even snow, which depending on how much snow we get could delay the finishing of the golf building. We are happy to see Karl and his wife here today. We are all teasing them asking if they brought the snow with them. They play along and tell us that they just want to share the wealth, and snow is the only thing they have. Our newest members all say they are very glad that they were able to find warmer coats, hats, and gloves on the way up here. They just didn't think they would need them this soon.

Our lessons today are on tithing and fast offerings. Heber is teaching this lesson. When he explains what it is several of our group members say that we are already doing much more than a tenth. In our groups everything that is grown or hunted goes to what we could call the bishops storehouse and divided amongst us all depending on our needs. We do that with everything we get. Joseph tells Heber that he really did a good job of teaching today. Heber laughs and tells us all that he wishes all the lessons in the gospel were as easy for us as that one. For the rest of our meetings today we discuss how we can live the gospel better.

After church the temperature has dropped at least a couple degrees and you can just about taste the snow in the air. Actually we are excited about the possibility of snow for Christmas. We just hope it doesn't snow too much between now and then. Today my rocker-recliner feels so comfortable I think I will stay here for a while anyway. I must fall asleep because one minute I am listening to the ladies in the family talking in the kitchen and the next I am hearing Karl's big voice asking what we are having for dinner. Dayna figures she will mess with him a little and tells him we are having tripe cooked in tomato sauce.

She wasn't expecting his reaction to that comment. He tells us that he hasn't had that since he was a boy, and starts asking how we fix it. Luckily Junior and Trey are here as usual and they explain how they make it. Not only that, we have a pan half full of it in the refrigerator. Karl never was exactly shy, he goes over to the pan on the stove and sees it has spaghetti sauce in it and says he has missed the sauce we make here so if we don't mind he will eat some of the tripe some other time. Dayna smiles and says that sounds like a good compromise.

We have a very nice dinner with our old friends. We ask them about the trip down and they tell us it was pretty boring except for one day going through Pennsylvania. We ask what happened there. Karl tells us that they stopped for the night in a parking lot that was once one of those shopping centers. They didn't notice a car with some people in it parked in front of a store that used to sell liquor. They slept in the van, but when they got up next morning and were getting ready to leave they saw the car with four people in it.

They say they walked over to it and looked closer and all four people were no longer alive. I have a feeling about this so I ask them what kind of car it was. They say it's funny, but they could swear it looked like one of those we brought back on one of those trips up north. They say they remember it because the color was not something you see every day. I ask if they know how the men died. Karl says it looked to him like maybe they drank themselves to death. Who knows how long some of that alcohol sat on those store shelves and what might happen to it after so many years. They tell us we wouldn't want that car back anyway. They didn't even open the doors. They left it just like it was.

29

We explained to Karl and Sherry, his wife about the men that were sent away from our settlement. At least we don't have to worry about them coming back here and making trouble. We talk about more pleasant topics like the projects we are working on and those that we are in the planning stages on. He tells us that they are more than willing to help anywhere they are needed. Since they are in another group we will let the leaders of that group decide where they can be best used.

It has been a very nice Sunday afternoon. It is snowing outside when we walk Karl and Sherry back to their house in Ryan and Carol's group. Dayna and I just like to go for a nice walk in the evening and this was a good excuse for us to get out. When we get home there are just about two inches of snow on the ground. That's not enough to keep us from working on our project. We will just have to be careful and as cold as it is we may have to take turns working on the inside. By morning word has spread throughout the groups about the men that we had to ask to leave. Unfortunately no one misses them.

Today the Christmas spirit is really in the air. Everywhere we go we hear people singing Christmas carols or if they don't know the words they are humming them. We even sing some carols while we work today. We have a tendency to be rather loud in whatever we are doing and some of the people working on the inside of the building ask if we could at least sing the same song they are because we are confusing them. They say it with a smile so we ask them what song they want to sing. Now we are singing the same song, but now they say something about singing in a different key and singing too fast.

When we go home for lunch we tell our wives about all the critics we have working on that building. Misty, who is Sara's daughter and our son's girlfriend, says that her mom had a suggestion for our singing. I know I am going to regret this, but I ask her what that could be. She can hardly get the words out she is laughing so hard. She says that her mom said we should sing sweet, low, and far away, the farther away the better. That gets everybody laughing including me, even though I am trying not to show it. I go back to work trying to act indignant, but I just can't quite pull it off.

When we don't sing as much in the afternoon several of our friends ask us if they offended us with their comments. They say they were joking as much as they were serious. We tell them that they didn't offend us. We are just singing inside this afternoon, but if they would prefer we could serenade them. They are quick to tell us that won't be necessary. They wouldn't want us to go to any trouble for them. We laugh and tell them to sing a little louder so we can enjoy the Christmas spirit as well. We get a lot of work done, Harmon's son Orrin , tells us everyday how much he enjoys working with us and how much his family enjoys being part of this amazing group.

We always tell him that we enjoy having them here as well so it works out great for all of us. Today after work he comes home with us because his wife is at our house making fudge for the holidays. We make it with honey, but it doesn't come out bad at all. All the young people told the ladies making it that if it doesn't come out quite right, they will keep the rest of the family from suffering by eating it all. From seeing how much is on the little ones faces I think they are doing their best to eat all they can to protect us old folks.

We can't wait until we can refine the sugar from sugar cane that grows down in Cuba and other island countries down there. We have looked into it and feel that we could refine enough sugar for all of the settlements in a very short time. We have some sugar, but we would like enough to use for things like fudge. That's another project that we are planning to work on over the winter along with about twenty other important projects. It would be easier if all of us had the same intellect for doing some of these projects. Unfortunately people like me are good for projects requiring manual labor and sometimes planning. But when it comes to the more scientific or engineering projects we have a limited number of people capable of them.

Our younger people are always surprising us at how quickly they learn. Our scientific people are always looking for those that have an interest and an aptitude for learning the engineering processes. That will definitely be needed if we are going to continue growing and advancing our world. We finish up making the fudge and our friends tell us they have to go, they are expecting company for Family Home Evening tonight. I ask where all the noise is this evening and Dayna tells me she is a little worried because some of the older young people went hunting and haven't gotten back yet.

I tell her that they had a lot of game to get this trip. Sometimes it takes longer to fill that many requests. I am saying that, but I am also getting my coat on to go looking for them. Dayna tells me I am not going anywhere without her, so she grabs her coat and we are heading to the parking lot to get a small truck. Nickie comes out onto their porch and tells us that she just heard from Teddy. They are on their way back, but they found something that they feel they should bring back with them. We decide to wait for them while we visit Nickie and our grandson Little Jon.

I'm not sure what we were expecting, but we see the headlights pulling into the parking lot in what seems like just a few minutes. The trucks carrying the animals continues on to the large barn where the meat will be processed. I can see Rod, Ken, Steve, and Jerry heading that way to get started as soon as possible. We are heading down to the parking lot to see what our hunters found. We are almost there when we see someone get out of the van that does not look familiar to us at all. From here it appears to be a woman, fairly small in stature, and she is not really dressed for the weather.

When we get to where they are standing we can hear her ask if there is any way back. I am a little confused because I am not sure if she means back to where she was found or back to somewhere else. Teddy and Timmy see us coming and tell her that here is someone who can answer all of her questions. She turns toward Dayna and me and I can see she is really quite young and very pretty. She sighs and says it will be great if I can give her some straight answers. I tell her I will be happy to try, but perhaps we should get indoors where we can talk without being so cold. She laughs and says she is numb from the cold so she hardly notices it anymore.

I take my coat off and wrap it around her shoulders, then Dayna and I ask her what kind of questions does she have that we may be able to help her with. We get in the house just ahead of Lillie, Izzie, and Carmen. They tell us that they had a really successful day of hunting. I tell them that we have company right now, but we are really interested in how they did. Perhaps we can talk about it over supper. Our guest says that she saw the trucks with the animal carcasses in them, she was wondering what they were hunting. It takes the next ten minutes for them to tell us all about the hunt. It sounds like it was very successful.

I ask the young lady what questions she has for us. She looks around and asks me what year this is and where are we. I ask her first off how did she come to be here. She tells us that we will never believe her because she doesn't believe it herself. She is a lot like our twins in her mannerisms and the way she talks. They just happen to come in while she is getting ready to tell us. Naturally the introductions slow down the process just a little. Finally she can tell us.

She starts by telling the twins that if they ever get invited to a Christmas party by your boss, even if he is married don't go. She continues saying that he told her they were not going on a date, they were both coming to the party anyway, they may as well ride together. That lasted as long as it took to walk to her office where he tried to corner her and tell her that she could move up quickly in the company if she knows what he means. She is getting angry as she tells us all this. I can't blame her, I am getting angry and I don't even know the guy.

She tells us she told him she knows exactly what he means and his wife was going to hear about it on Monday. Then he tried to tell her she was mistaken about what he meant and tried to put his hands around her shoulders. She says she wasn't born yesterday and knew exactly what was coming so she kicked him where it hurts, grabbed her computer, and left. She says she grabbed her coat, but as we can see it was not made to keep you especially warm. It was made to make you look good. She laughs and says from now on she is choosing warm over good looks.

There is some conversation about her boss, but I want to get over and help the guys with the animals so I have to ask her to keep telling us about how she got here. She is really relaxed now, so she is talking more animatedly, just like Tammy and Tina. Actually all the girls within a couple years of their age talk like that. She tells us that she hailed a cab and told the driver to take her to her home. She says they no sooner stared driving when it started snowing so hard the driver couldn't see and crashed into a parked car. The driver told her he would go for help and left her there. She thought about walking, but in the cold and it was snowing so hard she couldn't recognize any landmarks or anything to even tell her where she was.

She says all of a sudden she was exhausted and couldn't keep her eyes open any longer. When she woke up it was no longer snowing so she got out of the car and it looked like a ghost town, but even with all the snow earlier there was barely an inch or two on the ground. She started walking toward where she thought her apartment was and nothing was familiar at all. In fact there were old cars parked all over the place and when she back tracked her steps the car she had been in was gone. Now she was totally confused so she decided to look for her apartment. She walked all over the city and never did find anything familiar or alive.

She thought maybe the city had been evacuated for some reason and started walking toward where she knows there is another city not too far away and that's when she ran into our hunters. She asks me if she is in the Twilight Zone or something. Even our children have heard of the Twilight Zone because we found old tapes that had most of the old TV shows on it. I have to laugh and tell her sort of. I explain how many of us came to be here and tell her as much about our world as we can. I have plenty of help with that part.

Dayna asks her if she is leaving family behind. She says that her parents passed away when she was ten and she got passed around foster homes until one of her foster fathers would expect her to take the place of their wives and she would hit them with whatever happened to be handy. When she was old enough to go to college she earned a scholarship and learned how to design computers. She graduated two years ago and found this job right out of college. She loved the job until last night, or whenever that was. I ask the ladies of the house to help make her comfortable and I will go help the guys quarter the meat and get it hung. As I am leaving I hear Tina tell the young lady that if anybody tries to take advantage of her here, Daddy Jon will read to them from the good book.

They also ask her what her name is, which is something I forgot to do. Anyway she tells them to call her Dede, her name is Deidra. It really was a good day of hunting. It's a good thing that some of us decided to come down and help, otherwise our regular meat cutters would have been here half the night. As it is it only takes a couple hours and we can all go home. When I get home we have quite a bit of company to meet Dede. I expected it so it is no big deal. The family had Italian sausage sandwiches so I do the same. I knew that

Mike and Morgan, James and Jenna, and David and Kimberly would be over here as soon as they heard about our newest member.

They are fascinated with the computer she brought with her. I wasn't sure it would even work in this world, but it is explained to me quickly that the computer will work, but there is no internet. Dede is very upbeat considering she just found out she has landed in a totally new world with people she doesn't even know. At least she has some warmer clothes now, it looks like the younger ladies in the house found some that fit her. Tomorrow we can take her to the clothing warehouse and she can pick out a whole wardrobe including a good warm winter coat. Jenna, Morgan, and Kimberly ask her if she thinks she could put together a computer or possibly more than one if she had the right parts.

She tells them that she built the computer she has from parts that were left over from other projects. It is still the most powerful laptop computer she has ever seen. She continues to tell them that it would be best if we could visit somewhere that made computers for that time. She says that if the war took place in 1969 the odds are that any computers are going to be quite large, but that doesn't mean we can't use them. They will just take up more space and they won't be very powerful because the technology just wasn't there. Our scientific people know of some companies that manufactured computer parts that are no more than a couple hours away. Apparently they are not far from the chocolate factory and since there is a trip planned to go there anyway, they may as well look for computer parts.

Everybody in the family room agrees with going tomorrow, I am sitting in the kitchen talking to Dayna and eating my sandwich when Jenna comes in and asks me what time we are leaving in the morning. I ask them what they need me for, we have plenty of good men in this group that can defend them just as well as I can. I tell them I have to get the roof finished on the golf building before Friday and if I take a day off it will not get done. Now LT and Orrin get involved, I didn't even know they were in there. They tell me that they can get it done by Friday even if I take a day off. Heber and Joseph said they would like to help out on that project.

Sara tells us all that we can take the helicopter and probably be back around lunch time. That way I can get at least half a day in. Dede hears helicopter and says she will take a car or some other vehicle that does not leave the ground. She is shaking her head when she says it. She goes on to say that her parents were killed in a plane crash. She doesn't go anywhere she can't drive. Dayna brings up that we could take one of the electric busses to go over. Everyone agrees to that and Dede is excited because she has never seen an electric bus before. We agree to leave at first light, but in order to do that we have to take Dede shopping for clothes tonight.

I'm sure it looks more like a parade going to the clothing warehouse. Teddy and Nickie came along because they helped stock the shelves and know where just about everything is located. The girls tell them what she needs and they find it for them. When it comes to the more private clothing she whispers in Nickie's ear and she takes Dede and a couple of our daughters to where they can find it. Finally she has all the clothes she needs and we can go home for the night. Dayna and I are sitting in the family room when Dede and the girls come down stairs. Dede tells us she cannot thank us enough for making her feel welcome here when we don't even know her.

She tells us she will do everything in her power to help us progress and to continue growing. She asks if it would be too much to ask for a hug goodnight. She says our daughters told her we always do that and she wants to feel like part of the family. Just about then two little whirlwinds come running into the room and jump into my arms. It's Jenny and Tiffani, they call me grandpa and tell me they will miss being able to give me a hug all the time when they marry Junior and Trey. I tell them that just because they don't live with us anymore we will still see each other all the time and we can hug any time they want to. Dede is smiling, but there are tears running down her face. She says she loves hearing those two talk, it's so cute.

As usual the puppies follow them into the room. They are not as little as they used to be, but they think they are still puppies. They jump up on me and I have to tell them I refuse to hug them until they do something about their breath. Like always they sit down in front of me and tip their heads to the side like they are really listening. My little friends run out to the kitchen to get some ice cream and naturally the dogs follow them. Our daughters say that sounds good tonight and tell me to get my hug quick before the ice cream is all gone. I get my hugs and so does Dayna. Dede runs after the other girls and tells them to save some for her.

With so many people in the kitchen Dayna and I decide to go right up to bed. It sounds like tomorrow is going to be a full day as usual, but it should be very interesting as well. When we are finally alone Dayna turns to me and asks me what a computer is. I try to explain it in terms that she will know so I use the fact that they are doing all of the families genealogy by hand. If we had a computer they could type it and save it to either the computer or a disc and print it out whenever they want to. I tell her they could even make corrections without erasing it on the paper and rewriting it over the weak spot left in the paper.

She tells me that would be great for the others, but she never makes mistakes that have to be erased. I start to remind her of just last week when she almost said a bad word because she made a couple mistakes in a row. She jumps on me and tells me it must have been someone else and she is going to tickle me until I admit it wasn't her. We must be making a little more noise than we should be because our daughters come and knock on our door telling us it's time for people our age to be sleeping, not roughhousing on the beds. We can hear them laughing in the hall. Dayna tells them if they were in their rooms where they belong they wouldn't have to listen to us. She also tells them she will tan their backsides if they are not careful. The door opens and as many young lady backsides that fit in the doorway are filling it now. Naturally they have pajamas on. Dayna and I laugh so hard we have tears in our eyes. We tell them all we love them and say goodnight.

30

In the morning we load one of the electric busses and one of the gas burning vans and head out for the chocolate factory. Sara decided to fly the helicopter there anyway, but the only one flying with her today is Gary. Our daughter Amy, Misty, and Bobbi want to go along today to learn as much as they can from Dede. She is about as excited as any young lady I have ever met and that's saying something. She told us this morning that she has never slept as soundly as she did last night. She says she is sure it's because she finally feels safe and comfortable around our family. Dayna tells her that she never slept well until we met. Then she just knew that she was safe.

The electric bus drives very nicely, it just doesn't go very fast, which is not necessarily a bad thing. Dede is looking out the window while she talks to the girls. She says it's really difficult to believe that there are only a small percentage of the people that once populated this entire world left. She changes moods very quickly because now she is asking if we have a certain store anywhere near us. They were always too expensive for her budget, but now she can afford anything she wants. The girls tell her they have some clothes from that store. They don't see any real difference between those and the less expensive ones.

Dede tells them that's because they don't work in an office where everybody judges you based on the clothes you wear and how you wear your hair. Misty tells her that her mom told her it also depended on how your bottom looks in those clothes you are wearing. Everyone laughs and Dede says that she was trying to be a little less honest than that. Amy tells her that Misty's mom is seldom less honest when she says something. She usually just says what is on her mind. Misty agrees totally, Dayna and I tell them that Sara is careful around young children. We hear the helicopter above us and then Sara's voice coming over the radio telling me to get the lead out of my butt and get moving.

We all laugh and tell Dede that's Misty's mom. I tell her that she used to be a pilot in the other world. In fact when Tim, LT, and I were seals we rescued her after she was shot down in the Middle East. Dede asks if we were in on a lot of rescues. I start to tell her we were involved in a few when Dayna and the girls start telling her about some of the adventures we have had here. Sara breaks in again telling us that she is going to go on ahead and get everything ready for when we get there. We remind her to be careful and we will see her in a little while.

The girls keep us entertained with stories about out settlement and our family. Dede says it all sounds so exciting, she wishes she could have been here for some of the adventures. Dayna tells her it sounds exciting, but if they didn't have the knowledge we do about tactical warfare the outcome may have been totally different. The girls have done such a good job that we are already here. We can see the place the guys were talking about that may have the parts we need to build a couple of computers. Personally I am not getting my hopes up, but then I probably won't use a computer very much anyway, if at all.

Everyone wants to see the chocolate factory and see just what goes into making one of all of our favorite foods. Sara and her team have it down to a science now. They have cocoa beans fermenting while the last batch is being turned into chocolate candy. We are all treated to a small sample that we all wish was about three times as large. Sara asks me to stay behind while the others go looking for computer parts. Dayna and I help her load the boxes of chocolate into the helicopter so she can get them back home before Friday. We still have a couple of days, but why procrastinate when we can get them today. We are loading through the back entrance so that we are not seen by the others. When we are done we head back to the front of the factory and decide to go see how the others are doing.

When we get outside I notice that something is not right as soon as I see a car that was not there when we got here. I am remembering those men that stole the food of the group down in Florida. I tell Sara and Dayna to wait here while I go and check this out. I have a gun with me, but with as many people as we have in that building, it might not be a good time to start shooting. I am hoping that maybe the people in the car are only looking for a place to settle. When I get inside the building I know that I am wrong.

I can hear a man's voice telling the men that they are going to take the women that they want and if they don't start any trouble nobody has to get hurt. I hear another voice saying that they will let them go when they are done with them. I can hear what sounds like four or more men laughing. I also have my K-Bar knife with me so if I can get in close, I have a chance to stop these guys. I cannot see what is happening, but apparently one of them pushes my daughter Amy and she tells them to keep their filthy hands off of her and everyone else. She tells them that her father will be here any minute and then they will all be sorry. One of the men says if I'm no tougher than these guys, referring to James, Mike, and David, they have nothing to worry about.

I figure I can't ask for a better time to start the ball rolling so I take out my Sig and my K-Bar and walk into the room planning to put my gun on whoever seems to be the leader. As soon as I step into the room I tell the guy near Amy that if he touches her or any of my other daughters he is a dead man. They can see the knife, but not the gun. I can't tell who the leader is, they all seem to be about equally dirty. They have guns, but by the way they are handling them they don't have much experience using them. The one near Amy gets a belligerent look on his face and reaches over and touches her. I was hoping this could be avoided, but I guess not.

I raise my gun and shoot him in the chest. The look on his face is one of disbelief. They never think they will be the one to die. He actually does us a favor because he tries to raise his gun to fire at me I guess, but he pulls the trigger and the bullet strikes the guy closest to me. I am happy to see that the girls and the scientific people drop to the floor when the shooting starts. I know you are not going to believe this, but that guy gets off a shot that hits another one of their guys. The last one is so confused that he doesn't know who to shoot at. I start to aim at him when I hear a blast behind me and see the last one blown against the wall. I turn to see Sara with a shotgun in her hands.

We check to see if any of the attackers are still alive. Unfortunately they are not. It bothers me more and more to have to take another life. Dayna always reminds me that if I wouldn't have, what they would have done to the girls would be far worse that anything I did to those men. Sara tells me that we only sent two of them up to meet Heavenly Father personally. Their buddies didn't want to go alone so they asked them to join them. Gary tells me that we should look at it as doing missionary work. We prevented those poor souls from sinning any more in this mortal existence.

Amy comes running over and throws her arms around my neck. She tells me that just like her mom she knew she would be okay as soon as she saw me walk in the room. Dede and the others say they felt the same way and are waiting their turn to get a hug. James, Mike, and David tell me they are sorry, but those guys totally surprised them. They never expected to have anyone accost them here. I tell them that they really have to start being more careful. I know that they are all good fighters, but if someone shoots you before you can do anything about it you are out of luck. I tell them I will bury these guys while they continue looking for what they came here to get.

In just the quick look around I have I can see a lot of parts that look like they are for electronic devices. The guys help me drag the bodies outside, then we look for a backhoe or something to make digging easier. Dede asks if we should call the police or something. I don't mean to be callous, but I tell her there's a phone, I really don't think there is anyone to tell except each other. Dayna tells her that we don't like having to kill to survive either, but that's the only choice some people leave us with. In this world, at this time, we are the law. Often we have to be judge, jury, and executioner or we will be the ones being buried.

At least she understands what we are saying. She just says it is going to take a while to get used to her new life. At least thanks to her new family she will have a life to live. She continues looking at the supplies here. We men find a backhoe that is indoors at a construction equipment place. It doesn't take long to get it started and it doesn't take long to dig a grave. The men have no identification on them so we mark unknown on the wooden cross we put over the grave. We go back in and there are several large boxes of electronic looking things waiting to be loaded into the van. Dede says that most of what is here is nothing we can use for computers, but there are some components that she knows she can use.

We load the boxes and promise to keep looking for a place that has the things we need. Sara recommends that we think about going to Washington D.C. because politicians always have the best of everything. At the last minute I decide to drive through the city we are in just to see what else may be here. The others may have done this before, but I never have. We see some places that we definitely want to investigate further. We actually find the store that Dede was asking about earlier so we stop while the girls, all the girls, go in to do some shopping. Actually they do not take as long as we expected. They just bring out half the store saying that if they don't use them they know someone will.

We are getting ready to leave when we go down a small street to turn around and there we see a sign that says State Senators office. We figure it is worth a look so we all go in. As soon as we get in the door we find a computer and a printer that was obviously here for his secretary. Dede and the others say that this is definitely more advanced than our world was in 1969. We continue looking and find five more just like the first one. Those all go in the van along with all the printer paper we find, and spare ribbons, as well as anything else that our people feel are important. We are on our way out when we see a sign that says, County Engineers Office.

We are thinking that this may be one of the biggest finds of the day. We go in and find two more computers that look like twins of the other ones we found. The big prize is the computer that is in the Engineers office and the other three that are in what appear to be his assistant's offices. There is also a pen plotter, don't ask me what that is, it's what James and Mike called it. There are several large rolls of paper that look like they go with it and several boxes of pens that are apparently why they call it a pen plotter. We now have the van full as we head for home.

There is a lot of excited talk on the way about the items we found today. We will have to let our experts try them out and decide the best way to use them. When we get home naturally Sara and Gary ask us what took so long. I tell them we stopped for lunch at this little roadside café that I have been dying to try. The air is filled with an odor that I do not recognize. Teddy tells me that they are smoking a whole bunch of that alligator tail. I make sure that they waited until the pork we were smoking was done before putting that other stuff in the smoke house. Teddy laughs and tells me he supervised the unloading himself.

There are still a few good hours to work so I go to the golf building and get to work with the others. They must have been working their tails off because we can probably finish putting the roof on tomorrow. That would be great because it would give us Thursday to get ready for Christmas. When I go home for supper I am half afraid Dayna will tell me we are having alligator tonight. Instead we are having one of my favorites which is basically breakfast food for supper. No one in this house is complaining so it must be a popular choice.

We spend a quiet evening reading and doing a little talking before we go to bed. I dream again about building a temple, only this time I am told that Wyatt will be given the instructions for the temples design. I am also told that there is a man out west that will be getting in touch with us. As usual there are no timelines or dates discussed. I wake up ready to finish that building, but when I look outside it is snowing pretty hard. LT comes over as well as the other guys that have helped on this part of the project. We discuss it and decide that as long as we are careful we should be able to work today.

Today we all make sure we are using the proper safety harness and that it is securely fastened in case one or more of us slip. LT and I take the outside and Orrin and Heber take the inside. When we put a panel in place we put the bolts through the holes in the panels and the framing and the guys inside tighten them up. We get all of the panels into place and hold the bolts on the outside while they are being tightened. When the last nut and bolt is in place we are relieved because it is snowing so hard that we can barely see the ground. Our only way down except for falling is to be brought down by the crane we have been using to hoist the panels into place.

There is a basket that we use for this sort of thing and when it gets up to us we climb in before we release our safety lines. I climb in first and fasten my safety line to the side of the basket as usual. LT is climbing into the basket when the foot that is supporting his weight slips on the snow and he starts to fall sideways away from the basket. I have to grab his coat to keep him from falling and just about pull him into the basket. It is snowing so hard that no one down below could see what happened and LT asks me to keep it that way. It scares Kathy enough with him just getting up here.

It is a big relief to know that at least the building is all put up. Now we will have to insulate it so that it can be used in the winter. When we go inside with the other people that have been working on the inside, it doesn't feel bad at all. This is one huge building. I think it is just about the same size as the hangar we put up for the C-130. David reminds us that we promised the Missouri group that we would help them obtain some buildings and put them up. They do not have the resources that we have when it comes to man power.

Christmas Eve is finally here and it seems like everybody is full of the Christmas spirit. There is enough food being prepared today to more than satisfy everybody in our groups. We always wait until Christmas Eve to put the presents under the trees. Dayna and I got up before anyone else and did that already. Dede, Summer, and April were kind of surprised to see that there are several presents for them under the tree. They look at me and I just tell them that Santa must know where they are this year. They all laugh and say that he never seemed to find them before, but they are not complaining.

The day goes by quickly with all the preparations getting done just in time. Before bed time we read the story of the birth of Jesus from the bible so that our young people learn the true meaning of Christmas. We just finish the story when we hear a knock on the door. The children all say that maybe it's Santa. Dayna and I are a little worried because everybody we know is home doing what we were just doing. I answer the door and find a man, a woman and two small children standing here and they look like they are just about frozen. The man asks if they might come in long enough to get warm and to talk to someone about a home.

We welcome them in and pour them some hot cider with cinnamon in it. That's something we all like to drink. The man says they saw our light and since it's the first one they have seen in their travels they are hoping they have found the settlement. They heard us on the radio, but couldn't respond so they started out to find us. That was two weeks ago, they had a car, but it quit running about an hour ago so they have been walking since. He says they thought about sleeping in the car tonight, but it was so cold they decided it was better to walk. They were pretty sure they would find a barn or something to spend the night in.

When they see the decorated tree they ask if we are having some sort of celebration. I start to explain, but the children tell them all about Christmas and about this being Jesus birthday. They say they remember their parents telling them about it, but they had no idea when it was celebrated. I start to ask our daughters if they can share a room for the night so our guests will have a place to sleep when Billy and Ramona walk in and tell our new friends that they have plenty of room for them if they need a place to sleep. They saw the people come up to our door and figured what had happened. They go with Billy and Ramona and we invite them to our Christmas service in the morning.

Billy tells them that they will make sure they have the proper clothes for this weather in the morning. We turn in for the night wondering how many other people are out there alone and in need of some friends and family.

31

Christmas at our house is always a noisy affair, but today seems to be some sort of record for noise. The noise usually comes from the very young ones, but this year it is primarily the upper teen and early twenty demographic that is the source of most of the excitement. Dayna and I have to laugh because this is really April and Summers, as well as Kristi and Jill's first Christmas. Dede has had many Christmases, but this is the first one that she has had a family to celebrate with since she was nine. The older girls are handing out presents and the smaller children are happy to take any that are passed to them.

Dayna and I don't usually get too many gifts because we have pretty much everything we need. This year our daughters got us some gifts and our newest family members also got us some presents. Our daughters give me a beautiful cap and ball antique pistol along with a powder horn and some lead balls. They even have the mold for the bullets to go with it. I ask them where they got this and they tell me that it is kind of from the entire group. Jenna and Sara found it in one of the old buildings in one of the towns we went to in England. They know that I will appreciate it and take care of it the way it should be.

I also received some nice tee shirts that are from that expensive store we were at the other day. Dayna gets some clothes from there as well. The girls tell her she needs to dress more like the attractive young woman she is than a grandmother. She reminds them that she is a grandmother so it is not all bad looking like one. I have a special gift for Dayna, but I will wait until everyone else has opened their presents. The girls open theirs and find out that Dede gave them and the other girls in the group all the clothes she got at the fancy store. The funny thing is that our girls gave the clothes they got from there to Dede and the other girls who weren't with us.

There is sure a lot of hugging and crying going on this morning. When everybody has their gifts opened I ask the twins if they would please get me Dayna's gift. They tell me that they decided to keep it, so I have to look for another present for her. They are only kidding because they are on their way to get it. When they bring it out Dayna says it looks kind of big to be a new pair of boots. Everybody knows what it is except Dayna, the twins are not very good at keeping a secret, but at least Dayna didn't find out about it.

She unwraps it and is still not sure what it is. Dede comes over to Dayna and tells her that this is a word processor. She continues telling her that it is kind of like the predecessor to the modern day computer. The main difference is that this one is strictly for writing on. Dayna says that it is awfully big for a typewriter. Dede tells her that this is similar to a typewriter, but on this you can correct any mistakes without erasing and when you are satisfied that you are through you can print what you typed on a printer. Dede tells her she will help her make some templates for genealogy. That should make it easier and neater.

We tell Dayna that we brought back enough of these from the amusement parks for all the people working on writing the history of our family and genealogy. She can't wait to try it, but now we have to get dressed and go to church. We no sooner get back downstairs when Junior and Trey are here. I almost forgot all about the weddings today at least that's what I tell them. That gets me smacked by just about every female in the house. When we get outside there is about two inches of fresh snow on the ground. We wish everyone we see a Merry Christmas.

That's a lot of wishing because everybody in our group is headed to church. We see our guests from last night walking with Billy and Ramona. They are dressed quite a bit warmer than the last time we saw them. They make their way over to talk to us and the man tells me that they were part of a group until just before they heard us on the radio. They say they were living in some houses in a small city and that one morning they woke up and the others were gone. They waited for a couple of days before leaving, but there was not much food left and they couldn't see freezing to death in the house they lived in.

They ask if there is any way we could see if their friends found another settlement or if anyone knows what may have happened to them. We tell them after church we will ask around for them. It is great to see so many new people joining us. We would not mind if we doubled our size every year. In church today we talk about the birth of Jesus. Many of our newer members have never heard that unless they have read the scriptures. When the service is over Wyatt, who was teaching today, tells us all that we have two weddings this morning as well. Junior and Trey start asking who that could be and both get smacked for their efforts at humor.

Heber tells the ladies that they are starting their marriage out right, establishing who is boss from the very start. All the married women and most of the single ones agree with him. I figure we better get these weddings started before we lose our spirituality. I already asked them if they would prefer to have two ceremonies or both get married in one. They both said that one will do fine. I call the couples up to the podium in the chapel. Junior and Kristi are one couple and Trey and Jill are the other. When they come up I call Tiffany and Jenny up with them.

We do not have a written ceremony so I kind of take one from the teachings we have had so far. Mainly I ask them if they are totally committed to each other and to their very special children. I commit them to work towards a temple marriage even though we don't have a temple yet we can still live our lives as Christ like as possible. To conclude the ceremony I pronounce them by name as a family. I have to hand it to our groups, they are still being reverent at least until we get outside the chapel. Then everyone congratulates them and asks them where the cake is.

Actually the women surprise even me when they open the doors to the kitchen and there must be a thousand cupcakes there. Wyatt comes over after making sure his little ones get a cupcake, and tells me it's funny that I should mention a temple. He says that he heard through the grapevine that we found a computer the other day in a county engineer's office. He says that if that computer has some kind of drafting software he can possibly use it to do what he has been told to do in his dreams. I tell him that as soon as Dede and our other computer geeks figure them out we will know for sure. I add that until then we brought back a nice drafting table if he would like to get started.

He laughs and says he has done some of both and prefers using the computer. It's much easier to fix mistakes and to make sure you have room to put everything you need on a drawing. While we are talking my little buddy Ephraim and his sister Ariel come up with frosting all over their mouths to tell me a secret. Ephraim looks up at me and motions with his finger for me to bend over so he can whisper in my ear. When I do he tells me that his mom made me a Christmas present. He says it loud enough that I would have heard him even if I was standing up five feet away from him. I tell him I won't tell his mom that he told me.

He wants a hug after telling me, then Ariel wants a hug as well. Now that I have almost as much frosting on me as they do Sara comes up and tells me that she knew she should have gotten me a bib for Christmas. Everybody is laughing which is not a bad thing. It's a nice walk home after church with all of our friends. We make arrangements to drop off the presents we got for our friends in a little while. When we get home the young ladies in the family have a small list of items that they would like to talk about. I tell them that it will have to wait until we help four members of our family move into their new homes.

They do not have much, but in our world you don't need much because we will furnish what you need and don't have. My little girlfriends Jenny and Tiffany start to cry when it is time for them to go to their new house. I give them each a hug and promise to see them every day and besides they will be back in about two hours for dinner. The girls volunteered to baby-sit for the two little ones while the newlyweds get their houses arranged the way they would like them, but they told them that they want the whole family to have a say in how they decorate their homes. We couldn't be happier for them all.

When that is done our daughters bring up the topic again only this time they have ten other young ladies approximately their same age and even some of the young married ladies in the group. Dayna tells me I better listen before the mob starts getting ugly. The funny thing about that is Sara walks in with Gary and Misty right at that moment. I look at Dayna and tell her it's too late. Sara walks over and hits me, she says she isn't sure what I meant, but she is sure it was something derogatory about her. Now that we have a good portion of the female population present we can begin.

I ask them if I should be taking notes. Tina smiles and tells me I can have her list when she is done with it. Tammy comes over and hands me a copy of the list, she says they don't want to give me the only copy that they have so she made one especially for me. I ask her if that means they think I lose things a lot. Our daughter Amy tells me not all the time, only on days that end in d a y. Dayna smiles and tells me I have been known to forget where I put things at times. I know when I'm beat so I look at the list and it isn't all that bad. I look over at Dede and tell her this must be her doing. These girls were never interested in these things until now.

She starts to get defensive so I tell her it's perfectly all right. All these things are great for them and a whole bunch of other members of our community. I tell them that when they start these things they realize that a whole bunch of people are going to want to participate as well. They say that they are hoping that everybody wants to, especially two oldens that could use some exercise. We begin discussing some of these items when Wyatt and Tori come over with Ephraim and Ariel. Right behind them are Nickie, Teddy, and Little Jon. The little ones give Dayna and me a quick hug and run to the kitchen to see if Dayna has baked any Christmas cookies.

Everybody already knows what we have been talking about. Teddy tells me that we can move some of the workout equipment in the building we have for that to one end and get some more mats from the high school in town for us to start learning Yoga and doing some aerobic exercises until we can get a new building put up. The girls say that they would like to start the martial arts classes again during the winter. Dede asks if there is anywhere we can get some exercise bikes for what they call spinning classes. Even I remember taking some of those classes. It is beginning to look like it is going to be a very busy winter.

Tori comes over and puts a beautifully hand knitted hat on my head and says Merry Christmas. She has one just like it only smaller for Dayna. The little ones come into the family room carrying as many cookies as four and six year old hands can carry. Their moms ask them if they are planning to eat all those cookies before dinner. We can see that they are thinking, then Ariel says that they brought some in for us. All the women say that they better get going if we are going to eat on time. We are having dinner as a community today and every family is bringing some of the food.

Everything we are all bringing is done so we head over to the community building that we use for occasions like this. Our newest friends are here with Billy and Ramona along with our son Timmy and their daughter Bobbi. Tim tells them that he made some calls to the other groups and even broadcasted a message to anyone within hearing that they are welcome to join us as long as they are willing to be part of the community. He tells them he mentioned their name also in case their other friends are listening.

The tables are set and the food is set out kind of cafeteria style only with so many people we have three locations with all the same foods on them to speed things up. The food is kept hot or cold whichever it should be because we have basically three kitchens in this building. When we built it we planned for it to hold a little over a thousand people and we planned to be able to add on when it becomes necessary. The noise levels do tend to get a little high when we have one of these meals, but the ceiling is high enough and we put some sound deadening insulation in the ceiling. The conversation and food are both excellent. Our newest friends are still in shock that we have been living this way for so many years.

The meal is winding down when Tim comes over to our table and asks our newest friends if they would like to talk to some friends of theirs on the radio. They are so excited that they have trouble getting away from the table. I go with them to see if there is anything we can do to help them. There is a radio right here in this building. It's in a small room of its own so if someone calls they can be heard. It sets off an alarm in the main room. I stand far enough away from the conversation so that they will have some privacy. They talk for a few minutes when Pete, that's the father's name, calls me over and asks if we might be able to go and pick up six more people to live here.

Now we have several people here asking where we have to go to get them. Actually from the description of where they are we can get there and back in just a few hours. It is still fairly early in the afternoon so we can be back shortly after dark. LT, Gary, Billy, and Pete all want to go along. We take a pickup truck and one of the fifteen passenger vans. Luckily there is not much snow on the roads, but the van and truck have good snow tires on them anyway. On the way Pete tells us how they became separated. He says that these four men came into the small group of homes that they were living in. He says after seeing how we are living, he should say existing in.

They ran and hid from the men because they knew what they were after, but the men decided to stay in their homes so they ran to find new homes. They became separated and couldn't find each other after that. Then they heard our radio conversations and decided to try and find us. By the grace of Heavenly Father they were able to. We get to where his friends say they are and sure enough they are here. Very cold and very hungry so they are happy to see us. We load them into the van and head back. We brought winter coats, hats, and gloves just in case. On the way back we see smoke rising from what was once a restaurant. We stop and find five people living here. They say they are not doing too badly, but if we have room they would prefer to have some neighbors and friends.

When we get home the women have dinner ready for our newest friends and some moving around has taken place so that they will have a warm place to live until we can make more room. That's one thing that our people do well is take care of each other. Some of the new people are young ladies approximately the same age as some of our young ladies, so they are going to stay with us. We have had an empty room for almost eight hours now. When everything has settled down for the night at least, Dayna and I start to make a list of the projects that we have before us this winter.

We still have the amusement rides to be put up and if possible put inside so that they can be enjoyed all year round. David and Kimberly reminded us today that we said we would help them move a couple of large buildings to their settlement in Missouri right after the first of the year. The museum is coming along nicely, but still needs work to make it just right. The girls come down to get some cookies and milk and remind us about the new building for working out in. They want to do Yoga, aerobic exercise, stationary bike riding, and martial arts. That will not take long, but is still a fairly major project.

We are planning to build a facility for the factory we want to bring back here. That is definitely a major undertaking. Frank and Tom told me this morning that we may need a new tractor or two in order to accomplish as much acreage as we want to plant. Again it is no problem getting them, but it will require some time finding what we need, then get it back here. Wyatt comes over with Heber, Joseph, and Max. They want to talk about the temple that Wyatt has been commanded, I guess the word would be, to design the temple then when the design is acceptable we can build it. I'm not sure exactly who will decide if the plans are acceptable or not, but we have faith that it will happen.

We also have the train that everyone is excited about getting the track run and the train engine running. Someone said that if it is possible that we should run the track all the way around our different groups. That way everyone can enjoy it and it will make our groups even closer together than we are now. We have another trip planned to that area anyway so we will see what we can do. We know for sure that some of the other groups are going to want some of the trains and tracks as well. One of our young people was checking the train engine out and found a metal tag on it that tells where they were manufactured. Sounds like another adventure to me.

The list is a long one, but no longer than we have faced every year since coming here. One thing that we have come to realize is that if it doesn't get done today, there is always tomorrow. The important thing is that we all work together and play together so that we don't lose sight of what is really important in our lives. The way we are able to accomplish as much as we do is because we work together. We all have the same dream, that's to make our lives better and to help anyone that we can every day. Dayna is telling me that it is time for bed. It has been a very good day. It will be exciting to see what tomorrow brings for us. If you run into anyone who needs a home, they as well as you are always welcome. Love you all, goodnight.

Other Books by Ed and Eunice Vought

Best Friends 1: The Beginning

Best Friends 2: First Summer

Best Friends 3: Sophomore Year I

Best Friends 4: Sophomore Year II

Best Friends 5: A time of Maturing

Best Friends 6: Junior Year I

Best Friends 7: Junior Year II

Best Friends 8: Third Summer

They Call Me Nuisance (Published 2010)

2nd Earth: Shortfall

2nd Earth: Emplacement

2nd Earth: Adversary

Made in the USA
Monee, IL
15 April 2021